Foxhead Books

Shaken in the Water

Jessica Penner

Foxhead Books

Penner, Jessica.

Shaken in the Water / by Jessica Penner. 384p. 20.11 mm.

   ISBN-13 978-0-9847486-8-6

   1. Fiction. 2. Fiction—Short Stories. I. Shaken in the Water.

Cover Design by Christine S. Lee

Cover Photo by Alex Koeleman

Author Photo by Ron Rammelkamp

Contents

for Helen

SHAKEN IN THE WATER

Und der HERR wird Israel schlagen, gleich wie das Rohr im Wasser bewegt wird, und wird Israel ausreißen aus diesem guten Lande, daß er ihren Vätern gegeben hat, und wird sie zerstreuen jenseit des Stromes, darum daß sie ihre Ascherahbilder gemacht haben, den HERRN zu erzürnen.

1 *Koenige* 14.15

For the LORD shall smite Israel, as a reed is shaken in the water, and he shall root up Israel out of this good land, which he gave to their fathers, and shall scatter them beyond the river, because they have made their groves, provoking the LORD to anger.

1 *Kings* 14:15

… und sie hatten Haare wie Frauenharre, und ihre Zähne waren wie die von Löwen.

Die Offenbarung Des Johannes 9.8

… and they had hair as the hair of women, and their teeth were as the teeth of Lions.

Revelation 9:8

Shaken in the Water, Part 1

1923

Agnes had a birthmark that crossed her back from her left shoulder to her right hip. The midwife who had brought her into the world once whispered to her that it was a *Tieja Kjoaw*—Tiger Scar. It was thin and delicate, with a slight swirl to each end like the underscore of a signature. It was slim and sensitive to touch. Usually she wore her corset to bed to keep it protected from the maneuvering sheets. When her husband, Peter, touched it on their wedding night she gave a little gasp of pain. He stopped caressing her back and curled his fingers around the back of her neck. It was completely dark; even the curtains were drawn against the feeble light of a mid-cycle moon. All that could be heard beyond their stifled breath was the lonely echo of a cricket somewhere downstairs.

Peter's hand fell away from Agnes' neck. *Daut deit mie leet*, he whispered. Forgive me.

Agnes knew she should fumble for that hand, press it against her breast and whisper any sort of lie to explain it away. That would end his embarrassed conjecture; it would help make their milk-fed marriage stronger. But she could not lie to him just yet. She wanted to be married more than a half of a day before she began lying to her husband.

Aufpausse, was all she could force through her lips. *Aufpausse.*

Wait, he whispered in anxious agreement. *Aufpausse.*

Agnes had tucked her nightgown beneath her pillow so she would not have to find it in the dark. She slid it over her head. It was made of a light silk that she had sewn months ago during an ice storm; she was not surprised by how cool the threads felt as they slid over her August-soaked body.

Peter had not been so prudent. He shook the sheets and felt the floor for his pajamas. Had they been in love, this would have been shyly hilarious. Agnes lay down on her side of the bed and let him search alone. Finally, he found the pajama bottoms and struggled back into them. The bed swayed, creaked and bumped against the wall beneath his shifting weight. Peter's parents' bedroom was below; two of his unmarried sisters slept across the hall. Nearly everyone in the Harder household would breathe a sigh of relief and believe Peter was now truly married.

Tarred

1943

Agnes' daughter, Huldah, was in Elder Fast's east pasture when she saw a funnel cloud touch the earth and charge toward her on an otherwise clear day in January. The moment her feet left the ground, she felt the wind press a finger to her throat and curl itself around her, growing tighter as she rose higher, until she felt the throb of her heart on the outside of her body. Her last memory was the sky through the top of the finger. Its peaceful blue shocked her, as if nothing in the world was wrong.

Elder Fast's son found Huldah lying in a shallow gulch near his father's farm. Though her body was unbroken and unbruised, he turned his tiny face from what he saw, for every bit of clothing was gone and her hair fell in swirls around her naked body.

Huldah woke when she heard his feet brushing through the grass towards home; she felt the air wander over her thighs, stomach, breasts, throat and forehead with softened hands. But it was her hair that fascinated her. For the first time in seven years her hair lay open to the sun. When she'd joined the church it was banished from sight, rolled and pinned beneath the gauzy-white prison that held her purity with God.

The winds had brushed her hair clean. She decided she would never wear her head covering again, but let her hair hang free.

She knew the wind was from God; it had told her it wasn't a sin to swing her brown-red mane as she sang on the women's side the following Sunday.

There were angry mutterings throughout the service. Most Mennonites in the area had given up head coverings and plain dress a few years before, but Gnadenfeld *Kirche* would not be moved. There was talk of Meidung, though no one had been shunned since the village had left their Milk River on the Steppes of the Ukraine.

Agnes and Peter begged the elders to let their daughter's actions be ignored. She is *fe'rekjt*, they said. Crazy! You know she has spells. Every spell makes her a little crazier!

The next Sunday Elder Fast pleaded with Huldah to obey the community's demands.

Do you not understand this covering represents our separation from the world? he asked. That if we give this up we are one step closer to becoming like the *Englische*? We would no longer be

Mennonite.

We have already become *Englische*, she said. We drive cars. We use harvesters and tractors.

The elders decided such things are not materialistic; they are needed, he argued. Horses are more expensive to maintain than vehicles. We share these new things among each other. The *Englische* way is selfish and worldly. They tout their cars freely. Enjoy standing out.

I understand. I'm not asking the Grossmuttern to bare their heads. Just me.

Elder Fast opened his Bible and swallowed several times before reading the words Huldah had memorized when she joined Gnadenfeld *Kirche* seven years before: *So jemand zu euch kommt und bringt diese Lehre nicht, den nehmet nicht ins Haus und grüßet ihn auch nicht. Denn wer ihn grüßt, der macht sich teilhaftig seiner bösen Werke*—If there come any unto you, and bring not this doctrine, receive him not into your house, neither bid him God speed: For he that biddeth him God speed is partaker of his evil deeds.

Huldah only understood what she had chosen at breakfast on the morning following the pronouncement. She stopped short before her place at the table, now occupied by Gretta. Gretta's neck grew scarlet as Huldah paused behind her.

Was machst du?

She looked at Momma. Her mother's eyes remained on the

floor, her mouth in a rigid line. Poppa's eyes were to the ceiling.

Was machst du?

She had never seen anyone shunned before. She had thought her family was exempt from the Elder's command. Huldah saw the little table at the end of the long one. Set were a plate, utensils and glass; the milk poured, the eggs and toast arranged on the yellow plate she had loved as a child. A brown dishtowel served as a crooked table cloth. It was only an inch away from the family table, but as Huldah stepped towards it she felt she was crossing a field newly shorn, her bare feet cut by the stubble, miles from comfort.

Poppa began to pray. The family linked hands. Out of habit, Huldah reached out, only to see the circle close.

Christe, du Lamm Gottes—

Was machst du?

Poppa's head remained bowed. Momma's eyes were fixed on someone other than her daughter, the tendons in her neck standing out. The little ones hands struggled out of the older ones' grasp, breathing into their fingers.

—der du tragst die Sund der Welt, erbarm dich unser—

Why are you doing this? She spoke in careful English. Why do you listen to the elders—do what they say to do about your own daughter. I am still your *Dochta.*

Raus! Poppa's head rose and his eyes locked with hers. Raus! Leave this house; take your dirty *Englische* words with you! You are dead to us!

That evening she carried her things to a tiny house behind a trellis that would be covered in morning glories in the summer; Poppa had built this for his parents before she was born. She still ate her meals with the family, but always an inch away from their circle.

~

The Voice came as Huldah was leading the cows past the burned-out barn that had once belonged to her Grandpoppa Funk. An acid of fear on her tongue came first, followed by a foul smell that penetrated her nostrils, then the rain in her mind that came softly at first, crawling on each blade of grass with lightened feet before it became prickling hail, studding the dirty snow before her eyes. She lifted her face to the sky and saw a wall cloud tower over the earth, as if it were a humid afternoon in August.

The wall cloud crowded close, its insides swirling a single finger that pulsed within, ready to burst upon the earth.

Aufpausse, said the Voice. Wait.

She opened her eyes to see the barrel of a gun pointed at her head.

Aufpausse, the Voice growled, her breath hot on Huldah's face. Wait.

For what?

They need you. Just wait.

Then she heard a sound echo against her ears: the roar of a tiger.

Huldah knew who would lend her a gun and teach her how to

use it: Kaleb Wiebe. He'd never joined the church but stayed in the community. She had seen him target practice in the neighboring pasture.

Hold this, he said, tossing the metal shaft into the air. Huldah caught it easily with arms as round as a man's. He grinned at her strength and continued cleaning the tiny workings spread around him.

She balanced the gun's barrel on her right arm and wiped it clean with a soft cloth, then took a long brush and cleared the inside of caked powder. The gunpowder flew into the air each time she drew out the brush, a dark glitter that littered her dress and fingers. When she swept stray hairs from her face, she felt it smudge against her forehead.

Next? she asked.

Now we put it together. It's like a puzzle.

Huldah watched as he carefully assembled the parts of the gleaming hammer and barrel, so that in a moment what had been independent of one another became a glowing whole.

Here, he said, giving the shotgun to her as if it were a newborn. Hold it.

She cradled the being in her hands and watched her fingers wrap around the barrel. The power and the heat of the sunned parts drove the index finger to the hammer.

Boom, Huldah said, glancing at Kaleb.

He laughed. Not quite yet. No boom yet.

He took it from her hands and grabbed a box of shells. He jerked his head to the east. Let's go to my target.

For a moment she hesitated, sensing what she was about to learn was very nearly a sin.

A bare cottonwood stood at the rise of the pasture and a target hung on its branches. He dropped the box of shells to the ground; the lid popped open and the resting bodies scattered on the wilted grass. Cracking the gun in half, he pushed five of them into small nests made just for them.

Now it's ready. Watch.

He pulled himself up and posed for Huldah, his body taut, the gun melding into his shoulder. She jumped at the shout of the gun as one of the shells exploded from the muzzle.

The gun dropped to Kaleb's side as he turned to face her. There. That's how you do it. Now you.

His arms nestled around Huldah's hands as she assumed the pose he had shown her. Okay. Okay, he said, breathing into her hair that draped over her shoulders and past her waist.

She cocked the gun. The shock of the report would have made her stagger if she was a smaller woman, but her buttocks were appropriately relaxed and her thighs ready to spring back, so she only briefly brushed against Kaleb's chest.

Very nice. Very nice.

Let's see if I hit it, she called over her shoulder, galloping away.

Upon arrival, Huldah considered the well-used target. How do you know if we hit it? she asked. Each hole seemed the same to her.

You have to feel them, see which is hotter than the others. His hand brushed over the pock-marked wood. You can see the powder as well, see which is newer. There, he said, pausing at one hole. And there, his voice surprised. His hand stopped on the target's upper left-hand corner.

Who did what? She turned to face him.

Kaleb laughed. We'll never know.

Can I shoot again?

As much as you want.

Don't you know why I wanted to learn?

Not particularly, Kaleb said. I figure I'll know someday.

The following morning, Huldah found a note slipped under her front door. Huldah couldn't read English; her master of German was that of a small child, so her momma wrote in symbols rather than words. It contained the usual sybols of chores for the day as if she no longer knew the rhythms of her family; one more was added: *Ulysses fabric Poppa.*

Huldah and Poppa were crossing the street in Ulysses when they saw Mrs. Herbert Carr. Huldah tried to hurry them to the other side of the street, as if that side would protect them from Mrs. Herbert Carr's buxom frame. Poppa seemed to walk slower.

How about buying some bonds for the boys? Mrs. Carr asked.

No. I apologize, Poppa answered in his schoolbook English that always embarrassed his children.

And why not?

I don't participate in such things, he said. To—

Poppa, don't, Huldah said. She wanted to touch his shoulder, to remove him from this place, but she gripped the fabric she had just purchased instead.

And why not? Mrs. Carr drew herself up. You did not send your sons over there, so the least you can do for this country that took you in is give money to the effort.

One of the Lord's commands is to not murder.

Murder? Do you say my son is a murderer? It's them Nazis, them Japs, that're the murderers.

Yes they are, he said. And your son as well.

Mrs. Carr lunged at Poppa, who stood his ground. You should be ashamed for such things! she screamed, clawing at his face. Mrs. Carr stumbled and fell. Poppa reached out to help her up, but she slapped away his hand.

Huldah dropped the fabric and crouched down to face Mrs. Carr, whose face was streaked with tears. Mrs. Carr, she whispered. Let me help you.

Mrs. Carr opened her eyes. Help? You help me? You're crazier than they say if you think you can do anything of the sort. You belong nowhere. Not with us. Not with them.

On the ride home, Poppa drove blindly, his left hand running up and down his beard, talking to himself: *Denn sie trachten Schaden zu tun und suchen falsche Anklagen gegen die Stillen im Lande*—they do not speak peaceably, but devise false accusations against those who live quietly in the land.

His words streamed through Huldah's body as if she were merely a wall of air.

Tell me, *Dochta*. I will let myself sin for a moment and speak with you. Tell me the truth: was I wrong?

Huldah rolled his words in her mind. It was a sin to even speak to a being he and her momma had made. She wondered what he had thought in that moment she had been imprinted in her momma's womb; if the act of creation even entered his mind.

You were wrong, Poppa, she said. You shouldn't have called her son a murderer. You were not the quiet in the land this afternoon.

You are right, he gave a cheerless laugh. Yes, you are right. He smiled with a sadness that nearly brought her hand to his shoulder. Why won't you confess so I can bring you to life again? Why is your hair such a barrier between us?

It is not my barrier. I did not build it.

I cannot pull it down. Where would this family go if I did? We would all be shunned. We would become *Englische*.

It is not the worst that can happen, Poppa.

You saw how I act around the *Englische* already. I say the wrong things and sow hatred for all of us. Besides, he said to himself, I would have to shave my beard. That would be a hard thing, to have a naked face. He smiled at her sadly.

Huldah saw that he was as frightened of the world as she. There was nothing else beyond this little circle of people for him. It would be harder for him to fall in the world than for her; she had been an outsider long before the church turned its back.

You should leave, *Dochta*. Your presence tempts all of us to sin; the little ones, your mother—myself sin.

I'm waiting, Poppa.

For what?

I don't know. Something is going to happen.

The Voice came without warning. Huldah struggled to open her eyes against the rushing wind borne by a white striped beast. She ran away, zigzagging across the empty field, crying for someone to hear her, to wake her from this. She would not survive this time. Once it swept towards her it would break her open, its jaws filled with her stretch of skin. She fell against a wall of rough wood. She felt her way around the wall on palms scratched by brush, and she crossed a threshold. As she shut the door she realized the building was on fire—she felt the flames lick up her legs, crawl over her breasts until it surrounded her face. But her body felt nothing.

The Voice wailed against the wood. And then fell silent. She could feel the chest of this beast heave against the wall, its muscles tensed to pounce.

≈

The men came as the family sat down to supper that night. She heard them coming. It was one of those rare nights on the prairie without wind, so that a person could hear the roll of wheels from miles away, the stillness of the ice-laden grass letting the sound glide between each blade.

Her family sat quietly with their fear. Poppa gripped his beard and mumbled an indecipherable prayer.

Momma propelled them into action. Peter, we must hide. Huldah, gather every quilt and line the floor to muffle the sounds upstairs.

No one moved. Each eye fixed on Poppa's hands, Poppa's beard.

Now! Momma thundered. They leaped and rushed around Poppa's stillness as if he were no longer a man.

Peter. Peter. Momma's words tried to reach Poppa's stillness. Peter, we must do this. This is the only way.

The thunder of the vehicles began to separate until Huldah could count each of the voices that rang through open windows. Fifteen, she muttered. I think there are fifteen.

Now! Momma hissed and fumbled in the darkness for Poppa's hand. Huldah found Poppa's shoulder and gave him a gentle push. Something she'd never done in her life. Poppa's body obeyed his women, and moved towards the stairs. The trapdoor of the attic had just been shut when Huldah heard the cars reel into the yard. The headlights swept the frigid air and glowed up to the attic window. The twins, Tobias and Johan, not even a year old, coughed and whimpered. Momma snatched a quilt and dropped it over their nest.

The engines remained running as car doors creaked open. Harder! one of the men shouted. Peter Harder!

Huldah crept towards the trapdoor on her behind, dragging a small blanket with her. One of her brothers stirred at the sound of her movement. She reached for his face and pulled him to her.

Stille. Stille, she murmured, and waited for his nearly impercep-
tible nod before letting go.

We know you're in there. We just want to talk. A chuckle rum-
bled among the men. Huldah was sure she knew that voice. She
waited until his voice rang again: Look how brave you are right
now.

Huldah grasped the handle and swung it open. She left the
blanket between the trapdoor and frame to silence it shut, and
slipped her thick frame through the house.

She pulled the rifle from its hiding place and loaded it, her
hands icy and awkward. One of the shells slipped from her fingers
and hit the floor. She fitted the last of four and cocked the shotgun
as feet found the porch steps.

The voice pounded on the unlocked door. Huldah aimed the
gun and waited for it to open.

She was as tall as their *Englische* neighbor, Mr. Herbert Carr,
so the sighting piece lined up just to the right of his bent nose. Her
entire body focused on his face, the crinkles around his eyes that
showed him to be a decent man. She could smell his onion-laced
breath aimed against her face.

Hey there, Huldah, Mr. Herbert Carr said genially, as if they'd
just met on the road on an anonymous afternoon.

Hey there. Huldah felt an echo of an alarm behind her eyes.
The taste of bile, the scent of metal was coming. The alarm grew
louder. The Voice was coming. She widened her eyes, moved her
tongue back and forth on the roof of her mouth, tried to keep it at

bay; she knew it would find her soon.

You know, I don't have business with you. I got business with your father.

He isn't here.

Are you sure?

Yes. They're all gone.

Your car is under that shed. Are you saying your whole family's gone but you? Just walked down the road on a night like this?

I am. The alarm swelled into a cry of terror. She felt her body demanding to fall to the floor, the shivers sneaking through the back of her mind, like scouts on a mission.

Mr. Carr let out a growl of a laugh. If you're telling the truth, you wouldn't mind us poking around inside?

No, you can't. Tell them to go home, Mr. Carr.

And if I don't I expect you'll shoot me. He shifted his weight in a friendly manner.

Maybe.

Isn't the whole reason your father won't buy the bonds is because he takes Thou Shalt Not Kill a little too seriously? That he wouldn't send your brothers to war like my son?

Huldah nodded.

So why are you holding a gun just now?

More Voices had joined the Voice. The Voices began to shout a prayer: *Christe, du Lamm Gottes*—

They don't let women pray out loud in church, she shouted over the Voices, her voice skittering over the porch rails and onto the frozen grass. Even our benches are lower, so a giant like me won't sit higher than a man. Why would I follow what the men of my church decide?

Christe, du Lamm Gottes—

Lamb of God, Huldah heard her trembling voice say. You take away the sins of the world, have mercy on us—

Mr. Carr's face studied hers. He reached out and rearranged a strand of hair that hung in her eyes. He smiled with pity. There, he said. There.

Go home for the night, Mr. Carr said softly to his men.

When their wheels distanced themselves enough, Huldah lowered the gun to his gut. She saw his pistol, quietly sheathed. She saw what the men had left behind: two buckets of tar, a bag of feathers and kindling for a fire.

She heard the Voices approach on a rush of wind that wanted to dampen all other sound. Huldah fell to the ground as the elders and their wives cheered within the cloud, husking themselves of their beards and head coverings and letting the roiling wind carry their Voices:

Christe, du Lamm Gottes—

Lamb of God—

—der du tragst die Sund der Welt erbarm dich unser—

—you take away the sins of the world, have mercy on us—

Herein! Come in! said the Voice.

Who are you?

Your way home, purred the Voice. Behind her closed lids, Huldah saw its flashing white and black hide, its tiger's grin.

Shaken in the Water, Part 2

1903

When Agnes was born, her momma was worried about the long, thin birthmark that crossed her firstborn's back, but the Poppkje Matia, Ruby Hiebert, was unconcerned. It will fade, I'm sure, she said. Thank the Lord she is healthy and strong—don't worry about outward things. It smacks of pride.

On her way home that evening, Midwife Hiebert stopped at her sister's farm and described the birthmark. You know what our momma would have called such a mark in the Ukraine, she said, leaning on the barnyard fence while her sister milked the last cow. She would've called such a mark the *Tieja Kjoaw*—Tiger Scar.

Is that a good or a bad thing? her sister asked, stripping the last of the milk from the cow's udder.

Midwife Hiebert shrugged. I've heard both: that it's the mark of possible greatness or the mark of disaster. But, she laughed, of course all of that is nonsense and rather pagan; Momma listened to her Russian maid a bit too often for a pious Mennonite.

Her sister agreed.

Agnes' momma was still worried, but after Midwife Hiebert's reproof she didn't say anything to anyone else. She noticed that the birthmark was sensitive to the touch, and if any cloth was too rough, Agnes would writhe and scream until the offending material was removed. Only the softest cotton worked. One of Agnes' aunts, Lola, got hold of a length of silk and made a shift out of it. They could instantly see the comfort the child felt as it brushed over her back. However, as Agnes grew, her momma couldn't afford soft cotton or silk. When her momma and poppa were doing chores and she was alone, she wiggled out of her clothes and ran around naked. She soon forgot that she shouldn't be seen or heard during these times, and would whoop and scream and roll in the soft grass closest to the house like a horse just in from the field.

No matter how many times her momma and poppa punished her, she could not be stopped. They took to tying her up on the porch when both of them were needed on the farm. Finally, Lola came up with a solution: she made undershirts out of soft cotton and silk that had tucks in the sides like the hem of a dress that could be let out as she grew.

This way, she said, you don't have to replace the undershirts as much. Perhaps our *Ssockaschoote* will stay clothed now. Right, sweetheart? she said to the deceptively complacent three-year-old.

Although Agnes' actions mortified her momma, it amused her aunt. She wondered what it was like, to have such a freedom with one's body. She had seen Agnes exploring the fields and pastures, the birthmark bouncing through acres of wheat and grass like a lip of a torch in darkness. It reminded her of the photos of the people who were native Kansans. Perhaps there was something in the air of this place that made some feel that the plants and air were enough. In the memories of her childhood in the Ukraine, the air in the Molotschna Colony had always had a violent feel to it. You would not want to wander about that part of the country without something on the shoulders.

Eventually there were no more incidents. Though Agnes often had to be reminded to button her blouse or pull up her stockings, she stopped wandering the farmyard naked. As other sons and daughters entered her family, her momma and poppa became more distracted by the babies and the farm. Every time a baby came out of her womb, Agnes' momma would ask the *Poppemutta* the same question: Does its back have the mark?

What her parents did not know was that Agnes had a spot she went to when the need to let her skin breathe became unbearable. There was a creek a mile away from the farm that only became a true run of water when it rained for days or after a snow dissolved. Around that creek there was a small valley and a copse of stunted trees. An abandoned barn leaned toward the creek as if it longed for a drink. The barn was built on land that once belonged to an *Englische* family that gave up farming and returned east. Agnes' poppa had pulled down the soddy and would have pulled down the barn as well, but many neighbors had protested, because that barn had been the first meeting place for the Gnandenfeld immigrant community. The *Englische* had let them meet there until the community raised enough money to build a proper church a mile to the south.

The hymns we sung there are still in the air, one of the elders had said.

It was there that Agnes would go when even the fibers of silk felt as though sand was being rubbed into her flesh. Winter and summer she would run there for an odd hour or more, her bare feet numbed by the snow or chafed by the dead summer grass. She sneaked away an old quilt and stored bits of food in the barn. In winter, she would build a small fire inside the barn. One time the fire had nearly gotten out of control because she had not made the pit deep enough; she solved that by digging the pit deep into the earth and lining it with stones from the creek.

It was there that Agnes met Nora.

The day she met Nora, Agnes had fought with one of her brothers, Zeke. It was one of those arguments that had turned into a screaming match. She knew she was too old to fight, but Zeke had a way of making her feel a wild violence she could not control. Their poppa shouted. She began to run from her poppa. She was a nimble fourteen-year-old; her poppa was a man fettered with a weeping child on the ground, another wailing in the house and a wife two miles away, visiting her blind grandmomma with their latest baby. Agnes easily outstripped him. The run did her good. The rage that had encircled her vision slowly receded. Her stomach uncoiled itself. Her thigh muscles surged beneath her as if she was coursing down a wild river. By the time she reached the barn her fury was forgotten and an unconscious smile played on her broad face. She ran two circles around the barn before she stopped in front of its yawning mouth. She unbuttoned her blouse, stepped out of her underclothes and stood in the bright August sunshine.

The sun seemed particularly brilliant to Agnes that day; the sky was a heady blue without a cloud to temper its color. The wind whistled through the shaking brambles and drought-hardened branches of the stunted trees. The creek was nothing but a stagnant puddle, but she could sense the seasons that had overflowed its banks and caressed each grain of the sandy soil beneath her feet. She stared at the slight rise that hid the barn and its inhabitants from view. It seemed as though she was standing before a mountain like the ones she had seen in books at school. She breathed in the heat that radiated from this sudden mountain, began to march towards it and spewed the hymn she always wanted to beg for when the elders asked the congregation what to sing in church:

Ein' feste Burg ist unser Gott,
Ein gute Wehr und Waffen;
Er hilft uns frei aus aller Not,
Die uns jetzt hat betroffen.

Der alt' böse Feind—

A howl and several grunts interrupted her anthem. She stopped, crouched to hide her nakedness and scanned the yard for the sound. The howls and grunts continued. Finally, Agnes saw a thin blonde girl sitting at the window of the hayloft. The noises she made clashed with each other; it seemed to Agnes that the girl had never heard a laugh in her life. She dashed to her dropped clothing and started to get dressed, but the howls turned into hoots. When she looked up, the girl had pulled off her own dress and threw it at Agnes' feet.

Agnes saw the firm stitches in the dress that lay in the dust before her feet. She thought it strange that there was no attempt to hide the fact that the dress was patched. The pale blue pattern was interspersed with browns and grays that seemed to need patches of their own. But one patch caught Agnes' eye: beneath the arms of this toss-away dress were two strips of bright fabric. They were bright and pure, as though they had never been worn before. There was no red in the Mennonite world anymore; the elders had decreed this to be too bright for the community.

Some had disagreed: Why do we want to shun a color the Lord Himself has made. Sunsets shine this color, birds carry it on their wings.

The elders stood firm: We are aware of the beauty of this color— that's not why we shouldn't wear it or decorate our homes with it. It is expensive. It will make those who are too poor to have it ashamed, will bring the wealthy pride and distrust of those who cannot buy it.

That is the reason why we must put this back to the earth.

So, this *verboten* color was stowed away in secret places or had taken residence in hand-braided rugs that were shoved into darkened parts of houses. Agnes knew that color's name: *knaul'root*. It was to the ear a sharp bang of a door in the wind; to the eyes a slam of sunlight after a day of shadow. A glaring, unashamed red.

A parcel of underclothes hit Agnes' bowed head. She looked up. The girl stood proudly naked before Agnes, who laughed.

Komm! Agnes shouted.

The girl continued her odd laughter. *Komm!* she shouted again with a wave. Come down!

The girl disappeared for a few seconds. Soon she stood eye to eye with Agnes, smiling and spinning her sunshine body in the puckering August wind.

I'm Agnes.

The girl's back was to Agnes when she spoke. She reached out and grabbed her shoulder. I'm Agnes, she repeated.

The girl stared at her Agnes' lips with sudden concentration. She made a quick motion with her hands.

Agnes.

The girl made the motion again.

Agnes!

The girl hooted and nodded her head. She began to make several motions with her hands. Agnes realized the girl was deaf. There were plenty of older people who were partially deaf in her church, but she had never met someone completely deaf. She stopped the girl's hands and shook her head. She got on her knees and traced her name into the dust. She pointed at her name and then pointed at herself. The girl crouched down and drew her name beneath it: Nora. She looked up at Agnes and made another sign: her fingers spread wide and swept over the right side of her face. She pointed at her name, made the sign and pointed at herself.

Ah! Agnes grinned and mimicked Nora's sign.

Agnes wanted a name that needed no voice; something that only the air would feel as she swept it through the speckles of dust the way Nora's name did. She wondered how she would define herself in one twist of a joint and brush of her skin. Perhaps the straight spine of an A would do. She pointed to herself and drew the capital letter in the air. Nora spun an S in the air instead. Agnes shook her head and repeated her sign. Nora shook her head and repeated her sign. Agnes was frustrated; she stomped her foot and made an A. Nora shook her head briskly, a faint line appearing between her eyes. She clapped her hands onto Agnes' bare shoulders and turned her around. With one finger she traced Agnes' birthmark.

Agnes screamed. She felt as if someone had touched her with a burning piece of coal. She jerked away and tried to grab Nora's arm, but Nora ducked and ran into the barn. Agnes wanted to follow her and make her feel what she had felt, but at that moment the sun shifted a little farther west and made the shadows stretch a little over Agnes' bare back. There was an odd mixture of warmth and coolness that sponged down her back, as though someone had just slipped a cool silk garment over her head and down the length of her body. Agnes closed her eyes and could see the shimmering bearer of the gown as she stood before her, a scant smile on the visitor's lips. Agnes felt fingers like prickles dance up her body and crawl through her snarls of hair. The bearer of the gown stepped closer and gave Agnes the tenderest of kisses on the corner of her mouth, her cool hands gently tracing her scar yet again. This time Agnes didn't scream, but she breathed in the bearer of the gown's shadow and saw the outline of the S mist before her eyes.

Ah! Agnes opened her eyes. She looked up at Nora, who still stood in the loft, her ivory body gleaming, her blonde hair scattered by the wind. Agnes smiled and traced the S in the air. Nora stared, then traced the S back at her. Then, she spread her fingers out wide and scraped the air before her as if to say: I am Nora. Agnes scraped her S in return, as if to say: I am Agnes.

1923

No one was in the house to give Agnes a chore when she came down the morning after her wedding night. She had never been unoccupied in Peter's house before. Before they were married, she had been the hired girl, always put to work baking, washing dishes or scrubbing floors the moment she crossed the threshold.

Only a week before, Alma Harder had seen Agnes searching her shoes for the dime she received each Saturday in the heel of her left shoe—money never traded hands in the community but appeared folded in someone's pocket, under a hat or in the heel of a shoe. Agnes had worked for three years without pay; for the past two years Alma had granted Agnes a salary.

There's nothing to look for, Alma said from the kitchen, her hands full of clean dishes that Agnes had just finished washing. I figure we're spending several times that for the wedding supper. Besides, she added, you'll be a married woman soon. You don't need to have pocket money to buy candy anymore.

Agnes wanted to throw her empty shoes and scream at this woman who knew the ten cents did not go across the counter of the candy store. It bought flour and sugar and shoes for her siblings. She wanted to grab each dish she had just washed and throw it to the floor she had just swept and mopped. Agnes felt the color of her temper cloud her eyes and threaten to blind her. Alma stood watching her closely, holding the dishes out from her body, as if she could sense what Agnes wanted to do. Some of the dishes were very old. They had been served under arbors of grapes on the banks of the Milk River in the Molotschna Colony in the Ukraine. They had been packed in sawdust and carried over an ocean and half a continent. They were scraped by knives and plunged into steaming water each day as if they held no worldly importance. But Agnes and Alma knew better. They both knew that breaking one of these dishes further increased the distance between themselves and their past; that the day the last dish was broken would be the day they would have nothing that was held by hands that knew the river's every bend, plucked the grapes and let the fruit brush lips that were now dust. Agnes turned and exited the house without putting on her shoes. She was glad for the shocks of pain that coursed through her feet as she walked down the gravel road to her poppa's house two miles away.

Agnes reached into the icebox and poured milk in one of the blue glasses from Russia. She took a fresh *zwiebach* and placed it on a solid yellow plate. Agnes laughed, because the thought that crossed her mind was the fact that Alma Harder imagined that she was going to get the services of her new daughter-in-law for free until death. But Agnes knew that Alma and Abram would eventually move to the small house Peter had built for them. It stood behind the wash house and was surrounded by a lattice shrouded with morning glories. Agnes would have no responsibility to the granny house. She would have charge of the big house that she and Peter would swarm with children. Those dishes, those glasses would belong to *her* to do with as she wished.

The Circle of the Earth

1955

Tobias didn't break the glass; he simply didn't catch it as it fell. Momma had been washing dishes when the telephone rang their number—their party line was six. She left the glass she had just dipped into the sink on the counter. Her feet stomped by Tobias, who was on the floor, reading, and faded into the hall. He watched the glass move slowly across the counter top like a glacier headed towards the end of the world.

This glass was a special glass. This glass had come across the ocean long before Tobias was born. This glass was a mottled blue that felt strange in your hand, because its surface wasn't smooth like other glasses. Instead it rose and fell in tiny waves, your finger tracing the waves of the miniature ocean. Tobias wondered if it had always been that way, or if it had been shaped by that voyage.

The glass continued to skate towards the edge on a tiny bubble of water. Tobias knew it was going to fall, but he couldn't bring himself to disturb its journey.

Then it fell and shattered, each molecule of the time-frozen water setting off on its own. Only the glass bottom remained whole and revolved on the peeling kitchen linoleum like a top Tobias once owned before Johan threw it into the fire. He slid out of his hiding place and grabbed the nearly perfect circle of glass. Momma reappeared.

Tobias Harder! What have you done?

Nothing!

You broke my glass!

No, Momma! I didn't do it! It fell off the counter!

All by itself, then?

Yes!

Momma pulled Tobias by the back of his shirt. Don't you ever lie to me! Understand! Never!

But I'm not lying, he screamed. Momma was holding him tight against her chest. He could not see her face. I'm not lying, Momma.

Momma muttered something in Low German: *Ekj wenschte dü weascht nie jebuare. Ekj wenschte dü weascht nie jebuare.* Momma and Poppa never spoke Low German to Tobias and Johan. It was the language of rage in their house.

He felt something wet against his chest. He tried to look down, but Momma only squeezed him tighter. He realized his chest hurt, and the wetness was warm. He craned his neck lower. His right palm held the blue circle. Momma's hand was pressed over Tobias' hand. Blood seeped out beneath it, spreading like the molecules of glass had seconds before.

Momma. She only pressed him closer. Momma. Momma.

Be quiet! Tobias felt her angry breath against his neck. The pain pushed his tongue again: But I'm bleeding Momma! My chest is bleeding!

She turned him around and screamed at her hand that had held the circle's jagged edge to Tobias' chest. My God. My God, was all she could say.

The circle of glass created a mirror image in his skin that shrunk and softened over the years. It never disappeared though. When hair grew on his chest, it stood out even more, like a brand that claimed his life for someone else.

Fifteen years later, when his wife saw him without a shirt for the first time, she reached and brushed its surface like a bather testing the water. Tobias felt the vibrations of that touch fill each fragment of his body. She stepped closer, her eyes nearly level with the circle. This time her lips grazed his skin. His hands curled like tree knots; his biceps stretched until he could feel the base of his neck spasm. Please. Please. Please, was all he could manage.

Does it hurt?

Yes. No.

I should stop.

No. Please.

∾

Momma swabbed the wound with harsh medicine for days after; her fingers pressed into his flesh as if they could erase what had been done. For penance for breaking the last of a half dozen similar glasses, Tobias had to dust and mop the church every Saturday for three months. While Johan and every other boy within a five mile radius rode their bikes into Ulysses, Tobias trudged to the tiny weathered building surrounded by a parched expanse of a parking lot. He smeared oil on every wooden surface and wiped it clean; he lifted up each pew cushion and turned it over so that one side wouldn't be paler than the other; he swept the aisle twice before he mopped it; after he mopped he waited for the expanse of wood to dry, because he would sweep it once more. Momma tested his work the next morning before the others came—she would know if he had not followed her strictures.

The last Saturday of his punishment was in late August. Tobias was excited; he got on his bike and sped to the church early. He hummed to himself nosily as he opened the unlocked door and headed for the broom closet. He was glad the weather was sure to be good for a long time yet. There were many Saturdays left for Tobias to finally speed his bike past Johan's into town and be the first to reach Ulysses' water tower. He would leap off his bike and slap the side of the tower twelve times at a heated run before taking off again—this time to the grain elevator on the other side of town. That next Saturday was going to be the best of his life; that next Saturday he would leave Johan behind for a very long time.

The early morning sunlight piled upon the narrow church windows, creating bright strips of light and gray shadow through the sanctuary. She was standing so still that Tobias didn't notice her until he nearly ran into her heavy frame. She had fiery hair and an ugly dress. Her face was drawn together as if someone hadn't brought enough flesh to fill the empty space. Had Tobias not been twelve years old he would have run away. Had his sister not held a red book in her hands, Tobias would have shouted at her presence. Instead he asked: Why are you stealing that?

Huldah grinned. I'm not stealing it.

But it's one of our hymnals!

I'm one of you, right?

But they need to stay here. Where people can use them.

I need to use them.

For what?

My collection.

Tobias set down the broom. You collect hymnals?

No, not just hymnals. But these are a great example.

Of what?

Of the color I'm looking for.

Tobias wondered if he'd ever really noticed the cover of a hymnal before. It was like paying attention to the calm sky. It's red, he said, noticing for the first time how the edges of the cover were muted from the hundreds of times the members of his community had held them. He saw the cracks in the spine were filled with the dust and sweat of people that maybe no longer sat on this side of the earth.

Not just red. Huldah held the hymnal in the strip of morning that crossed them. *Knaul'root.* I've started a collection of books that are this color.

Why?

Now that's a secret.

Where's this collection at, anyway?

My house.

Tobias had never been to his sister's house. The house, like his sister, like the scarred ring on his chest, was never talked about. Can I come see it?

Huldah grinned. Sure. But we'd better clean first.

Huldah's house in Ulysses wound up in its corner like a sleeping snake; the surrounding trees stood a ragged guard around its flaking gray siding. Inside, the worn wooden floors creaked beneath Tobias' feet as he walked in. A set of straight backed chairs and a table gathered on one side of the living room. A shabby sofa and an ottoman slouched in the other. Their presence was overwhelmed by mountains of books. They filled the walls and even parts of the windows. Slim and fat stood side by side in a jagged line. On one side of the room it looked as though Huldah had put more thought in the ordering of books, then gave up and slid them in wherever there was space. Frayed tails jutted out above texts with the fore edges pushing out; spines were shelved with their titles upside down. The two sides of the room seemed to lean away from each other. One had a spacious breadth to it; the other reminded Tobias of the jungles he had seen in school books. Tobias preferred the jungle. The one thing that each book had in common was the color of their bindings. Tobias had never thought there were so many red books in the world. Even though the room was dimly lit by the early afternoon sun, the colors seemed to pulse at him like a giant heart. They gave off a heat all their own. He approached the books carefully, placing one foot directly in front of the other. When the only space between him and the books was less than an inch, Tobias stopped. He chose one book to examine. It was a middle-sized one. Not as flashy as its neighbors, but held its own quietly. He breathed in the title: *The Secret Garden*. Its binding was cracked, as though it had been opened hundreds of times. The lettering had once been black, but had faded into a muted brown. Tobias touched the spine, surprised at how cool the coarse cover felt.

Go ahead, pull it out.

He rested his hand more firmly on the spine. He looked at Huldah. How many books do you have in here?

She cocked her great head to one side. Her hair swung to the side as well. I guess about two hundred, more or less. Plus one, she said as she slid the newest tenant onto a shelf near the front door. She grinned at Tobias. He smiled back, and pulled out the book.

Have you read this? he said, lifting the book for her to see the title.

A faint line shadowed her wide forehead that was without a single wrinkle. I can't read, she said.

No one ever taught you?

They tried. I'm trying again, now. But I'm slow, you see. I can't keep anything in my head for enough time.

Tobias studied her face. There was a boy in the church whose face was like Huldah's. He'd heard grownups say he was slow. Some of the kids would laugh at Matt and pushed him away when he tried to play with them. Tobias had even done such things. But Huldah didn't act anything like Matt. She seemed perfectly normal.

You don't act slow, he said. You must be wrong.

Maybe. But sometimes I fall asleep without meaning to—

I do that all the time!

And then I have these dreams that chase me around until I wake up.

I have one bad dream sometimes, Tobias confessed.

Yeah?

I dream that Johan is dead. That he's drowned. That he's drowned and I could've saved him, but I didn't. I just stood there while he drowned.

Huldah nodded her head. I've had those before—about other people.

Oh? Tobias felt relieved. He wasn't the only one then.

Yeah. I think a lot of people do.

He looked down at the cover again. He looked up at the sea of red that surrounded Huldah's living room. Tobias wondered if they were alive, if they were listening at that moment, and wondering what he was thinking.

I think they're very—beautiful, he said.

Huldah nodded her head. I think so, too.

Can I help you—with your collection?

Huldah laughed. Tobias liked her laugh. It was light, like little bells on a string. Of course, she said. That's why I came to the church today.

Tobias heard other boys shouting. He saw Johan speed past Huldah's open door. The crowd of boys followed. He knew where they were headed. I need to go, he said, running to the door. Can I borrow this? I'll bring it back. I'll be back. I'll be back again.

He tucked the book into the back of his pants, jumped on his bike and veered to the left while the voices echoed right. Then Tobias only heard himself breathe, his body sucking great drafts of air through his body and out again. Then his eyes only saw the road ahead, the way his bike tire navigated the bumps and rocks along the way. He knew a shortcut he'd held secret for weeks now; he'd found it while wandering around town one day. This was the first time he would use his bike on the shortcut. There was an overgrown alley on Jackson. A shaded path between the First and Second Baptist churches. A ragged bridge over a ditch that used to be a creek. Then he was in the clear, only a few brief yards from the water tower that loomed like a warning shot over Ulysses. He saw the others trundling towards the goal, Johan in front. Johan saw him. Tobias pumped hard. Johan pumped harder. They were flying towards each other. Tobias leapt off his bike just before it crashed into Johan. He rolled towards the side of the water tower, reached out his hand and struck the hollow metal with a satisfying thwack. The others circled their bikes around the tower and began thumping the water tower ferociously. The sound rose gloriously into the Saturday air, like a pounding hymn from an ancient land. Tobias leaned against the water tower and watched them race. He imagined they were praising his victory over his twin.

He looked for his brother. Johan was pulling himself out from beneath their tangled bicycles, his face filled with rage. His shirt was torn and flapped against his heavy belly. Tobias laughed. Johan strode towards him, a fist shaping in his hand. Tobias jumped up; felt the summer warmth of the water tower hold his spine in place. Johan stumbled, cursed, and looked at his feet: Huldah's book. He picked it up and held it in the lowering afternoon light. *The Secret Garden*, he mouthed. *Was ist das?* Whose secret garden?

Tobias moved to take the book. That's mine—I mean it's not mine. I borrowed it from somebody.

Johan had opened the book and squinted as he read: Mistress Mary. *Scheisse*, Tobias. Are you reading a girl's book?

By this time the other boys had stopped running, their plaid-covered chests heaving, and surrounded them.

Tobias is reading a girl's book! Johan shouted.

A girl's book a girl's book a girl's book, his friends echoed, their voices a mix of English and German.

Give that to me! It's not mine! I borrowed it!

He borrowed it! He borrowed it! He borrowed it! Johan crowed, his voice a sharp falsetto. How's that any different from owning it? You chose it!

It just is, Tobias said quietly, seeing his defeat in the eyes of everyone there. Give it to me.

He held out his hand.

Oh, okay Toby, here you go. Johan took a step forward, offering the book. When Tobias moved to take it, Johan whipped it back, pulling pages out and tossing them into the air. Here you go! He ripped every page out of the book, and then tore the cover in half.

Tobias tried to remain strong, but a tear ran down his cheek. Then another. The laughing stopped. He knew it was in anticipation. That every boy was waiting to see if he would cry. His chest felt tight. He thought it was going to explode unless he let out the cry that was building. He remembered the day they showed a film in school about nuclear bombs. Over and over the same explosion filled the stifling classroom, the powerful mushroom cloud reflecting on the pulled shades. He remembered the wind that came after: a grainy force tore through houses and brick buildings as if they were made of cotton. When the teacher turned on the lights, she told them in a solemn voice that for protection, the government had erected a horn that would warn everyone. If they were in school when the horn sounded, the students had to crouch beneath their desks and pray for their country. Tobias had never understood how their tiny desks would protect them from such a storm.

By the time the explosion ended, he was alone. Bits of ragged paper clung to the grass, helplessly awaiting the wind's final tug.

∾

Momma was waiting on the porch when Tobias came home. He had to push his bike the entire way; the front wheel was bent and the spokes had loosened. He carried a fistful of pages from Huldah's book in his right hand, and the torn cover was clamped beneath his left armpit. Tobias stopped in front of Momma, biting the inside of his cheeks.

Momma sat on the top porch step, so she and Tobias were nearly eye level. She was the tallest woman in their community. Her covered head and plainly dressed shoulders rose like a mast in full sail during church. Johan, Huldah, and the rest of his brothers favored Momma; their young shoulders sprouting up in her shadow. Tobias and his sisters favored Poppa. Poppa was small and thin but for his belly. Poppa's head always rested on one side. Nickolas, Tobias' oldest brother, joked once that it had become that way from the number of times he had to crane his neck to kiss their mother. This was only conjecture, of course. Momma and Poppa never kissed or touched each other in their children's presence. Momma's voice matched her size. Her children claimed they could hear her voice by a half a mile. Her voice thundered in song, a broad alto that struck each note decisively. Tobias had often heard Poppa speak about their people being *die Stillen im Lande*—the quiet in the land. He had decided a long time ago that Momma was not really one of the community, since he had never known her to be quiet.

Where have you been? Her voice rolled out and wrapped around Tobias' ears.

In town.

Did you clean the church?

Yes, ma'm.

So if I walk there right now I won't find a speck of dust?

Yes, ma'm.

Where did you get those papers?

Tobias was too tired to lie: It was a book. One of Huldah's books.

You were at Huldah's house?

Yes, ma'm.

Why did you go to Huldah's house?

Because I saw her at the church and she said I could come.

You know she's shunned. We are not to speak or think of her.

Yes.

So why did you go to her house?

Because she's my sister.

Momma rose and took a step towards Tobias. He backed up; his feet tripped on a crack in the sidewalk and he fell backwards. He let the pages fly from his fingertips. But the red book cover, the cover Huldah had called *knaul'root*, stayed in place.

She is nothing to us, Momma said evenly. The church has said so.

He opened his eyes and managed to look at Momma, who was looking at the ground. Tobias wanted to hit her, to force back those words she had spat out into the evening air. He wondered what he should do. He couldn't decide on anything else, so he dropped the cover in front of Momma.

Here. Huldah said it's *knaul'root*.

Momma didn't move. Tobias picked up his bike and went into the shed. He sat on an oil can and waited for night to come. Just as true darkness had fallen, he heard Momma's step on the porch, then on the sidewalk, then on the gravel. He heard her open the car door. He waited until the growl of the engine was far away down the driveway before he emerged. The pages that had littered the yard, the remnants of the book cover were gone. He knew where Momma had gone.

Tobias began to run towards Ulysses.

∾

When Tobias and Johan were older and on the Gnadenfeld College cross-country team, they would run together almost daily, shouting derisive comments about each other's skills, or singing old German hymns:

Ein' feste Burg ist unser Gott,
Ein gute Wehr und Waffen;
Er hilft uns frei aus aller Not,
Die uns jetzt hat betroffen.
Der alt' böse Feind,
Mit Ernst er's jetzt meint,
Gross' Macht und viel List
Sein' grausam' Ruestung ist,
Auf Erd' ist nicht seingleichen.

Whoever dropped out of the song first from lack of breath had to buy the pop at the end of the run. They would sit on the bench outside the IGA, layered in sweat. Their last run together was on an August day, one day before Tobias was going to announce his decision to leave Gnadenfeld and go to the state college. He hadn't told anyone yet, least of all Johan. They never spoke of anything beyond going on a run, or farm work, or girls. Anything else was beyond the bounds of their relationship.

Johan finished his pop in four solid gulps, let out a groan that ended in a burp, and stood. He pulled off his stained shirt and used it to wipe his face. I think Merv will think we're ready when school starts, don't you? he said to the coffee shop across the street.

Yeah. I guess so.

Johan turned, smirking. Come on, Toby, that's our best time, for either of us—even if you lost.

Tobias didn't answer, but sipped his pop, keeping his eyes on the ground.

Toby, what's eating you anyways? Did I say something? If I did, I'm sorry.

Johan was always sorry in the aftermath of anything he'd done. Tobias was sure he meant all the apologies he'd gotten from his twin. He always apologized profusely, and Tobias forgave him, just like he had always forgiven him before. The only problem was that Johan was incapable of remembering his sins the next day.

You didn't do or say anything. It's me who's done something.

What'd you do, knock a girl up?

No danger of that, unless I slept through it.

Johan's face split into a grin. That's a good one. I'll have to remember that.

I'm not going to Gnadenfeld anymore.

You're joking. Johan's grin stayed on his face, but his eyes were shocked. Why the hell not?

I'm going to Kansas State. I've made all the arrangements.

But Momma and Poppa paid the tuition already!

I know. But I talked to the registrar last week. I'm leaving Wednesday.

Why are you doing this?

Because I need to. I can't stay here anymore. I need to go somewhere else.

What's wrong with Ulysses?

Nothing. I want to be a vet. They've got a good program there.

Good grief, they've got a good vo-tech school in Garden City. You could go there after school's done.

No. I'm sorry. I just can't do it.

I still don't understand why. Why are you all leaving me? Why do I have to stay?

Tobias and Johan's brothers and sisters had left the farm for their own lives when the twins were still young. It had always been assumed that Tobias and Johan would take the farm. Even Tobias had thought it was inevitable for most of his life.

You don't have to stay. You can leave. But you'll have to leave on your own.

He knew Johan would never leave; unlike the rest of them, he was tied to the land. When they were very young, Momma said the two of them tried to eat dirt. She said Tobias had spit it out in disgust immediately, but Johan chewed it thoughtfully before swallowing. Johan had ingested the land like none of them did.

Tobias poured the rest of the pop on the cement. It fizzled and ran down to the cracks in the sidewalk. He looked at the bottom of the bottle. A few stray bubbles trapped air huddled inside the bottom. He wondered how old the air was within those glass houses; how many times their world had been filled and emptied by anonymous beings who could destroy their habitat with a slip of gravity. It was a little like being God of a world that lay too far away to really see.

~

As he ran after Momma, he mapped in his head the quickest way to get to Ulysses without being seen. He stumbled through an empty pasture, slipped past the remains of a burned-out barn, and then came upon the road.

Tobias' heart was thumping so hard he felt his body lurch with each beat. He hurried off the main road once he reached town and headed for the railroad tracks. He came up behind Huldah's house through the alley, where Momma's car was parked. Her backyard had an unbelievably tall fence. All the climbable trees lay within; Tobias was afraid of heights, anyway. He stepped towards the fence and laid both hands on it. The heat of the day still reverberated through the boards. He imagined he was blind and began to brush the wood lightly, hoping to find his own Braille. He found what he was looking for: a knothole nearly eye-level. Cupping his hands around his right eye, he looked into Huldah's yard.

With the light from the streetlamp in front of her house mostly blocked, Tobias could only see patches of the yard. The center was bare; the corners were shadowed with hedges and trees; a clothesline with sheets still hung. Lights burned faintly inside Huldah's house, and he thought he could see the silhouettes of two people.

Herein, a Voice growled.

Tobias leaned harder against the fence. Huldah? he whispered.

Herein.

Momma?

Herein! The Voice's power shook the fence.

Where is Momma? I want to see Momma.

The voice exhaled a *poof!* of hot breath. Your momma's inside.

Who are you?

Nora. Herein—come in!

What are you doing in Huldah's yard?

I live here.

A woman lives in Huldah's house?

Nora chuckled: I am no woman.

How do I get in?

There's a gate. A gate in the front. Nora's voice exhaled again, and was gone.

Tobias scrambled through the bushes to the front of the house, but he found only more fence. He wanted to pound against the wood, force this Voice to let him into the sanctuary. But then he heard his momma's voice.

He crept towards the open window. Through the screen, he could see her back to him. Huldah sat next to her, her hair like a copper cape. Momma's hair was undone as well; her graying black hair swirled down, looking lost, unsure of what to do with its freedom. He could see pages piled in front of them; the dusty red cover of *The*

Secret Garden lay beside his momma and sister.

They were speaking a mixture of German and English, the voices low with the German, letting the deep consonants hold the higher English notes to the ground. Tobias tried to decipher the mix, but he couldn't understand, until his momma spoke clearly in English: Now. Read.

When Mary Lennox was sent to—Momma, what is this?

Misselthwaite Manor—I don't know if I'm saying that right. English is *ubergeschnappt*. Just remember that.

Huldah and Momma both laughed high and light as they bent over the pages again. Tobias had never heard Momma laugh like that.

Herein, Nora's voice said in Tobias' ear.

Tobias kept his eyes on Momma and Huldah. I can't find the gate!

Look again.

This time he found the gate with a sweep of his hand. He carefully lifted the latch and let himself in. Huldah's yard was several degrees cooler than the rest of the world. The streetlamp was hazed by a thin cloak of mesh that stretched among the branches of the trees. A few birds stirred at Tobias' presence. A waddling dog sniffed his feet and sat on them.

Where are you? he said, ignoring the dog.

Lie down, Nora's voice commanded.

Tobias couldn't decide where she was, because her voice echoed on all sides.

Look above you.

The grass was unlike any Tobias had experienced. It nestled

around his neck and supported his head. It was not damp yet; like the wood of the fence, the heat of the day lingered in its roots. The dog flopped by his side, and nudged his hand until Tobias began scratching its ears.

What do you see?

The sky.

What else?

Stars.

Stars are made up of billions, maybe more, of bits of gas. Can you see that?

No.

No. Does that mean the stars aren't important?

No.

No. Think about your skin—think about that scar.

Hot anger filled Tobias' chest.

Skin is made up of millions of bits of cells. Can you see them?

Tobias brushed the scar beneath his shirt. Strange shockwaves pulsed through his body unlike anything he had felt before. It hurt, but it was a pain he couldn't describe. A pain that he didn't want to avoid.

They're important, but you can't see them. That's the way God sees us.

God sees everything.

Yes. But he doesn't see you, or me, or anyone in the singular. It doesn't mean he doesn't care. He just doesn't see.

That can't be true!

Tobias pushed the dog away and jumped up, shaking his fist at the shadows. A loneliness he had never felt before crept in between his shoulder blades. Nothing Johan had ever done created this lonely fear. The sky was dark with stars. He tried to see them each on their own, see each pulse of light individually, but he couldn't.

Isaiah once said, *Who hath measured the waters in the hollow of his hand, and meted out heaven with the span, and comprehended the dust of the earth in a measure?* Nora's voice was booming inside his head until he felt each hair within his ears tremble at her breath's power. *Behold, the nations are as a drop in the bucket, and are counted as the small dust of the balance.*

Tobias' ears rang. He tried to enter in the silence that had been his before, but he couldn't reach it anymore. Nora's voice had pressed itself in each cell and laid her footprint: *It is he that sitteth upon the circle of the earth, and the inhabitants thereof are as grasshoppers; that stretcheth out the heavens as a curtain, and spreadeth them out as a tent to dwell in.*

That's why I'm with Huldah. That's why I was with your momma long ago. That's why I'll go to someone else, when the time comes. Some people need a little more attention—attention God can't spare.

Why can't you protect me? Why won't you pay attention to me? Tobias wailed. His voice was enveloped by the arms of the trees, by the cloth in the air.

I'm sorry, Tobias. You'll have to do it alone.

Tobias swirled on his axis and shouted into the prison of air. He pulled leaves from the trees and threw them to the ground. He stumbled over the waddling dog and slammed into the grass that now prickled his skin like steel wool. Tobias wondered why no one had decided to hold him against their chest in love. Johan hadn't, Momma hadn't, and now the great voice called Nora didn't want the job, either. As he lay in the grass, he heard heavy feet tread towards him and stop. The breath of Nora blew like a hot wind from the south before a storm. Tobias forced himself to stay still beneath such power. Nora settled next to him and released a fountain of purrs that shook the earth. Tobias couldn't stay awake.

When he woke up, he was alone. He called for Nora, for Huldah, for Momma, but no one replied. Tobias found the gate and slammed it shut. Tobias did what he knew he could do with ease: run.

Poppa was on the phone, shouting: Where is my son? Why haven't you started looking for my son? He is young and small! Don't you even care where he is? Several cars were parked around the yard. Every light in the house burned. Shadows moved behind the pulled shades. The sun had just reached the horizon, pushing the purple night away with its arms.

Momma was seated on the front porch. When she saw Tobias, she stood, and then sat down again.

He saw his mother as if it was the first time. She was one of the chosen. She had been like the one piece that remained whole when the blue glass was broken; a circle of clear earth that might have just been a glimmer in God's eyes, but was the whole world for the Voice that had chosen her.

Where have you been?

I've been running.

All night? Where did you go?

I was looking for you.

Well, here I am. Right here.

No, you weren't then. You were at Huldah's house.

I was not!

You read with Huldah. You laughed with her.

Momma stood and towered over Tobias like she always would. She leaned towards his left ear that still felt Nora's voice. You saw nothing! she whispered, her hand taking hold of his shirt, her fingers brushing the circle on his chest. Tobias lurched forward in the pain that stroked his body. He took a breath he thought would never end.

I met Nora, he said when he exhaled.

Now Momma took a breath. She dropped his shirt and peered into his eyes. Nora? she said. How do you know that name?

Tobias found himself very tired. It's a secret, he said. Mine. Not yours anymore.

∾

The day after his father was buried, Tobias found his mother burning her journals in the trash barrel behind the house. She had piles of other things waiting for the flames: several yellowed head coverings, photographs, a box of old letters. He walked up to her, collecting his thoughts, wondering how he should deal with this; how long it would take before he could climb into his car and disappear to the other world he'd created in South Dakota when he'd left Ulysses. Although he'd often seen her journals lying among her sewing or knitting, he'd never seen the pictures. He bent to pick up one of the photographs. He immediately recognized his mother as a young woman, but he didn't know the pregnant woman beside her.

Who is this, Momma?

Momma did not turn. She continued to rip the aged notebooks that held her entire life: some of them had childish scrawls, others showed her mature handwriting. Nora, she said.

Nora? Tobias tried to keep his voice level.

She was your father's sister. She passed away when we were young.

You were close, then?

You could say that.

Finished with the journals, she reached for the box of letters. She dropped them into the corroded barrel one at a time. Tobias wanted to grab her hand, but forced himself into stillness. Why are you doing this, Momma?

I'm just getting ready, is all.

Getting ready for what?

Dying.

Tobias laughed. Momma, you aren't dying anytime soon. You're healthier than any of your kids!

Don't be silly. I realized when I got your father's suit out for burial that I don't want certain things to be lying around for you boys and the girls to find when I'm safely in the dirt.

The letters were gone. She reached for the photographs, including the one Tobias held. Without even looking, she tossed them into the fire. For a half a second, he saw his momma's face wreathed in smoke. She was smiling. Momma had never smiled for a single photograph during his childhood. As the flame licked Nora's face away, he saw her hand nearly curled around Momma's waist. Tobias cousld see the movement in her fingers, as though she had done it in the camera's flash; they were lilted just enough for him to see light between her touch and Momma's waist, like a pianist about to stroke the keys for the first time.

Priscilla's Tiger

1968

That summer a rumor went around the neighborhood. The rumor said that Miss Priscilla had a white tiger in her backyard. Ellen Groening doubted it immediately.

Ellen, believe me. I *swear* it's true. Brice saw it yesterday through her fence, Jacob Myers said, proudly saying the banned s-word. I *swear* it on my grandmomma's dentures.

She has a wood fence, Ellen said. How did he see through a wood fence?

Through a knothole, of course, Jacob said slowly, as if she wouldn't understand.

Miss Priscilla was a mystery to the kids who lived in the neighborhood surrounding her little gray house. Even though everyone *knew* she was Huldah Harder, she was called Miss Priscilla by anyone under fifteen for reasons long forgotten. She wore plain dress like the Mennonite women outside of Ulysses, but she didn't wear the usual head covering—she let her hair flow down her back. Since she was, by the definition of the neighborhood, an *old lady*, Ellen and her friends found this freedom with hair weird and exciting. All women in Ulysses wore their hair in sensible bobs; to have hair flow after the age of thirty was unheard of. More than once Ellen looked at her hair with sadness, knowing its time of freedom neared an end.

But you didn't see it yourself, Ellen said.

No, Jacob admitted slowly, ashamed at his lack of courage. But I did hear a growl once. That could have been a tiger.

I'm telling my dad, Megan Richert said. He'll shoot it. Tigers don't belong here.

Don't you dare tell your dad, Ellen insisted. I want to see it first. Then we'll decide what to do.

The main problem with looking into Miss Priscilla's yard was that she didn't have a predictable schedule—she could be seen any time of the day prowling the streets. Miss Priscilla was notorious for weeding other people's gardens without permission, harvesting their tiny stands of corn and leaving the ears on back porches, gathering loose crab apples and dumping them on her compost heap just outside of her fence. After a thunderstorm, she put on her galoshes and went through the neighborhood, picking up branches and piling them neatly at the curb for the garbage man. Ellen once asked her Aunt Delores about this behavior, and the fact that no one seemed disturbed by it.

She's always done it, Aunt Delores said as she dried the dishes. She isn't hurting anyone—I'm kinda hoping she comes our way before I have to go and finish off the string beans.

Then there was the fence itself. It was higher than most and had gauzy white netting draped on top of her back yard, for it was said that Miss Priscilla rescued injured birds and kept them in her yard while they healed. Once Macy Brier and Ellen were about to put a struggling robin out of its misery with a trowel when Miss Priscilla came out of nowhere, hissing: *Raus, raus*, don't hurt that bird! She put it in her apron and disappeared around the corner with it, mumbling words of encouragement in the *Plautdietsch* Ellen's grandmomma had used.

So, what're we gonna do? Jacob asked.

We could break open the gate, Ellen suggested.

Our parents would be *pissed* off, Macy said, enjoying the ever-forbidden *p*-word.

Or we could spy on her, Ellen said. Try to get to know her habits, and then when she's gone, we'll get a ladder and look inside her yard.

That might take forever! You know she doesn't do anything at the same time.

Everyone has habits. We just need to follow her close, Ellen said, flipping her doomed hair over her shoulder. We've got plenty of time. Do you think she can take a tiger out just like that?

~

Ellen was all too aware of her habits. They included getting her father out of bed and making breakfast with everything in place before he set foot in the kitchen. By the time Ellen came home from school, Aunt Delores was in the kitchen, baking bread or a pie. Ellen would hang around to watch Aunt Delores bake for a while, then excuse herself and find Macy. She'd return for supper at exactly six o'clock.

When Ellen was younger, Aunt Delores would stay far into the evening, sometimes tucking her in bed. But Aunt Delores had gotten married that spring and had her own house to care for. She was out the door as soon as supper was ready, her hair sometimes dusted with flour. Ellen and her father ate alone. Sometimes it would be an easy meal: he would tell funny stories about how much dog food Gertrude Hamm had bought one day or how Denny Eitzen showed up with a bit of bird doo in her hair. Other times he would brood over his food and barely look at Ellen.

Things were trickier that summer. He was laid off at the grain elevator and like everyone else couldn't find work that didn't require an hour's commute, which seemed to him too much of a burden to bear. He went on unemployment and hovered in the house all day in his underwear or disappeared for hours at a time. When he came home, he swayed and mumbled to himself before flopping on the couch or the floor. If Ellen spoke to him, he would stare at her as though he'd never seen her in his life. He grew thinner and had a wasted face that seemed to house a spirit that needed an escape. When he was clean, he referred to his heroin as the God of the Veins. That summer, he had found his God of the Veins again.

When Aunt Delores was around, he perked up and became the joking self he was with everyone else. But he returned to his true self the moment she left, her cotton skirts making a little breeze by the fluffed dandelions. This true self sat in the cool wash of the television with the sound off; this self cranked up the stereo and curled up on the floor; this self forgot where his shoes were, but never the Hiding Places that held his God.

On one of his clean days, he took Ellen to see a rodeo outside of town. He was jubilant each time another rider was thrown the moment they came out of the cage.

Those bulls know they're really free, he told Ellen.

How? She draped herself on his arm, watching the sunset shoot light through the clouds. They're the ones in the corral. Not the riders.

He cheered again, his voice crashing into her eardrums as a rider in white was flung from a bull's back into the muck of dirt and manure. Because, he said, his voice roughened by shouts, God tells them, whispers in their ears that they are tied down only in body, not in spirit. That their souls are free.

But bulls don't have souls. The preacher says they don't.

Baby, the Bible don't ever say nothin' about animals not having souls. Which means it's always a possibility. God let all those animals know they should go on Noah's ark, right? Now, why would he do that otherwise? He coulda just made more animals.

Ellen hadn't thought of that before. She thought about the tiger in Miss Priscilla's yard. It too had a soul then.

How can we know for sure they have souls, that we have souls? Ellen asked.

She thought of her mother, a woman she'd barely known, lying in the ground without a soul. Dead as a robin in a gutter, with nothing to rise up to the sky for.

He sat silent at her question, ignoring another rider as he flew through the air from the bull's back. Ellen wondered if he was thinking of her mother too.

Faith, he finally said in a whisper. He stroked her hair once and let his hand rest on her scabbed right knee. We just gotta have faith.

Through her curtain of hair she examined his forearm; watched the faded scars interspersed with fresh ones, like feet tracking the escaping sunlight.

∾

Your momma was *Englische* through and through, Aunt Delores told Ellen more than once. From what Ellen could gather, her mother was the exact opposite of the ideal Mennonite woman in every way. She drank, swore, shot things beyond vermin and worked at the grain elevator on the edge of town—bizarre behavior for even an *Englische* woman. It was said around Ulysses that the elevator's manager, Ken Schlehuber, had hired her as a joke when she'd applied, but she ended up being his ablest and most loyal employee.

That was where her parents met. He was hauling grain for his poppa and she was working the giant floor sieve that funneled wheat up into the white elevators that towered hundreds of feet so that a person could tell where a town was from twenty miles on a clear, dry day.

It was the first summer we had the big truck, she said. Your poppa was so proud to be driving it, showing the *Englische* what we had.

When the truck glided into the shed that sheltered the sieve he gave a nod to the fellows—*cool as a cumber*, Aunt Delores said. She knew this because she'd ridden into town with him that day. He fiddled with the throttle and the grain bed began to slide up gently on its greased axels. That was when he saw Ellen's momma. She wore low-slung jeans and a man's undershirt. She held a shovel in her right hand and leaned towards it, her grain-dusted face watching the bed reach for the ceiling.

He stared at her so long the co-op boys had to shout at him to turn the thing off. After the dump finished, Ellen's momma turned her head and caught his reddened face in his side-mirror. Aunt Delores said she wasn't sure, her angle of sight wasn't very good, but she thought she winked at him.

Whatever it was, it distracted him enough that he gunned the motor and ran smack into the back of somebody's jalopy.

Ellen's father became *Englische* when they married. Her momma said she'd die before she'd ever wear a bright-print cotton dress even when it was ten below, and she'd always kept her hair short, so a head covering was ridiculous. Ellen's parents are dressed alike in the only family photograph ever taken, their expressions nearly identical; unless a person looks at it carefully it isn't clear who's who.

It didn't take much for Momma to make herself the man of the house. He had a falling out with his poppa when he left the Mennonite church and quit the farm. He couldn't hold a steady job. Ken Schlehuber only gave him a job after her momma died. Ken always ignored his failures until the local milk processing plant closed and business at the co-op went slack. Though her father wasn't the only one laid off, he was the first.

It wasn't until the summer the white tiger appeared that Ellen realized for the first time why Ken Schlehuber had kept him on for as long as he had: guilt over her momma's death.

Ellen was eight the summer her momma went to the top of Elevator Three to gather samples for a buyer. That afternoon Elevator Three had been nearly cleared of grain. She had been told it was Elevator Two that had been emptied.

The thing about wheat is that it forms a shell over the rest of the load. Someone is supposed to go and shatter the crust before the grain is siphoned away. But no one did. She walked right onto the false ground and broke through.

Ellen often wondered what she thought in that moment of weightlessness. If she was scared, or just shocked. If she imagined herself a bird searching for an upward draft that could carry her away before gravity grasped at her ankles and pulled.

A scraggly elm in Harold Diener's backyard stood across the alley from Miss Priscilla's yard, and was a comfortable perch for the neighborhood kids to witness her comings and goings. No one used their front doors in Ulysses, so Ellen knew she'd see her whenever she left the house. Everyone in town used their back doors as they went about their day; even friends dropping by used them. A front door was only used on more formal occasions, like a graduation party or a meal after a funeral.

The others lost interest after half a morning and headed to the public swimming pool. Talk about tigers on the iron-hot playground didn't matter when you could spend the day in blue water with a candy stand nearby. Macy was the last loyal hunter, but even he begged off the next afternoon, blatantly wearing his trunks; a worn beach towel snaked around the handlebars of his bike.

Ellen had a new idea, so his abandonment meant little to her. The plan was this: to pick the lock on Miss Priscilla's gate. The idea came to her the day before when her father was recounting a story to Aunt Delores about how he'd picked the lock of Obediah Fast's garage and took his brand-new Chevy for a joy ride.

And how old were you then? Aunt Delores asked dryly.

Fourteen or fifteen or so. You know me, Del. I was deep into *rum springa* at the time.

We don't do that foolishness in our community. Never have. It's ridiculous how those Amish let their kids run heckish all over creation.

Ellen stared at Aunt Delores. She had never heard her say anything close to the *h*-word before.

Well, okay. In my head it was there, though, he said.

So, what you're saying is you're still in *rum springa*?

How'd you learn to do it? Ellen asked.

What, how to pick a lock? I can't remember. I'd been doing it so long by then. Why do you ask?

Could you teach me?

Well, I don't know if you should be asking those questions when Del is around, he whispered.

Aunt Delores shook her head and murmured: I may as well be talking to the wall.

I think that means permission granted, he said.

Aunt Delores did hang around for the lesson, though. By the time it ended, she could do it as well as Ellen.

See, Aunt Delores whispered later, stroking Ellen's hair. Just keep him happy like that, and things'll get better.

Ellen wanted to believe her, to believe that her father would abandon his God for good and be like all the other men she saw. The men she saw had arms that were browned into firm leather; calloused hands; muscles that could swing a girl up without a pause; hair that hid beneath straw hats or baseball caps every day but Sunday. But Ellen figured she'd stay on her search for Miss Priscilla's tiger in case that didn't work out. She had decided that morning that anyone who kept a tiger *and* survived was a person who would protect her like her father never had. That a woman who rescued half-dead birds would take in the daughter of a drug addict.

That afternoon, Ellen decided it was time. She climbed as high as she could go up the tree and waited. Half an hour later, Miss Priscilla emerged, trundling a little wooden wagon. She wore her hair completely free, the strands of leftover bronze outshining the whitening gray that surrounded it. As soon as she exited the alley onto Myrtle Street, Ellen climbed down and dashed to Miss Priscilla's gate. She had never been this close to her yard before, and felt a little out of breath as she touched the sun-brushed boards, resting her cheek against the grain. Ellen thought that this must be the way her ancestors felt when the boat docked in New York. A kind of modern Holy Land, this New World.

But it had been a myth. Great-Grandmomma Groening had told her the women wept when they arrived by train and saw the place they would be forced to call home. They had left their lush Ukrainian fields and their Milk River for a windswept desert.

Ellen wondered if the tiger in Miss Priscilla's backyard was a myth. A story meant to pull an ignorant fool to a dusty alley.

She examined the lock. It was a cheap drugstore brand, which was disappointing. She was sure she could crack it, but it seemed too ordinary a lock to house a magnificent creature. Ellen pulled out her tools—a large paper clip and broken half of a pair of tweezers—and fiddled with it for a few minutes; each second that drew away time making her more and more anxious. She could hear movement inside: a dog's quiet bark, the bleat of a goat. Then there was a click! and Ellen's fingers pulled the shank free.

Her hands were shaking. She grabbed hold of her left wrist and stood for a moment to feel the pulse, then switched hands. Ellen breathed deep and looked at the lock; considered closing it again. What if there was no tiger? What if there was? She was not afraid of the tiger itself—she was afraid of what she would do next, after she had made the discovery.

Herein, said a gruff voice.

Ellen looked around, and saw no one.

Herein. This time it sounded a little nearer. It was coming from the other side of the fence.

Miss Priscilla?

Nein. Mir ist es. The Voice was impatient. Don't you speak German?

No.

Well, okay then. Open the door, then, the Voice commanded.

Who are you?

You won't believe it.

I would, too!

Ellen sounded as impatient as the Voice.

The Voice chuckled, and said, a little less annoyed: Trust me on this.

Ellen slowly pushed the lock from the gate's teeth and swung it open. She slipped in and pulled it shut. The sun had a speckled quality from the gauze above. The fabric rose and fell on the fingers of the wind that caressed its folds. The air had dropped ten degrees. Swirls of the mischievous breeze caught each individual hair on Ellen's arms and wound themselves up and down each muscle.

Something brushed against her. Ellen held her breath and looked down to see a small, grinning goat bumping its head against her thighs and glancing up to see the reaction.

Are you the Voice? she whispered. The goat bumped her legs again and skipped a few feet away with a bleat. Birds called from their perches in the trees, and squirrels ran around the branches, searching for the crop that would sustain them in the winter. Two cats were settled in the shade, flipping their tails, eyes only half open. A mountain of puppies gathered around their mother, who had spread her body wide on the back porch.

Ellen saw no tiger.

Are you here, Voice?

Oh, she's here, a different voice said. She's resting from the day.

Miss Priscilla had appeared by Ellen's side, the little wagon filled with bags of groceries. She cradled a gallon jar of milk with one arm. Instinctively, Ellen reached for the milk. The hand that held it was cool and thin; veins and spots of age settled on the top. Her hair swirled over her left shoulder.

So, what do you think of my *Arche Noah*?

Arche Noah?

An ark—Noah's Ark.

Arche Noah. Ellen pronounced the words carefully, letting her tongue get used to the vibrations.

Exactly. Bring the milk inside.

Inside was cool and silent except for the gentle tap of a clock. Miss Priscilla left the wagon in the mud room and set the groceries down with a thump! The refrigerator's over there, she said, motioning with her head. The refrigerator was covered in scraps of paper that had tiny drawings of food and had their names in German and English underneath, written in block letters that were smudged with eraser marks.

Oh, wait. Keep it out. You want some cookies? I bought some at the store, she said, pulling a box of chocolate chip cookies with a smirking cow on the front.

Ellen was a little disappointed that she hadn't a stash of homemade cookies like Aunt Delores. She expected *Englische* Macy's mom doing such a thing, but not a woman in plain dress.

They sat at the kitchen table and ate the cookies in silence, the groceries only half put away. Ellen noticed she had a loaf of bread sitting beside a jar of generic grape jelly. She couldn't hold back her surprise: You don't bake your own?

I used to, long ago, Miss Priscilla said, once she'd wiped milk from her lip. But that was in another lifetime. That's dead to me now.

Ellen noticed how her careful words were somewhat stunted by her voice. It was low and gravelly, as though she had a mouthful of candy stuck in the back of her mouth. Her eyes were closer together than most people's, and her face seemed slightly squished together.

Miss Priscilla, do you really have a tiger here?

A slow smile spread across her lips. Who did you think was talking to you just then?

But tigers can't talk.

Have you ever seen a tiger before?

No, just in pictures.

Then you have no proof.

No one's ever said it on television.

Of course not. They're very choosy, the tigers. And the people they do talk to keep it a secret to protect them—and to keep people from thinking they're crazy.

Miss Priscilla sipped her milk and looked at Ellen. You've obviously been chosen.

But it's never met me!

Yes she has. She knew you've been in the tree longer than anyone else. She knows how hopeful you are.

Did you know I was there? You never said anything to me.

I figured you'd let yourself come out when you wanted to.

I'm too old to believe this, Ellen said, placing my cookie down firmly. You're too old to believe this.

You're right. She stood up. But old people are supposed to be a little *fe'rekjt*—crazy. And people always said I was slow. She reached inside a cupboard and took out a small key dangling on a thin chain.

Here, she said, putting it on the table. Come back anytime—evening's best to meet her. She rests during the day.

Part of Ellen wanted to snatch the key and run out the door, but instead she said: Why do you keep all these animals here—in this uh, ark?

I don't keep them. They've found me. I'm just holding them until they are ready to leave.

How did a tiger find you all the way out here? She's supposed to be in Africa.

They've always been here. There used to be thousands, millions of years before.

What happened to them?

I don't know. She's never told me. I think it's difficult for her to remember.

She's not that old. No one can be that old.

Well, she's that old.

How did she find you?

A long time ago I needed someone to save me.

From what?

When I was young, the church shunned me.

Why?

Miss Priscilla touched her hair and let her fingers flow down as though they were strands of hair as well. I wouldn't cover my head, she said. So they shunned me.

What did you do?

My family would've kept me, but they wouldn't speak until I brought my hair close to my head and pinned it away. So I came here—she spread her arms out wide.

You came alone then.

No. Nora was waiting for me at the door.

That's the tiger's name?

She was waiting and kept me from being alone. She saved me from this empty house and helped me build it on the inside to make it my own.

～

When Ellen returned from Miss Priscilla's, she saw the pickup was missing. He had gone to find his God. She stared at the ruts he'd made in their lawn one rainy afternoon when his truck careened off the driveway and came to rest against their oak tree. His bumper had bit deep into the oak; it took more than a tug to pull it free from its flesh.

Ellen wondered if grass and trees could feel pain. She wondered if the faint *swish!* of the grass and the rub of the oak's branches were really groans of agony. She sat in the ruts and felt the wounded ground swell up around her. The grass nestled up against her legs. The roots of the oak wrapped Ellen in its bristled arms; its calloused fingers tapped her cheeks and flicked the tears away.

Ellen realized he had always just been *father*. She'd never called him poppa or dad or daddy. Such names were reserved for a distinct zone of intimacy; an intimacy they'd never shared. One called a man with leathered muscles and a white smile on a sunburned face poppa. One never called a man with drug-tracked bones poppa. His heart strayed forever to a God in an unknown Heaven.

Ellen lay among the grass and trees and watched the faint blue sky melt towards evening. Finally she smeared the snot off her nose, sat up, ran to the front door and grabbed the doorknob with both hands. The door groaned from neglect and whipped stale air over her face. Ellen grabbed a paper bag and stuffed clothes and a hairbrush inside, and stashed it beneath the front porch. The front door remained open as though yawning from sleep.

Ellen realized that Aunt Delores hadn't come to start supper. Then she remembered it was Sunday. On Sundays Ellen was the cook, but most of it went uneaten, either because he was in withdrawal and declared the food *inedible as shit* or he had gone to his own service by the lake.

It was time to call Aunt Delores. Uncle Philip would usually come and they'd drive to the lake together until they found her father slumped over his steering wheel or muttering to the gravel beside the truck. Uncle Philip would drag him to his car after he cleaned off any blood or vomit. She'd sit in the back with him, cradling his head and checking his breathing.

Ellen didn't call this time. Instead she got on her bike and pedaled the three miles west to the lake, ignoring the streamed sunlight that tried to push her eyelids shut and rode the length of the three sections of road blindly.

She found him after an hour of searching. He was in a cove he usually avoided, because the sand shimmered invitingly in the August heat and drew dozens of people. He used to have the decency to hide his sessions in private. This no longer came to him as a thought. He lay half in the water, arms flung out as if he was doing the back stroke as he muttered to himself.

Ellen found the syringe nearly buried in the sand, the piece of dirty rubber flung a few feet away. The little lakeside cabins' lights had begun to twinkle. She dragged his devastated body that was too light beside the truck and turned him on his side. Ellen began to pour sand over him until his entire body except his head was immersed. By the time she finished the darkness was complete; no one remained on the beach. She crawled into the cab and slept.

~

The sweep of a flashlight woke Ellen; blue-red-blue bathed the roof of cab with abrupt strokes of light.

What's going on, honey? a man said when she rolled down the window.

Waiting for my father to wake up. He's passed out.

From drink?

No, from this. She pointed to the syringe she had placed on the dashboard.

Why didn't you get someone?

I figured he'd be okay. This has happened before.

Did you bury him in the sand?

Yeah.

Why'd you go and do that?

To keep him warm, of course.

You know, your daddy's a nice man.

Yeah?

He's a nice man. I'm going to have to arrest him though. It's illegal to do this. I'm sorry.

It's okay, Ellen said flippantly. He deserves it.

She couldn't see his face, but she imagined his shock at her cold answer. Ellen was glad.

~

Uncle Philip brought her father home from the county jail two days later since his truck had been impounded. He didn't even look up when he walked into the house; he headed for his bedroom. His profile was all nose and cheekbones. Uncle Philip laid a rectangle of pink paper on the kitchen table and set the sugar bowl on top, as if he was afraid a wandering wind would blow it away. His summons, he said. He'll be charged, will have to make a plea—his lawyer suggests he pleads guilty.

I know, Ellen said.

Del wonders if you'd like to come have dinner at our place tonight, maybe stay with us some more.

Ellen knew she should say yes, because for the past two days she had been combing the house, digging out each Hiding Place and sprinkling the garden with what she found.

No, Ellen said. I need to stay with him.

Uncle Philip looked like he wanted to say something. He barely knew Ellen's father beyond what Aunt Delores told him. He had always been Mennonite, out in the world yet hidden from view. He only knew her father had left that crawl space in life to marry a woman who wore jeans and cowboy boots like any man.

Ellen's father had once said as he held his forearm against his heart, his eyes glazing over with God, that Uncle Phillip's branch of Mennonites were too weak to live without cars and electricity like the Amish; too frightened of the outside to relinquish their cotton print dresses and carefully molded beards.

He emerged from his bedroom that evening. He sat down on the couch across from Ellen. The sheets had creased the skin of his face.

Baby, he said. Baby, I'm sorry.

Ellen had heard this before. It was as if they were about to follow an overused script: he apologized, she quieted his guilt with an *It's all right, I know you didn't mean it; we'll get through this together.* He would get better, for a time. Some times were longer than others. But more and more he looked to his God for Salvation. This God held him closely to his chest, looking over his greasy curled hair at her, smiling that benevolent smile Ellen had come to hate.

Most of Ellen's body wanted to throw itself in his arms, smooth out those wrinkles that were too long on his young face. She wanted to believe him. But she had seen his face as she poured sand over his body. That face held bliss Ellen would never feel; it reflected the bliss of a God she couldn't reach; it reflected a God who only knew victory.

Yeah? she said.

He stared at Ellen. She had thrown the script beyond his grasp.

Don't you hear? I'm going to be a real live poppa and make all of this go away and we'll forget about all this shit.

I won't believe you until you prove it.

I will prove it. Right now I'll prove it. He rose from the couch and headed to the Hiding Places. Ellen sat in her momma's reading chair and waited. Her favorite dim memory of Momma was listening to her read; Ellen's breasts, feeling Momma's voice deep in her body, the thump thump thump of her heart. Ellen knew she was ignoring the other memories: Momma's pursed lips as she pumped God into his veins, Momma's wild eyes as she held Ellen's arm so tight it bruised and she had to wear long sleeves for a week when she'd blabbed a story to Macy, who'd told his mother, who'd called the police. Ellen needed this memory for now, as she listened to her father throw shoes out of his closet and pat down each cupboard space. He swirled around the tiny living room where Ellen waited. As if he was saving the nexus of his universe for last. He panted his way to the doorframe and watched Ellen watch him.

Where is it?

It's gone, she said evenly. I threw it out.

Why'd you go and do that?

Ellen remembered the police officer asking the same question: *Why'd you go and do that?*

Because you're not the man you want to be, she said.

His eyes opened and looked as if he'd never seen her before. Wh'the hell you know about men, he hissed. You haven't been in the world long enough. All you know is your protected little house, your damn tree-hugging games.

I know men who don't shove that *shit* up their arms, Ellen said, feeling proud to say such a word for the first time. Who don't roll down their sleeves every time a neighbor comes so you can hide the scars.

He almost hit her then. She wanted him to. Then she'd have proof of what went on behind the ever-closed front door. Ellen wanted him to hit her and leave a mark so that she could wait for Aunt Delores and calmly show her the evidence she'd helped hide. She knew he wanted to. She saw his muscles flex from shoulder to fingers that curled so his yellowed nails cut his palm. But he knew what would happen next. He would no longer be a pitiful man, stunted by his wife's death, but an arm that struck his daughter with its yellowed nails. His thin, nearly imaginary cover would be blown. They both watched as he uncurled his fingers and loosened his arm muscle by muscle. He straightened his back and walked out the front door. The heels of his boots crunched through the brittle grass towards his missing truck and stopped.

Ellen opened the screen door. Miss Priscilla loomed behind our fragile oak. She cradled a trowel and a bag of mulch. Her white-bronze hair shifted under the speckled afternoon light. She did not look at Ellen, but kept her eyes trained on Ellen's father.

Evening. Miss Priscilla's voice sauntered over the grass and circled him lazily.

Evening, ma'am, he answered.

Everything okay?

His back shrank away from Miss Priscilla's stare. He dropped his head to study his shaking hands. Certainly, he finally said. Certainly is.

A small gate Ellen had never noticed before swung open, and a flash of white whisked through the bushes and disappeared into her shadow. She could feel Nora's warm breath on the back of her legs, her muscled coat searching for the caress of Ellen's fingertips.

Shaken in the Water, Part 3

1918

Agnes and Nora met every day. Most of their time together was spent with Agnes pointing at something: a tree or a flower, and Nora giving its sign. Sometimes there were things Nora didn't have a sign for. That was when she and Agnes developed their own signs. At times, they would argue over the signs. Agnes would suggest one sign, but Nora didn't like it because it was too much like another sign. Sometimes Agnes' rage would circle her eyes, and she would abruptly leave, afraid of what she might do if the rage filled her eyes completely. When a sign was finally decided on, however, she would forget the arguments. Instead she would feel a touch of evil pride, for they had created a stroke of language that no one else on earth knew. She wondered if this was how Adam had felt when he named the animals.

One afternoon, Agnes began by pointing at her toes. Nora pointed at her toes and wiggled her fingers. Agnes pointed at her feet. Nora pointed at her feet, then held her fingers straight with no space between them. Agnes pointed at her ankles. Nora pointed at her ankles and held her fingers straight again, only this time with them pointing up. Then Agnes' calves. Then her knees. She hiked up her skirt and showed her thighs. Soon both girls were holding up their heavy skirts, pointing their hips and attempting to sign. Laughing, they pulled off their dresses and ran in circles in the speckled sunlight, pointing at elbows, arms, necks that stretched like slender boughs of trees.

They finally stopped, panting, arms stretching up to the sky before dropping them to their knees, their backs curved towards each other. Agnes peeked at Nora, who was peeking at her. Nora straightened her back slowly, as if each vertebra needed to be stacked precisely in its proper place. Agnes stayed still. Nora turned and touched Agnes' birthmark carefully—the touch as light as the twitch of an eyelash. Agnes felt a stream of heat run through her back and down to her belly. A spasm of warmth exploded there for less than a second before racing to her legs and shooting out of her toes. Agnes was shocked. She had never felt such fire. How had Nora's touch done that? When she finally could move her neck and look at Nora, she saw that her friend still stood over her back, her finger poised as if the moment Agnes had experienced had not yet come to pass.

1923

On the second night of their marriage, Peter went outdoors after supper and stayed there. When everyone was in bed, Agnes decided to find him. It didn't take long. He was behind the barn by the slurry pit, smoking.

Was is los? she asked.

Peter jumped and almost doused the cigarette, but she stopped him, took it between her fingers and examined it. When she was younger, she had always imagined she would feel an utter dirtiness with such a thing. But she didn't. Agnes laughed.

What are you laughing at?

You, of course. At last I've found a fault in Peter Harder I can laugh about. She sat beside him and brought the cigarette to her lips.

Careful—it isn't as easy as you'd think.

I've smoked before, she said.

They sat in silence for a moment, passing the cigarette between them. Agnes smiled up at the pale half-moon that shone weakly over the dying grasses, the drying dung. How long have you been smoking here? It's a perfect spot.

I don't remember, Peter sighed, leaning his elbows on his knees. I think I saw one of Poppa's *Englische* workers doing it one day. Later, when I got my first one, it seemed an obvious choice.

It really is. I wish I'd thought of it.

And where do you go to?

Out to the old barn on my poppa's land—what's left of it, she said, nodding towards darkness.

All the way out there? Alone?

Didn't the elders once say that barn is under God's Own Hand?

They don't say that anymore, Agnes.

I guess that's true. Agnes paused. Don't worry though. We're alwys careful.

Peter turned. We?

Nora. Me, she said softly.

What did you just say?

Sometimes we smoke together. Sin together. Sometimes I just need to sit beside her and hear her heart beating.

He stared at her as if he had never met her in his life. Nora's dead, Agnes, he said softly, sadly. Nora's dead. Then he stood, dusted off his pants and walked away.

1918

September was coming. Agnes knew she would have to trudge away to school every day. Her walk would be even longer this year because the boundaries for the school districts had widened. Her poppa's farm was now included with the school in Ulysses, which was two miles away. The country school nearby had been closed.

Two days before school started, Agnes relayed the news to Nora. Nora seemed nonplussed by her reluctance.

I have sisters who go to school. I have a brother who used to go to school. I am going to go to school too.

You are coming to school with them?

No. But Peter is going to give me lessons. I can write and read, but he's decided to teach me something new: he is going to teach me how to speak.

Agnes stiffened. Peter was only five or six years older than Agnes, but he seemed decades older with his blond scraggly beard, his red-rimmed eyes that always squinted even in shadows. Nora had told Agnes that his bedroom was filled with books in German, English, Russian, French and Latin. When he wasn't working with his poppa in the fields, he was reading one of those books or the Bible. Peter was very devout, which seemed strange to Agnes, given his knowl-edge of the outside world. She had seen how he followed the elders' every edict from the pulpit. When they called on the men to wear longer beards, he let his grow out even longer. When they called on the women to wear more modest clothing, he would harass the female members at the door of the church to drop their hems and raise their necklines.

You speak just fine, Agnes said.

But only to you, to my family. Peter says this way anyone will know what I say. He has read about a woman who was deaf and blind who learned to use her voice. He says I could learn to speak.

Agnes pulled at the grass surrounding the crooked cottonwood they sat beneath. Nora reached out and lifted her chin. Why don't you want me to speak?

I don't know.

But she did know. It was horrible and selfish, Agnes knew. She wanted Nora to herself; she didn't want her to communicate beyond the walls of their universe. It was bad enough that Nora and her sib-lings talked among themselves. Once Nora stepped out of this world that consisted of a barn, a sometime-stream and stunted trees, there was no guarantee she would ever come back.

Peter says maybe Momma and Poppa won't be so embarrassed of me if I could talk like everyone else. He says I could improve lip-reading and I could walk into any store in Ulysses and ask and get what I want. He says maybe I could go to school.

Why would you want to do that? At school you must sit and listen to an *Englische* man or woman talk and write things and expect you to know these things every few weeks.

I would like that. I would like to be with other people, even if they are *Englische*.

Agnes stood up and began to pace. No, you wouldn't like it one bit, she muttered to herself. The rage begin to cloud her eyes. She shook her head several times, trying to erase those rings of red that were brightening and roiling through the veins. You don't know what it's like—you don't want to know!

Nora stood and paced back and forth with Agnes, trying to read her lips, because Agnes' hands were tucked underneath her armpits. What are you saying? Why don't you want me to go to your school? Why don't you want me to speak?

You do not want to go there. Go to Ulysses. It is a horrible place. It smells bad and is full of *Englische* that will stare at you. They will laugh at you, she added.

Why would they laugh at me?

Because you are deaf.

But I will speak. They will hear me. I will know what they say.

Agnes thought of her classmates, both Mennonites and *Englische*, and how they laughed at her stumbling gait, her broad face. *Horsa! Horsa! Horsa!* chanted the Mennonites. Horse-face! Horse-face! Horse-face! the *Englische* hollered.

They will laugh at you.

Why?

Because your voice will never sound like theirs. Your laughter is rough and doesn't sound like a normal laugh. Even if you learn to speak perfectly, you will still not sound like me or Peter or anyone.

Agnes could no longer see. The world was red. Agnes stumbled away, plowing the air with her fingertips, trying to force the red out of the way.

1918

The following Saturday, her momma handed her a basket full of preserves and two loaves of bread. Take these to Alma Harder, was all that was said.

Agnes noted the grim look on her momma's face. She knew that Abram had loaned her poppa money to pay for the war bonds that some *Englische* men were selling for the Great War that had begun that spring. Some members of the church quietly acquiesced, others said buying war bonds went against Thou Shalt Not Kill because that money went into the hands of soldiers in the form of guns. Two days earlier, Jack Carr had walked into their house, placed his hunting rifle on their kitchen table and sat. No one spoke. They had all just sat down to breakfast; Agnes still held her youngest sister in the air above the high chair. Momma had been about to lift the lid off the pan of scrambled eggs. She gripped the cover as though she didn't notice the heat. Poppa hand clutched the butter knife. Everyone's eyes were trained on the gun's muzzle, which was on the level of Zeke's chest.

Now, Jack Carr said, how about some coffee?

I cannot give you anything, Poppa said.

I'm only asking for coffee.

I have no money. I cannot buy anything from you.

You drink coffee, yes?

Yes.

Do you put sugar into your coffee?

Sometimes.

Do you grow coffee or raise sugar cane?

No.

How do you get these things, then, if you have no money?

Poppa said nothing.

I thought so, Jack Carr said, standing. He picked up his rifle and walked out the door.

That afternoon, Poppa walked over to Abram Harder's farm. When he returned, he had a small envelope. The next morning, Poppa walked with his children to school. After he had left them at school, he continued on to Main Street. Agnes stood at the school door, watching his broad back until it disappeared in Ulysses' only bank. She marveled how everyone surrounding him walked as if nothing had happened. As if this transaction was the most common thing in the world.

And now Agnes was taking bread to Alma Harder in thanks.

As she walked up the lane, she wondered where they would hide Nora the moment she appeared on the farmyard. She'd never been to their house. When she crossed the yard, she strained to hear the shuffle of feet, hoarse whispers behind the pump house. All she heard above the always-blowing wind was the lowing of cows being shuffled into the barn. A mottled gray cat sat in front of the house, calmly licking its paws. The house itself was almost cat-like. It hid beneath the shade of several twisted elms and had a stovepipe that ran up the side of the house as if it were the tail of a shocked feline. The porch was narrow and uneven; a porch swing tapped the siding expectantly. Agnes felt peculiar warmth emanating from this house. She had a sense that the house was merely humoring the presence of its inhabitants. That it knew better things and people would be along shortly.

Agnes tiptoed up the porch steps. The screen door had a jagged hole in it. She smelled baking bread. She could hear someone talking, but she couldn't discern any words. She considered leaving the bread on the steps and running away, but she wanted to see how Nora's family would react to her being in their house.

Finally she called out, Hello?

There was a pause in conversation before someone said, Well, go see who it is!

One of Nora's sisters, Evelyn, appeared at the door. Her pale eyebrows shot up in surprise. Yeah? she said. She did not open the screen door.

My momma sent me to bring this bread and other things, Agnes said, holding up the basket. The jars of preserves softly clicked against each other.

Why? We have more than enough of bread and other things, Evelyn said.

I don't know why. My momma told me to bring it and so I have. Agnes could feel her back begin to chafe beneath the silken cocoon her Aunt Lola had created for her. Every sound was slowly amplifying in her ears. She thought she could hear the blades of grass whisper in the wind, the rustle of leaves waiting to fall to the ground, the shuffle of the cat's feet as it crossed the yard.

That's when she heard it: the sound of someone pouring air through a rusted sieve crept quietly over the howl of the wind. Agnes couldn't decide where it came from; it seemed to come from everywhere at once.

Alma Harder appeared at the door. Did you bake this? she asked, jabbing a finger at the basket.

Agnes swallowed her angry reply and simply nodded.

Do you do laundry? Scrub floors? Alma Harder asked without pauses for a reply.

Tell your momma that she doesn't need to send bread to me. Tell her you'll come every Saturday until your poppa's debt is paid.

Alma Harder turned and walked away. Evelyn stuck her tongue out at Agnes before disappearing as well.

Agnes stood very still; threads of anger weaved through her and threatened to wrap themselves around her throat. She waited for the sound she had heard to reappear. Before Alma had appeared, she had recognized Nora's voice and understood what the noise intended to be: *wasser wasser wasser water water water.*

1923

The third evening of their marriage, Agnes unpacked her hope chest. She had begun this chest when she was twelve years old. She was surprised at how sure and firm her stitches were even then. Soon the room was filled with sheets, pillowcases, quilts, underclothes and nightgowns. She laughed at the whiteness of it all. Why anyone would sew anything so white in a place where dirt was constantly in motion. She pulled out a quilt; the first one she'd made at the age of fifteen. Beneath that quilt was a small package she had always known was there. She pulled the rough string and unfolded the wrapping. Inside was a set of curtains she had made years before. She spread them out on top of the pile of sheets and pillowcases. Age had seeped into them already; the folds were a brighter shade than the rest of the fabric; the places where the curtain had been torn and mended were rivers of white thread. Agnes stared at them, transfixed by a color she hadn't seen in a long time: *knaul'root.*

1918

Though Agnes was at the Harder farm from morning to evening, for weeks she never saw Nora. At first she wondered if they kept her caged up somewhere, but as time went on, Agnes had covered every inch of their house and saw no sign of a firmly latched door. Plus,

Alma Harder never tried to prevent Agnes from any particular place; she was often sent to the far ends of the house for one thing or another. She decided that it was Nora who chose to remain hidden.

One Saturday she was finishing the laundry in the wash house when she heard a wisp of a familiar sound: Nora's laughter. Then she heard another voice, amused by the laughter.

Agnes dropped the sheet she had been ringing and tiptoed out the door. It was always twilight between the wash house and the family house. A gnarled elm stood sentry between the two, and a large trellis covered with fading morning glories flowed behind it. It occurred to Agnes that she had never seen what was behind the trellis. Since most of the morning glories had finished for the season, she saw a narrow space between the trellis and the house. She slipped through and saw a small unfinished replica of the family house. It was unpainted, and the windows had no glass. Only half of the roof had been shingled. It was the granny house, where the parents would reside after their eldest, Peter, married and filled his house with children.

Nora's laughter drew her towards the open door. She saw Nora sitting on a box in an empty room, her knees touching Peter's knees, her hand on Peter's throat and Peter's hand on her throat. He had a Bible open on his lap.

The kingdom of heaven is like to a grain of mustard seed, Peter read slowly. He looked up at Nora. She nodded. He read the phrase again: *The kingdom of heaven is like to a grain of mustard seed.* Nora closed her eyes in concentration and began to speak. Her accent was thick; Agnes wondered if she would've known what Nora was saying had she not heard Peter's voice first. Peter seemed overjoyed at what Agnes thought as a failure. *Wundaboa!* he shouted. Now, he said. Again.

Agnes had never seen Peter so animated. In church he always had an expression that puzzled her. It seemed to be part happiness, part sadness and part fear. As though he didn't know which of the three was the most appropriate. She saw none of that now.

She crouched in the shadows of the decaying morning glories and watched Peter teach the first part of that passage to his sister. She wondered whether Nora even knew what she was saying. How had he taught her what the kingdom of heaven was? Had he found her a mustard seed? Did he point to the birds outside the window to explain who would roost in the mustard seed's branches? How would he teach her the words for foot? For knee? For thigh? Would he show her the way Nora had shown Agnes?

Agnes' legs were cramping. She rose to her feet slowly. Perhaps her body caused a shadow that fell across Nora's face; perhaps Nora felt an extra breeze in the wind; perhaps Nora had caught a whiff of lye from Agnes' hands; whatever it was, she glanced Agnes' way. Her eyes skated Agnes briefly before returning to Peter's face, as though Agnes had been nothing but a moth caught in the glitter of the afternoon.

1923

On the fourth morning of their marriage, Agnes found Alma in their bedroom, staring at the *knaul'root* curtains that Agnes had hung behind the heavier, beige curtains that looked out to the sky.

Take these down, Alma said.

Whatever for?

Elder Epp is coming for *faspa* on Sunday.

No one can see them from the outside! And he's hardly going to poke through our bedroom.

Alma reached out and tore down one of the panels of red. She examined it like a specimen of a particularly disgusting nature. *Knaul'root*, she muttered to herself. She tore it in half and let the pieces slide to the floor. It does not matter. I will know they are there. That is bad enough.

1918

It seemed to Agnes that Nora was now everywhere. She could hear her recitations in the wash house, in the kitchen, in the vegetable cellar; she would feel Nora's feet as they dashed through the bedrooms, too fast to be seen; she would discover long strands of pearl-blonde hair twisted through the hairbrushes she cleaned every week, letting the hair fly out of the window and into the breeze for the nests of birds.

Then one Saturday, late in October, Agnes arrived and found no one at home. The kitchen door was unlocked, so she let herself in. She sat at the bare kitchen table, tracing the grain of wood as it swirled out from its center like a flattened cyclone. The first time she witnessed a funnel that stretched from sky to earth she had wanted to run towards it, to let the arm of God lift her up and carry her to heaven. But her poppa had held her back with both of his human arms. *Je'fäadlijch!*

Je'fäadlijch! he shouted into her ear. She did not believe him. *Läajna! Läajna!* she screamed.

Poppa had to drag her to the cellar then tie her to one of the wall beams so he could get the rest of the family down as well. When he shut the door, Agnes screamed. Her siblings joined in; her momma and poppa shouted for silence; when she would not stop, her poppa struck her on the mouth. It was then that Agnes tasted blood for the first time. She ignored the pain that had opened in her lip; instead she drew them in and sucked each drop, marveling at the texture and flavor—it was hideous and delicious and over too soon.

Agnes scanned the kitchen for something to do—if Alma Harder returned suddenly, she had to be engrossed in something. But the dishes were washed, the week's bread lay on towels, the floors had been swept and mopped.

She decided to find Nora. She started in the cellar, pushing aside the wreaths of braided onions; she moved upward to the sitting room, feeling behind the shelves of books in English, German; she paused at the door of Alma and Abram's bedroom before she entered, but there was nothing there; finally, she climbed the stairs and strode through each bedroom—even Peter's, but aside from errant balls of dust, she found nothing.

Nüach! she shouted to the empty house. Enough of this! Where are you hiding your people? Did you eat everyone?

Who are you talking to? Peter asked from outside his window. He was perched in the arms of one of the elms, a book in his hands.

Before she could stop herself, she snapped, Your house, of course.

All you Harders hide from the rest of us. Why wouldn't your house do the same?

Peter laughed the laugh she had heard when he was teaching Nora. You're probably right.

Agnes scowled at him. Where is your student?

My student?

Your sister, Nora. I guess she never told you about me.

No, but I'm not surprised, he said, his voice attempting to sound as serious as hers.

Why?

Momma's tried to get Nora to come and work with you but she won't do it.

Your momma?

Yes. I believe she said once that you were a weird sort that would be an excellent friend because you would be so glad to have one you wouldn't go telling tales. She'd wanted do to this for a while, but didn't know how to go about it.

Agnes was so shocked she forgot to be insulted. That's why I work here?

Well, that and the fact that your father borrowed money from Poppa. Very convenient.

It was then that Agnes realized she was alone with a boy—a man, really. She'd never been alone with a man other than her poppa or grandpoppas. The way even the room smelled became strong with an unknown scent beyond sweat and dirt. Agnes wondered if Peter could sense it as well.

She began to back away, but couldn't help asking: Where's your family?

Peter closed his book: *die Bibel*. One of the elders is dying. They've gone to see him. I don't know where Nora is.

Why aren't you with them? You who's so devout.

Peter smiled a sly smile, one that Agnes saw rarely in the years that followed. It told her, when she'd nearly forgotten, that he was not so pure. If Elder Wiebe dies today, Peter said carefully, they will select a new elder tomorrow. I intend to be one, so I am sick with a cold today, and don't want to endanger him further. He waved the Bible at Nora as if he was signaling something in a code much like Nora's signs.

Peter rested his Bible in the crook of the tree and crawled into his room. Agnes backed away until she stood at the door. The scent rose as he walked towards her, his hands in his pocket, his Bible outside of the walls that surrounded them. He stopped a few inches away from Agnes.

Yeah, he said softly to himself. You'll do. Momma's right. His hand slid out of his pocket and reached for her cheek, but it never made it. As if he'd just been reprimanded for a deed yet to be done, he snatched his hand back, a blush growing on his face. He stepped past Agnes, leaning away from her so as not to let his body touch hers.

The scent dissipated on his exit. Agnes stood for some time, searching for the remnant. Later, when Peter asked her to become his wife, she closed her eyes and remembered that smell she now recognized—it had been the scent of two people, not one. Hers had married his that day. This was merely a formality, a loose knot that had tightened at last.

En Follboat

1971

After he finished his noon devotionals, Peter Harder shaved his head, beard, eyebrows, chest, even his groin. It wasn't easy. He was over seventy; his flesh had weakened and drooped so that hairs were sunk within him; his hands shook constantly and his eyesight was drifting away every day.

Peter had figured shaving in the bathtub while Agnes was in town would be the simplest way to go about it, though he suspected that the men of old were more public about the whole business. It turned out to be more difficult than he had imagined. While he shaved his groin, his buttocks kept slipping on the rim of the tub until he thought to lean against the wall instead. He couldn't see the back of his head in the mirror, so he was certain broad patches of hair remained.

He was most careful about his beard, slowly moving the razor over his sunken cheeks like he'd driven harvesters: careful to slice into each row with a little overlap on the previous pass. He had never so much as trimmed his beard since he was sixteen, unlike his sons, all of whom had been clean shaven since the first hairs sprung from their chins. The only reason there was a razor in the house was because Johan still lived at home.

By the time he'd finished, not only were small drifts of hair lining the bathtub, there were stripes of blood snaking towards the drain. He hadn't counted on the mess it would make—he'd figured it would slide away, since his hair was weak and seemed translucent these past few years. Instead, hair clumped on the far side of the bathtub, on the ledges for soap and even the tile walls he had put in when he was forty-seven. He would have to clean it. He could not leave this for Agnes.

Peter had never cleaned a bathtub. He crouched in the middle of the bathroom to look for whatever Agnes cleaned with. Nothing stood under the sink besides a plunger and a wastebasket. The closet next to the bathtub held only towels and rows upon rows of homemade soap. He had seen Agnes wearing an apron with several sizes of pockets that held various cleaning supplies just the day before. The cleaning apron had been her own invention; it seemed more sensible than dragging a dingy bucket from place to place, she said the first time he'd seen her wear it. He then joked that she should put an advertisement in the local paper; every sensible housewife would throw their buckets away for good, and Jim Franz would be put out of business since half of his store was filled with cleaning containers. Agnes only stared at him and turned away. They had been married for forty years at that point, and he rarely got a laugh from her.

Peter wondered where she kept the apron. He looked at his clothes crumpled on the floor. He looked down at his body, nicked and bleeding. He didn't dare use a towel or even toilet paper to blot his cuts—Agnes kept an eye on how much was used since she kept track of his bowel movements under doctor's orders—and even a drop of blood on his dark pants would somehow be noted. Agnes had not been gone an hour, and since it was a Friday she was visiting Huldah. Johan was in the field. He was alone for at least another half hour. Peter decided to risk it and search for the apron without a stitch on.

He chuckled as he opened the bathroom door and padded downstairs into the kitchen. This was why children did this, he thought. There was something freeing about the breeze of his movement swirling around each notch and shelf of his body.

He began opening cabinet doors above and below the counters. When nothing appeared, he moved into the pantry, where he found brooms and mops, but no aprons. He began to wonder if he'd imagined its existence. But he saw no bucket filled with soaps and metallic scrubbers, either, and Agnes kept the house too clean for there not to be cleaning supplies lurking in a corner somewhere.

Then he remembered that Agnes was in the midst of a deep cleaning session, which struck the house at random times during the year. This time she was focusing on the attic. Several boxes of books, toys and clothing had been steadily raining down from the trapdoor in the ceiling. Peter decided to look there.

The rope to pull down the ladder was worn slick by the sweat of the thousands of times members of his family had grasped its throat. Isaac Harder, Peter's grandpoppa, had only added the attic after his children had spent a winter shivering beneath the high rafters of the second floor. The house in general was an afterthought. For years, Isaac had figured the white-washed adobe was good enough for his immigrant generation and beyond. He spent his money on building a solid barn, then another, then a hen house and two pole sheds.

After the second pole shed his wife, Olga, put her foot down and insisted he build a proper house. We are not in the Ukraine anymore, she said. We're Americans, and Americans don't live with their animals! She pointed to the far section of the adobe house, where most of their animals had resided during those first years on the prairie; their body heat warmed the house just as much as their Russian oven.

Every other Mennonite family has built a real house, she shouted. I have been patient long enough!

Olga regretted her lack of patience, for her husband was no carpenter. The house leaned perpetually to one side and, unlike the solid mixture of sod and adobe that held an oven's heat day and night, only warped, thin boards offered protection from the harsh winter winds. As the years piled on, Isaac layered the house with additions until it resembled a multicolored snake, for he painted the additions only with whatever colors he had on hand at the time. It was Peter's poppa, Abram, who painted the entire house gray the summer before he married Alma. Like his poppa, however, he wasn't much of a craftsman. Bits of random blue, white and yellow still peered out in spots.

The ladder slid down easily, since Agnes kept everything well-greased in her universe. Peter pulled himself up the rungs, conscious of his shrunken penis that waved down at the floor below. When he reached the top, he had to crawl a few feet on the floor because he didn't trust his balance. He remembered being young and sprinting up carelessly, often with a younger sibling on his back. His brothers and sisters liked the feeling of great height on his shoulders compounded with the height of the attic itself. Alma was afraid of heights, so she never went into the attic. More than once Peter had dashed to the relative safety of the attic when trouble was afoot between him and his momma. As they grew older, his siblings stopped going to the attic, except for Peter and Nora. They would sit there for hours, reading or signing stories to each other. When he was young, the small, crooked windows cut into the attic looked down on the trees his grandpoppa had planted around his new house. Now the windows were blocked by the leaves of those trees in the summer.

No electricity had ever been pulled into this part of the house, so Agnes had a large flashlight near the entrance. Peter flipped it on; a strobe of light shot from Peter's hand to a mirror that leaned against the west wall and glared back into his face. He shouted and dropped the flashlight. For a moment he believed himself to be blind, and began to rub his eyes fiercely. Peter had always been afraid of the dark. Even as an adult the thought of a moonless night without a light terrified him. He tried to force himself to lose that childish fear, and for the most part he managed to push it below the surface, but he could not deny the fact that the idea of losing one's sight horrified him. When the elders spoke of hell, eternal fire and the moans of unsaved souls, it didn't move him. Peter's hell was black and still, the ringing of silence drowning every fiber of reason and thought.

But he hadn't gone blind—not yet, anyway. His eyes recovered when he opened them; the flashlight had rolled against a bolt of white cloth that now was lit like a snowdrift on a weak winter afternoon. He saw his reflection in the mirror that was cracked and darkened in places: a pale figure with boney knees, drooping belly and heaving chest examined him closely in the snow-light. He saw how his naked jaw was a taught wire under loose skin, instead of the round one he remembered. His now bald head made his ears stand out. His arms hung helplessly out of shoulders that had once held children without a thought.

When they were young, Nora would lean against his back and read whatever he read, her breath echoing in his ear. If she reached the end of a page before he did, she would make an impatient grunt until he turned the page. This irritated and amused him in turns.

Slowly, slowly, he would often sign against her cheek. You can't know half of what this book says.

Not so! she pounded into his back. I understand every word! I'm not stupid.

With that, she shoved herself off and ran downstairs to sulk, sometimes for days. But Peter never worried about her bruised feelings, because she always came back to him. One day or another he would be reading by the attic window and hear her shuffling behind him. He never turned, but waited for her to drape herself along his back, her baby-fine hair tickling his neck, her breath pulsing in time with his heart.

Their reading times ended one summer day when he was eighteen and she was fourteen. It was raining, and the harvest had stopped while the storm blew above bowed stalks of wheat. Peter grabbed his books as soon as he was done with his chores and ran up into the attic. Nora was already there, grinning and pounding along with the thunder she could not hear but feel. He settled down and opened a book he had just gotten at the library about a woman who was both deaf and blind. Nora flopped on his back as though he was a comfortable chair and wrapped her arms around his neck. Because of the rain, the window was shut, and a heavy, humid air draped around them. Nora's breath, somewhat sour that day, found its way beneath his collar and crept down his sternum before spreading out upon his chest like a myriad of spiders that Peter didn't want to control. He held the book open but he couldn't read. All he could manage was to smell her scent and feel her breath's fingers as they crowded out all other thoughts.

Nora, however, had finished the page and grunted several times, to no avail. Her grunts grew louder and she added pinches to his neck, which made him stiffen and struggle to remove her arms. She laughed her unmusical laugh and held on tighter. Peter yelled and leapt up, but the ceiling was low, and he knocked both his and Nora's heads on the rafters above. Her hands unclasped and she fell to the floor. She was up immediately, however, and shrieked like a wounded cat and lunged at him. The room was still spinning for Peter, and he didn't see her until she had landed on him and brought him to his knees and then the floor.

He was blinded by her curtain of white-blond hair that had tumbled from her covering. Each breath drew in strands of it. He realized he was drowning in a universe that had become filled with Nora: her hair, her breath, her small sweaty breasts that pushed against his ribcage.

He knew this was wrong. Every second they remained so enmeshed they were sinning more than the last second. But he did not want to move from this space and time that would race away before he could fully appreciate each sensation that rushed between each nerve. Peter tried to freeze every piece of it just as it was, so he could remember this moment at odd times for the rest of his life as he did now, standing naked on a similar day in July, watching a flashlight burn through the white-blond fibers of an innocuous bolt of cloth.

It was Momma who broke his moment for him. She pounded on the ceiling with her broom, so that Nora would feel her presence. Peter? Nora? What's going on?

Nora rolled off him and stood, her maze of hair threading her face, her dress twisted, her skirt hiked up above her knees.

Peter, answer me right now!

It's okay, Momma, he said woodenly, still lying on his back. We were fighting over a book.

Heavens! You're eighteen years old now, not a child anymore.

Yes, Momma.

Peter pulled himself to his feet, pushing away the sinful thoughts

Nora had incurred. He realized this had been coming for quite some time. They'd always been closer to each other than their other siblings, who often teased Peter for his obsession with books and Nora for the fact that she was deaf and made loud, guttural screams at any provocation. Only Peter ever bothered to develop a sign language from a book he had read—Alma and Abram were too busy to learn it beyond basic phrases. They never took her to church, so few people beyond immediate family knew of her existence. The Harders had never been sociable anyway, so no neighbors ever made unexpected calls and saw their invisible daughter. Peter and Nora clung to each other in desperation at first, but soon they found they appreciated each other's company above all others. They had touched each other more than they ought to have, Peter now knew. Been too easy with hugs and kisses. Unlike the other young men in the community, Peter never noticed other girls. He was too busy thinking of ways to make Nora smile.

That all had to end, he decided. She had to know that as well. But the moment he stood straight, she lunged at him, hugged him, and kissed his chin because he was too tall.

No, he said, pushing her away with one hand, steeling his eyes to her confusion. We should not do that, he signed with his other hand.

Why not? We feel the same thing.

It's a sin. He signed the last word letter by letter, since he didn't know what the symbol was for such a word.

Sin? What's that?

Peter realized that no one in his family had tried to save Nora's soul. Not even him. He hadn't wanted to. He'd wanted her to never feel the weight of guilt that knowing Christ brought. Whenever their poppa read the Bible to the family, Peter signed to Nora, but he left out anything even remotely sin-ridden.

A sin is something you shouldn't do, like stealing or saying something that isn't true.

How is this a sin? It feels right.

We are brother and sister. Feeling this way is only good when you are with someone who isn't a brother, an uncle or father.

Why?

Because God said so.

She laughed her grating laugh. God? Who cares what God says? God never wants us to have any fun.

Peter felt his jaw tighten. He dropped his hand from Nora's shoulder. We must be clean before God in everything. Life isn't about having fun. It's about serving God.

I don't want to serve God.

I do.

Peter stayed away from the attic for several weeks. Once, he heard a squeak above his head as he passed the trapdoor, but when he climbed the ladder there was no one there. His momma was at the bottom when he returned.

Don't, she said. Don't look for her there. You aren't children anymore.

What are you talking about?

You know what I'm talking about. I have eyes. I have ears. Leave her be.

She walked away with her basket of clothes. Leave her be, she repeated.

∼

Peter walked towards the image of himself in the mirror carefully. As they drew together, each fold of skin grew sharper. He crouched and then painfully kneeled before the specter with the coarse skin, the razor burns that crisscrossed his face. He figured the men of old had shaved with knives rather than razors. The men of old might even forgo the comfort of a knife and tear out their beards at times. The men of old knew how to beg forgiveness from God for their sins. They did not hide away their shame in a bathroom where only tiles and a toilet stood witness. They stood in the town's center and proclaimed their sorrow.

Und am siebenten Tage soll er alle seine Haare abschneiden auf dem Haupte, am Bart und an den Augenbrauen, daß alle Haare abgeschoren seien, und soll seine Kleider waschen und sein Fleisch im Wasser baden, so ist er rein—But it shall be on the seventh day, that he shall shave all his hair off his head and his beard and his eyebrows, even all his hair he shall shave off: and he shall wash his clothes, also he shall wash his flesh in water, and he shall be clean, Peter muttered to his reflection.

Peter did not feel clean the way the men of old must have felt when they denuded their bodies for all to see. Perhaps his sins could not be dispersed by water and blood.

That was when he saw the worn corner of a photograph peeking through the rim of a cardboard box behind the mirror. Peter drew the box out. Grabbing the flashlight, he peered inside. There were several photos in the box, but the one on top caught his attention, for it showed a young Agnes and Nora standing side by side, arms around each other's waists—or what was left of Nora's waist, for she was several months pregnant. Nora's grin was wild; Agnes' was more sedate, but the pleasure she was feeling at being alive in that moment shocked him. Here was the happiness Peter had longed to procure for his wife, but now he realized why he had never triumphed: he was not Nora. No amount of joking or gentleness could ever pull such a smile from Agnes' lips—he had been outpaced from the beginning.

How they had met, Peter did not know. For a time he didn't even know it was Agnes. But he knew that Nora had met someone else just from watching her across the dinner table, for she smiled to herself and sometimes laughed aloud suddenly. She would disappear for hours and return covered in sweat and dust.

He tried not to be jealous. It was good that she had found someone despite the tiny world their parents had forced her into. But he wondered if this person appreciated her as much as she needed to be. He began to wonder if this person was merely playing with Nora's feelings. Nora, he knew, fell in love with things so easily. He knew that she had named every animal her father owned, and she wept with true grief whenever one was slaughtered or sold. She treated books and common objects as if they were the bearers of souls. Peter began to be angry at this person. This person did not mean good for his sister. This person meant to break that spirit in Nora. He decided he had to find out who this person was.

One Sunday afternoon in August he sat up in his tree and waited. Soon she appeared from the side door and bolted east; Peter dropped to the ground and ran, keeping several yards distant from her. He figured where she was headed soon enough—Gerry Funk's pasture with that old barn and little creek. Once he knew where she was going he slowed to a walk and let her disappear behind the little ridge that kept the abandoned homestead from view. Soon enough he heard the laughter of two teenage girls: one was obviously Nora, the other he couldn't place. He was yet to crest the ridge. A few more steps and he would know who had taken his place. Peter stopped and considered going back. A girl was safe. A girl who accepted Nora should be acceptable in his eyes. He did not need to know who it was. But something kept him rooted there; it was not enough to be ignorant of his successor. So he crouched in the tall grass and crept forward, settling on his stomach when the barn and creek were in view.

Agnes Funk was his competitor, which didn't surprise him. What surprised him was the fact that she and Nora were unbuttoning each other's dresses, pulling their head coverings off their respective heads, and pulling their chemises off their shoulders. Once they were naked, they began signing to each other in a language Peter did not recognize, pointing at different parts of their bodies and laughing. Agnes was larger than Nora, with full breasts and a reddish stripe that swept across her back like the tail of a cat before it struck its prey. They ran in circles around the yard, stopping in intervals to sign chunks of information that led to more laughter, more running. Finally, they dropped beneath one of the trees, continuing the conversation. Peter could not understand what they were saying; they had developed their own language, one that he would never be a part of for as long as he lived.

He knew he should look away. He knew that he should never have let himself come there. He knew that God Himself might snatch away his life at any moment. He knew he had disregarded his momma's instructions: *Leave her be.* But as he lay in the heat of an ordinary August afternoon, he knew three things: one, that he loved his sister in the worst way possible; two, his groin was pushing into the dirt, searching for cover or relief; and three, he did not want Agnes Funk to have Nora.

～

Thanks to Helen Keller, Peter found his way back to Nora. Peter had read all about Helen Keller after Nora left his reading life. How a woman who could neither see nor hear, yet speak fascinated him. He walked around for days with his hand in his mouth to see how his tongue created vowel sounds and on his throat to feel the way that his voice moved. His brothers and sisters howled at him: *Räpel'tähn! Räpel'tähn!* See how the crazy man listens to his throat!

Nora, however, did not laugh. She watched him very carefully, and at times touched her own throat, as if that would explain what he was doing. Peter pretended to ignore her, knowing she would come sooner if he gave no sign in return to her blatant stares.

Finally, she could hold back no longer. Nora found him in the barn, tossing dirty straw out the door. He had devised a way to twist his right arm around the pitchfork so that he could do his work and feel his voice as he sang a hymn. He saw her stand just inside the barn door, but he did not stop:

Der alt' böse Feind,
Mit Ernst er's jetzt meint,
Groß' Macht und viel List
Sein' grausam' Rüstung ist,
Auf Erd' ist nicht seingleichen.

Nora strode over to him, pushed his hand aside and put her own hand in its place. Then she felt her own throat. Peter stopped shoveling, but he did not cease his singing. She did not look at him, but at the ground, her eyebrows twisted in concentration. She gave a grunt in frustration. Peter stopped singing. He echoed her grunt. She looked at him in surprise. She grunted again. He grunted back. Nora grinned. Peter sang the first line of the hymn: *Ein' feste Burg ist unser Gott*, then waited. What came out was a chaotic whine, but he smiled and repeated the line again. For a half hour he sang and listened to her attempt to mimic him, until something similar to true language came from her inexperienced throat. He finally had to stop; his voice was raw. Nora did not want him to stop. She growled at him. Peter returned her growl, which made her laugh.

Don't worry, he signed. We'll do it again tomorrow.

What are we doing?

Teaching you how to talk.

Nora looked surprised. So people will understand me?

Yes. Everyone will understand you.

Nora hooted and twirled before dashing out of the barn. He shouted after her: Where are you going? But, of course, she didn't hear. And, of course, Peter knew who she was going to tell.

～

Peter heard a car door slam. Agnes was home. As always, time had whisked past Peter Harder, leaving him lying in a field with an erection or naked on an attic floor with a faded photograph. Agnes would walk in, deposit the groceries and head for the bathroom first thing. She had an overactive bladder and used the toilet nearly every hour during the day, and often got up at night. She would see his mess; his ridiculous attempt to shed his sins that he had willingly taken hold of that day.

Peter listened to Agnes open the screen door four times before he heard the final *plunk!* of a paper bag full of groceries. He waited for her tread upstairs to the bathroom, but instead heard her head towards their bedroom. When they were first married, they'd shared his old room and narrow bed for as long as Abram and Alma lived in the main house. Peter expected several years would go by before his parents moved into the granny house behind the big elm, but days after Huldah was born, Alma announced they were going to Paraguay to help the Mennonites who had escaped the Bolsheviks in Russia. It was said that they were disheveled and hungry. Alma was sure her assistance was needed.

Off to save some souls then, Momma? Peter asked the morning they left.

She looked at him as though he had just confronted her with dirty language. We are not going there to save souls. I'm going to assume they're already taken care of. We're going to help them survive.

When they were gone, his two unmarried sisters moved into the granny house. Peter felt silly sleeping in his boyhood bed, but the thought of taking his parents' place unnerved him. Agnes, however, felt no such qualms. One day when he had returned home from town, every article of clothing and every book he'd ever read was removed to the wide downstairs bedroom. Agnes sat in a new rocking chair near their new bed as she nursed Huldah; she stared into his shocked face without blinking.

If you're going to be the head of this household, you'd better start acting like it.

Agnes always confused Peter, constantly changing moods and directions, but doing so with such force he was often convinced she'd been constant in her new voice. She confused him now with her strange behavior. He crept towards the trapdoor. No sounds breathed up to him. Maybe she was tired and had laid down for a nap. Maybe she had used the toilet before she left Huldah's house. Maybe there was still time.

Peter looked at the photograph clutched in his hand. The paper and the exposure were less than perfect. It was fading away, like so many things. What had once been an emblem of Agnes and Peter's painful ardor was now nothing but lines on paper that could disappear in a moment with no one aware of its existence. He gently set the photograph down on the floor. He crawled down the ladder and pushed it back into the ceiling without any more sound than a few molecules of air bumping one into another.

~

It happened the winter following the Armistice.

They continued their daily lessons, in the attic, wrapped in coats and stocking caps. Sometimes they could only be there a few moments, because of chores and other demands. Nora did not go to the barn and cottonwoods anymore. Agnes had been coming to their house to cook and clean away a debt between her father and Poppa, but Nora never went to find her. So every free moment she had was with him, no one else.

This made Peter shamefully happy. He never asked Nora why she didn't seek Agnes out; for fear that just a jostle of a thought would take her away again.

It happened after he had been denied eldership.

Peter stopped studying. Stopped talking. He sat in the attic and stared at the frost-bitten trees that tried to protect his poppa's house from the inevitable cold of the prairie. Nora would find him there, and would drape herself over his shoulders though there was no book. Her ice-tainted breath stirred him like no other. Not even God Himself had stirred Peter the way her chilly fingers did when they found a small breach in his coat and shirt and rested against his flesh.

The last time was long after they knew she was pregnant. Alma had screamed when she saw her daughter's rounded belly as Nora had climbed out of the bathtub: Who did this? Who did this to you? She ran out to the barn where Peter was milking the last cow. Did you do this to her? Did you do this? Didn't I tell you to leave her be?

Years later, hours before she died, Momma opened her eyes and looked at Peter, who had taken a turn to watch her. She hadn't spoken sense for weeks. Her eyes simply wandered frantically, as though she was searching for something precious—but at this moment they were clear and cold as she said in crisp Low German: *Ekj hab en Äakjel fonn di. Dü best Drakj. Hast dü kjeene Schaund? Ekj wenschte dü weascht nie jebuare.*

Then in English, a language she'd always hated: I knew. I always knew. I should've stopped you. You bastard. I always knew.

Peter stood in the upstairs hallway, and listened for his wife's movements. Each piece of wood in this house told the stories of its tenants. There were few secrets, if any. He wondered if his grandpoppa had actually done this on purpose; if his clumsy carpentry actually was a genius way to know what went on beneath the roof he grudgingly gave his wife. Sod and adobe were too quiet—they absorbed every footfall and whisper.

Finally, he heard a sigh and a squeak of tired bedsprings, then the careful tromp of her orthopedic shoes on the stairs. Peter did not move.

When Agnes saw him, she raised her eyebrows and said, quietly: What have you done?

I am clean, he said, hearing how ridiculous that sounded in the air of reality.

You were dirty?

This shall be the law of the leper in the day of his cleansing, Peter began, imagining that he was at last before a congregation that hung on every word. When he was young and alone in the fields, he would recite entire chapters and their commentaries, Christian and otherwise. He had figured he would need the practice when he became an elder. When that door was closed, he stopped until he had a family to speak to, but in the end they never took it seriously. His daughters left the church for congregations of Baptists and Lutherans. Huldah would have gone, had she not been shunned, had Peter defended his daughter. His sons stopped going at all—except for Johan. Though Peter suspected that he did it only out of weak respect, since he'd never grown a *follboat*—a dark, luxurious beard that would have exceeded Peter's transparent one.

He would have gone on, but Agnes interrupted him: I know some scripture—and that's about the cleansing of lepers. You had leprosy then?

Not of the flesh; of the spirit.

What is wrong with your spirit?

I need to tell you something—confess something to you.

Can it wait? I need to use the toilet. Agnes did not stop for an answer. She stood in the door of the bathroom and examined the hairy mess before her. She stepped in and closed the door. Seconds later Peter heard a stream of water echo against the toilet bowl. In all their years of marriage, he had seen her give birth and nurse their children, but he had never once heard her urinate. Usually she demanded he retreat or would waste water by turning on the sink full blast. It was as if Peter was no longer there; no longer of this world.

At last, she emerged.

I'm sorry about the mess. I couldn't find your cleaning supplies.

Is this your confession then?

No.

Now would be the moment he would say it—now he would tell it to someone who would shoulder the burden with him, and carry it on when he was gone. Somehow this comforted him. He didn't want it to be forgotten, as though that would protect others from the same sin. His momma hadn't counted, since she was dead before him.

It's about Nora.

He saw Agnes stiffen. He pushed on clumsily, afraid she would turn away from him. I was the father. It was me. All along. It was me.

She did not rage at him. Instead he saw a wash of pity in her eyes. She barked a tuneless laugh. This is news to me? You are confessing this?

You knew?

Always. Well, she conceded, not always. But almost always.

She told you?

No.

Did Momma—

Agnes laughed again. Your mother wouldn't have told me if Jesus had commanded it—we were not on those terms. But she didn't have to. I saw you together. It was easy to tell.

She turned and walked to a long, thin closet door that Peter had never seen opened. She took a broom and dustpan out, rolled up her sleeves and pulled the apron out. Agnes shut the door and walked into the bathroom, the cleaning products swaying like the dugs of a cow waiting to be milked.

How could you have married me then? If you always knew? How could you have stood the sight of me?

Agnes stood in the doorway, armed with the things that had always protected her. She looked younger than usual, as though the Agnes he had seen in the photo had returned.

You loved Nora. I loved Nora. You were the only link I had of her. Agnes shrugged. There was no one else for me anymore.

She turned and closed the bathroom door. Peter heard her begin to sweep.

Shaken in the Water, Part 4

1924

Agnes knew she had frightened Peter on their wedding night, and she would have to guide him to her this time. For someone that was so sure with the Bible and the land, he was nothing when it came to any of the women in his family. She had witnessed his interaction with his mother and sisters: they ordered him, he obeyed; they shouted, he listened, his head imperceptibly bowed. Abram was the same. Agnes knew that the women were the head of this family, not the men.

On the fifth night of their marriage, she waited up for him. When it was past twelve, she pulled on a bathrobe and walked out into the cattle rustler's moon. When she didn't find him behind the slurry pit, she made an ever widening circle until she came upon him sitting beside a campfire among what used to be the barn next to the some-times-stream. He dropped his book and stood up when he saw her.

So, I guess you come here, too.

Where's your head covering?

Can't I break any rules? she countered, sitting by the fire. You should be in bed next to your wife as you told God not so long ago, so I don't think you can be so high-minded.

Peter remained standing. What are you doing here?

Getting you to bed.

Agnes wondered how she was to go about seducing her own husband. It seemed so simple among the animals—rather violent, but to the point. She had heard her parents more than once. It was always slow at first, but grew faster and louder until she figured the neighbors could hear them. Sometimes they would stop, mid swing, as though they were thinking the same thing.

She thought about the scent they had shared, and tried to bring it back, but nothing came. Perhaps it was the fire or the night air. Perhaps it had disappeared after that one moment in October. Had they consummated their marriage there in his bedroom years before, would life have been different? She would not have loved Nora the way she had. Agnes would regard her love as nothing more than sisterly. She would've forgotten the heat Nora gave her. Maybe Peter could have excited more than children from her body. But it hadn't happened.

Agnes stood and held out her hand over the fire; the pounding of its heat made her bold. Come on, she said.

Where?

I want to show you a place.

We shouldn't leave the fire burning.

Agnes laughed. We'll be able to see it where we'll be. As they walked, she scooped up every memory she had of Nora in this place. She saw Nora struggle out of her dress; she saw her reach for Agnes' back, her bare arm trembling for what its finger sought; she saw her burning. Strangely, the scent of Nora's death raised her shoulders, her head and propelled her forward. She wondered if Peter was thinking of Nora at this moment—if the memories of her would be the linchpin for their marriage.

Demolition

1972

Agnes was out gathering the laundry, concentrating on the snap of the sheets as she pulled them off the line, when she looked up and saw the flashes of *red yellow blue purple* on the evening horizon.

She held the sheets against her chest. The usual string of lights that was Ulysses glittered on, but there was a separate universe now attached. Agnes wondered if they had always been there; if she was the only person who did not know about this new stretch of lights that blazed with audacity. She had been to town a few days before to run errands, and though she had crisscrossed the town for one thing or another, she had not noticed anything new. Had there been anything different she would have known about it, since something different in

Ulysses was an event.

Well then, she muttered to herself. I may as well go and see.

She dropped the laundry into the basket and walked to her car. As always, the keys were in the ignition. She backed the giant blue fish of a car out of the shed and drove towards Ulysses. The glitter of her own house lights followed her, though there was no one in it who would need her presence. Her husband was dead, her children married and moved away but Johan, and he was running a night haul of cattle to Colorado. Agnes made a left turn onto new 56 and the home lights disappeared.

When she reached Ulysses, the summer streets were abandoned. Agnes drove slowly down Main, looking for life in any of the storefronts. She rolled down the car window to get a better look.

That's when she heard it: the sound of engines roaring without their mufflers and the sound of metal against metal. Then she remembered the reason for the lights—the county fair had begun that night. When her children were young, the county fair became the center of their lives. The fair always opened with a parade that wound up at the fairgrounds outside of town. For three days judges in seersucker suits examined vegetables, quilts, dresses and stock of all species. Local talent provided entertainment, and a wandering band of charlatans and evangelists made their rounds.

The parades of the thirties and forties were small affairs: the high school band played the same two songs over and over; the sons of farmers and ranchers marched their prize-winning hopefuls behind; a float trundled by with local politicians.

During Tobias and Johan's youth, however, things had grown larger and more impressive: the high school band acquired uniforms and dancing cheerleaders; different floats holding more than politicians appeared and threw candy into the crowd. But just as Tobias and Johan deemed themselves too old to be seen at the parade, a new facet adorned it that brought them back for a few more years: the demolition derby. Each fair, young men from various parts of the county brought cars they had decorated with paint. Most of them had flames and various monsters on their hoods. Agnes remembered Otis Siebert's great-grandson's car had a well-rendered dragon spewing flames and smoke from its mouth. She wondered what Otis would have said to this dragon, had he still been alive. These cars would drive to the rodeo pit just outside of town and slam each other until only one car could move. Whoever owned that car received a cash prize.

Agnes' car drifted down Main towards the sounds of wheels grinding into a muddied field. She tried to remember who won the year the great-grandson of Otis Siebert entered the competition. She hoped the dragon had lost. It seemed a little out of the Mennonite church's custom to do such prideful parading. She had told her sons as much one day before they dashed off in their pickup truck to see the event.

I also think it's wasteful to destroy so much machinery, she had added.

Momma, Johan argued, they're going to the junkyard either way! They might as well have a good farewell party—and then it is less wasteful, since so many folks get entertained.

Agnes had only seen the cars on the parade route; she never actually witnessed one of these competitions. She, in general, had no interest in competitions of any kind. They seemed to be another way for the *Englische* to show off. But by the time Tobias and Johan were in high school, these acts of pride were common, even among the Mennonites, so she did not even have to power of the church to back her up. Agnes made a point of never attending any competitions, even when Johan and Tobias started running track and cross country for high school and later in college. Peter went whenever their team was running at the lake a few miles away, and would report the results. Often those results showed Johan and sometimes Tobias to be the winner. But even when neither of them won, Peter would still come home with a triumphant tone, and spew minutes and seconds at Agnes as she washed dishes or folded laundry.

But when they lose, they lose. They aren't the winners, she said.

It doesn't matter if they don't always win, Peter insisted. What really matters is whether they break their best times. They are running against themselves, more than against others. If they win, that's just an extra prize.

Agnes felt a little comforted by the thought of her sons competing against themselves. After all, the Bible did talk of running races. Maybe they were sticking more to the Mennonite truth than they realized. She still refused to go, though she listened with more interest when Peter came home, breathless and reddened by the autumn chill. She didn't want her sons to think they had won with her.

Agnes found a parking spot farthest from the fairgrounds.

She didn't want anyone from church to see her or her car. They would laugh in their sleeves at the fact that she had come to the demolition derby after her years against it. Or, she thought as she listened to the car's engine cool with its tiny taps beneath the hood, maybe they didn't even care. Maybe it was she who cared about such things anymore. Thirty years before they would shun the women who didn't wear head coverings. Now only a few remained covered, and the ones who had thrown them off sneered at those who minded the old ways.

She found herself leaning into the creaking arms of the driver's seat. She closed her eyes. More than once the cushions of this car reminded her of her dead husband. This car was the last he was to buy. Agnes had shouted at him when he drove it on the yard. It's too big, she yelled. It's a proud blue. When he managed to get her to sit in the driver's seat he told her to relax into the cushions.

Does it remind you of anything? he asked shyly, as if they had only met a few days before.

No, she said curtly.

Peter's smile disappeared. He backed away and ran his fingers through his thinning beard. His hair and beard used to be pale blond. Now it looked like dirty dishwater. When they first were married, Agnes would cut his hair on the front porch. When she was done, a ring of white gold surrounded them for a few moments before a gust of wind blew the locks away. She couldn't remember when she had stopped cutting his hair; when he had begun going to a barber's shop in town instead.

Agnes tried to think of what he could possibly mean. I'm sorry, she said. I really don't. What is it supposed to remind me of?

Me, he said softly. He smiled and patted his belly. Can't you feel how it curves into your back?

Agnes realized he was referring to the way they slept at night. For as long as she could remember, Peter would nestle up against her back, his protruding stomach fitting into the small of her back. It had always annoyed Agnes. She could feel every button of his pajamas, every wrinkle of fabric or flesh attack her skin with wire-sharp teeth. She couldn't sleep that way, so she would wait until his snores assured her he was asleep before she would move his arm from her waist and slunk to the far side of the bed.

Ah, she said. I see now.

I figured you would, he said, satisfied by her answer. He often said it was good to sleep like that, be in a position that they shared with no one else.

But it wasn't true, Agnes thought many years later, listening to the scream of metal in the darkness that covered the land. She knew it was his attempt to create intimacy that never existed. They had never shared it; he took it, and she gave grudgingly.

The roar of cheers woke Agnes up. She looked at her watch: nine-o-one. Before she could fall back asleep, she thrust open the car door and stepped out as gracefully as possible. She had never been able to exit a car with dignity; her skirt always pulled a little higher than was appropriate. Once she was out, she shut the door gently and patted the hood. Long ago, Agnes had heard one of her sons talk about "horse-power" in relation to cars. Ever since then she thought of cars in a different light. As she drove, she imagined small horses dashing beneath the hood. When she stopped, she saw them panting and pawing the ground, shaking their manes out of their eyes. Sometimes, when no one was looking, she patted the hood in praise of these faithful beasts whose pulses ran at the end of the drive.

She slipped into the crowd of onlookers easily enough, but she could not find a seat. She got quite a few stares at her head covering and plain dress, but no one offered her a seat. Agnes was tall, however, so she could see the arena.

There were only seven cars left; the defeated ones littered the outskirts of the field. The cars that remained had huge scratches and dents in them. Agnes wondered how they could even drive. The cars pulled to opposite ends of the field. Then a horn sounded, and they headed for each other, tires slopping through inches of mud from the rain the night before. As they smashed into each other the crowd gave a bloody howl of glee. Soon the cars crowded together; each gave the other short pushes that only ended in a closer lock. A horn sounded again, and the cars wiggled themselves apart. This action was repeated over and over, but no one seemed bored by this. Slowly, one by one, a car was disqualified because of various things: a fire, a displaced tire, overt cursing that would offend someone in the crowd. How anyone could hear these words was beyond Agnes' estimation. Finally, only two were left. Different groups seemed to be in favor of one of the cars. Agnes couldn't tell them apart. They both looked the same, bathed in mud and wounds.

One of the cars gunned its engine. The other car answered with a louder roar. They kept at this for a few minutes. Agnes figured it was for the audience's benefit. Then, the horn blew. The cars slipped towards each other. The thunder of the crowd nearly wiped out the screams of the cars. Agnes found herself holding her breath, waiting for the doom of one or both of the young men who so foolishly played with their lives.

That's when she saw the flash of pale blond hair bob its way through the crowd. Agnes forgot the cars, forgot the screeching bodies that surrounded her. She felt herself begin to float above the crowd towards that head of hair. The sounds below became softened, punctuated lightly by the scream of metal against metal, the shrieks of women, shouts of men. She did not care who won and who lost, nor if the roar she heard above all else was a mess of fire or the crack of thunder from the clouds that had hovered on the horizon all evening. She tried to pull her mind back, but the hair's force was too strong. Her body followed her mind and moved towards the entrance, which was where the blonde streak headed.

Agnes pushed her way to the exit, using her broad shoulders to move people aside. People muttered angrily around her. When she had broken free of the crowd, she breathed heavily and looked wildly around. Teenagers, women with heavy hips and children swarmed around her, the children eating cotton candy that stuck to their fingers and lips. The men stood aloof near the openings of the exhibition buildings, scuffing their worn boots in the dirt and adjusting their belt buckles under their spreading stomachs. A hundred yards away were the carnival rides: a rumbling tilt-a-whirl, a swaying Ferris wheel, a small bumper car rink and a miniature roller coaster creaked beneath the flashing *red yellow blue purple* lights that Agnes had seen earlier. Candy wrappers and popcorn boxes blew in circles by the wind that had begun to grow stronger. Agnes knew the clouds on the horizon were approaching; she could hear the electricity of thunder and lightning crackle in her ears. But underneath the cover of florescent lights, the world of wind and sound seemed far removed.

Her eyes searched through her thick glasses for that stream of blond hair she had seen. There was too much surrounding her. Too much sound and light and litter stood between them. Agnes scanned the crowd without any hope. She walked towards the carnival and passed the vendors and game booths. She looked at the men who stood behind the exhaust-laden counters, selling weary stuffed rabbits and cheap plastic toys.

She came upon the first ride: the tilt-a-whirl. The motor was idling; children and a few teenagers were climbing on, trying to keep their balance on the sloped flooring to the round cars that swung expectantly. Agnes had never been on the tilt-a-whirl. Her older children had always escorted the younger children to the carnival. She wondered what it was like, to see the earth move around her. She counted out some change from her purse and bought a ticket. The carnie looked at her quizzically before guiding her to the nearest car. She had been the last one in line, so she was alone on the broad curved seat. The carnie locked down the metal guardrail and walked to the edge of the ride, pulling the gate behind him.

At first, it moved slowly. The car swung back and forth, then around once, then back and forth again. Agnes heard the motor burp and wind up until she could feel its power flux beneath the floor. Then the ride began to speed up. She watched the world outside sway back and forth, then around three times, before swaying again, like a fishing bob in a current. Then the motor burped again before climbing into a rage that shook the car as it spun around again and again, until the world outside began to blur. Agnes clutched the guardrail. Every now and again she saw other passengers: mothers and children screaming and bumping up against one another, teenage boys and girls using the ride to let hands stray. That was when Agnes saw the blond hair flash past her.

The ride continued to rage. The faces of everyone on and off the ride continued to blur. Agnes clutched the guardrail as she craned her neck to see the blond hair again. The centripetal force held her body back. There. And again. There. Agnes bit her lips, tried not to scream for the ride to end. She felt a little sick. She would've closed her eyes, but she was afraid she would miss the hair.

As the ride began to slow, Agnes scooted towards the edge of the seat, examining each face, each head of hair that circled by. The flash of blond didn't resurface. Finally the car came to a stop. Agnes waited for someone to come release her. She saw that the children were unlocking themselves, and she followed suit. When she stood, the sky swayed.

She didn't feel herself fall. She didn't notice the twist of her body that tried to protect her left hip that had always given her trouble. All she saw was the circle of light above her; the way the dry lightning mingled with the splotches of *red green blue* purple red green blue purple that shimmered like a false sunset. All she felt was a tinge of heat flowing through her and exiting onto her very practical underwear that had been washed and dried in the sun over and over.

The next thing she noticed was several pairs of hands lifting her body. Hands that touched her where she hadn't been touched for years.

I'm fine. I'm fine. Her voice seemed detached from her mouth, as though someone else was speaking, as though someone else had stolen her breath.

You fell down, ma'm. We're going to have to put you in an ambulance and take a look at you.

I'm fine. I'm fine, she repeated with indignation. I'm not going to the hospital.

We'll just take you to the ambulance and see how you are, first. Then we'll decide.

They were off the ride, she thought. They were settling her onto a stiff board of some kind. They were picking her up and carrying her away. She did not want to be carried. She could feel the hem of her dress above her knees. She opened her eyes and saw between the arms of those lifting her. Several people watched her as she trundled past them. Her face burned with embarrassment.

I'm fine. I'm fine, she whispered to herself, pulling in puffs of air through her nose, as if those little breaths would cool what was inside.

Then they were scooting her into something. All she saw was the top of some kind of truck that reminded her of the types of trucks Johan drove. They were taking her to the hospital. They were breaking their word.

I thought you said you weren't taking me to the hospital! she shouted. I can't go to the hospital!

Ma'm, you have a gash in your head. You might have a concussion. We need to go to the hospital, one voice said. Is someone here with you? Maybe your husband?

No, she heard herself say. He's gone and buried a year ago.

The night Peter died, she had pushed his arm away when he was still awake. I can't sleep like that, she snapped. When she woke that morning, his body was pressed against the wall; his arms stretched in front of him, as though he had reached for her one more time.

After someone cut away a small circle of her hair, a doctor bandaged her head and told her she didn't have a concussion. They wouldn't take her to her car. You're too frail just yet, the receptionist said. We'll get someone to drive you home.

A young nurse just getting off her shift was found. Just take me to my car—it's at the fairgrounds, Agnes said, trying not to sound as angry as she felt.

Doctor said you weren't to drive for twenty-four hours, the nurse said.

I only live a few miles out of town. I can manage that.

I could get into trouble.

I'll take the back roads. Nobody will be around for me to hit. Besides, Agnes said, looking at her watch. It's late. I'm sure you're tired.

The nurse thought for a moment before she turned her car towards the fairgrounds.

∾

They came to the parking lot. The carnival rides were empty and dark; the auction barns were closed. The nurse circled the parking lot, looking for Agnes' great fish of a car.

Are you sure it's here?

Yes, by the shed over there.

They stopped by the shed. Nothing was there. For a moment Agnes thought she was going crazy; then she remembered. She laughed for the first time in quite a while. The nurse looked at her quizzically.

Someone must've stolen it.

We'll go to the police station then.

No, don't worry about it.

I would worry about it!

No, I left the keys in the ignition—like always. No boy in his right mind would leave it alone.

But your car's gone for good unless you tell the cops.

No, the tank's almost empty. They won't get far.

They might have money to fill it up.

They won't, because the cap won't come off unless you hit it just right with a piece of cut up tire I have in the trunk. They'll get frustrated and leave it. I'll have Johan go look when he gets home.

Agnes laughed again; this time the nurse laughed with her. The nurse's laugh was deep, like the roots of a tree that pushed against earth that wasn't used to being moved. It was a real laugh, not the kind of appeasement laugh that people made when they didn't get the joke.

Agnes watched the back lights of the nurse's car fade. She finished taking down the laundry and sat on the front porch swing. She wondered if her car with its mini horses was having an adventure; if this time it would not return.

It began to rain lightly and playfully. The wind made it mist onto the porch with each swaying breath. It played with her skirt until it caught the hem and rested it upside down on her thighs. She moved to turn it down, but something held her back. As if human fingers had pushed her hands back into her lap. She felt the wind tease her knees that hadn't been so exposed in years, reach up past her thighs and race down again, the unseen fingers nimble in their wandering; almost as if they knew her body well.

Very early in their marriage, Agnes knew that Peter's awkward thrusts against her pelvis wouldn't elicit anything more than children. One night after he had fallen asleep, she moved his arm from her waist. With her fingers, she drew an enlarging circle that began at her navel and pushed above her breasts and below her thighs. For several nights she did this; within a week she felt the tingling drip between her legs that was her own, not Peter's.

After Peter was buried and her children had returned to their lives, she went one night to his grave that already had notes of weeds on its chest.

I'm sorry, she said to the earth that covered his awkward hands, protruding belly. I should have taught you. You would've learned.

Agnes knew it was not Johan's truck that slid in the night towards her house. She knew the sound of her own engine too well. She stood and watched it curve towards her; she imagined the tiny horses racing those final yards, exhilarated by the adventure, but ready to be home.

A tall, lanky boy who couldn't be older than sixteen unfolded himself from the car. He was the grandson of Sam Hiebert. He smiled sheepishly at Agnes. I'm sorry I took your car, ma'am. It was just too hard to ignore, you know?

He cocked his head to one side, and a sweep of long, white-blond hair swung out into the porch light. Like Nora's, every thread shone like a prism: *red gold purple gold blue blue pink purple gold gold gold.* Had Nora lived, she would have had a brood of white-blond children who grinned that crooked grin and splayed their capable hands on their hips.

Yeah, I know, she said, laughing. Do you want a ride home? My son'll be here soon, I think, and he won't be as forgiving as me.

Ma'am, don't worry about me. It's only two miles to town.

He loped away like a tiger on a journey, not a hunt.

Homebody

1972

Johan put out a personal ad in the paper on his thirtieth birthday, and the only reply was from his niece. He sat on the edge of a booth at a truck stop, scratched the raw grain of the badly sanded table and held his breath, hoping she would disappear in the fog of lost oxygen. Her grinning face refused to mist away.

Johan, you've got to see the humor in all this! Imma leaned forward and touched his scratching finger. For a moment the scratching stopped. Johan drew his hand away to the seat of the booth; this time his finger found a rip in the vinyl to worry.

I don't quite see it. All I see is a very, very messed up situation.

He felt the familiar pull of anger that always rode behind his heart and pushed through him. This wasn't her fault, he knew. She had only been searching for the same thing he was. But his anger didn't listen.

Imma sat back and crossed her arms. It's not so bad, you know. I won't tell anyone, if that's what you're worried about. I'd never done it before, you know—the ads. Yours was just so hilarious I had to meet this man—you, I mean.

He had thought himself rather clever the night he wrote up the ad: *God Commanded Moses…to be smart, handsome, successful, witty, sensual, compassionate, energetic and blessed. Be his female match, 20-30, and share with him the Promised Land.*

What are you hauling, anyway? Imma asked.

He motioned to the city of idling trucks. See that one with the blue cab? That's mine. I'm trucking cows from Ulysses. Picking some up from Salina.

So you were going to give me a look-over and dash off with your meat?

Actually, they're Uncle Doyle's Holsteins. He's getting out of the business. It's too hard for him anymore.

I thought you were milking for him—that's what your momma said.

That must've been a while ago, he said, his voice low. I don't have much time. Since Poppa's died and I took over the farm.

Oh. That's right. I'm sorry.

Johan raised his eyes and forced himself to look at her. Though she was only twenty-nine, Imma had heavy creases by her jaw and a neck as thin as an exhaust pipe. Everything in her body had shrunk into itself. Folded inward.

She was so small, he thought. Had always been small. Unlike every other girl in Ulysses. Ulysses girls were large-boned with ample breasts and settled hips, whereas Imma's shirts slumped over her shoulders, caved in at her chest and flowed down to her hips like an unsettled river. Ulysses girls' hair was thick with curls or waves; Imma's hair was stick straight and so black it seemed purple. The only thing that Imma had in common with Ulysses girls was her eyes: they were wide and green with flecks of brown. Johan and all his siblings had those same eyes. It seemed to be the only physical hint that his brother had even touched his brief wife.

Johan realized he was staring, and dropped his gaze, only to be confronted with her hands. Her tiny nails were shiny from the clear nail polish she'd always worn so that each finger seemed to be the slender bearer of jewels. He had held those little fingers once to warm them up while they sat in a chilled truck.

Well, I need to go soon, he said, resettling his baseball cap.

So soon? she asked, holding a fork of oozing pancake near her lips. A little ring of pink lipstick clung to a white coffee cup by her plate.

Yes. I think it's best. I'll get the bill.

She flashed a grin and set down her fork. Johan, let's sneak out. Not pay. It'll be like old times.

Old times? That only happened once, maybe twice, Johan said, but he found himself peeking at their waitress. A bus had just pulled up and a stream of people was headed for the door. Imma slipped out of the booth and grabbed her purse. The waitress was shouting out to the cook behind the dented silver doors.

Johan, come on! Imma was already near the door. He grabbed his cap and shoved a few dollars under his plate. A tip for the waitress.

Imma was running towards the city of trucks, her tiny heels scratching at the grooved cement. She jumped up and down while he fiddled with the keys and unlocked the door. When she tried to climb in, her feet couldn't touch the first step. Without thinking, Johan boosted her up, his hand flat against her backside. He nearly dropped her when he realized what he had done.

Once Imma was inside, Johan slammed her door shut, climbed into the cab and tested the gas.

Let's go!

I can't just zip out. This isn't a car, he said. After a few minutes they pulled out of the lot. Johan was navigating through a maze of buses and cars; he didn't dare look back. Once they reached the interstate he looked at Imma. She grinned.

Where should I drop you off? I can't take you back there. There's a town nearby; you can catch a cab.

She laughed at his serious tone. Can I come along? Just to see the cows. I want to see what you do.

I guess so, he said. You have to lie low, though. I'm not sure if I'm allowed to bring company along on my routes.

∽

The first time Johan touched Imma surprised both of them. Johan had been fourteen; Imma was thirteen. It was as if a small, weakened section of a wall had caused the entire edifice of their friendship to crash around them, settling the dust around them artlessly. They had been eating stolen ice cream and were laughing over a private joke neither of them remembered the moment Johan's hand, aiming for Imma's shoulder in a gentle push, landed instead on her small, undeveloped breast. Hand dropping to his side, he turned away. Studied the rusting wall of Ulysses' only dumpster behind the town's only grocery.

Imma tapped his shoulder. Johan. It's okay. Don't worry about it.

He swiveled his head and saw her tiny grin, painted with a smudge of vanilla. Instinctively he touched his own lips. Imma read his signal and wiped her mouth with the sleeve of her t-shirt. They both giggled nervously.

Hey! Miss Janice, the grocery store clerk, appeared with a pack of cigarettes in one hand, a generic pop in the other, and an unlit cigarette drooping between her lips. What you two doing back here! This is private property.

We're just looking in awe at the dumpster, Miss Janice. Johan brought me out to see.

Miss Janice scrunched her face so her eyes were tiny slits. What?

Never mind, Miss Janice, we'll go, Johan said.

She looked at the ice cream they had stolen minutes ago. Where'd you all get that, anyways? I seen you walk out and not buyin' anything.

We got it at the Heavenly Delights. Imma waved down the street to the tiny candy store that was about to go under.

Didn't know they sold ice cream, Miss Janice muttered. Well, get outta here!

Imma grabbed the ice cream container from Johan's hand and began to run, laughing manically. He followed. When they reached old 56 she threw it into the air and watched it plunk! and splatter on the black-hot tar.

The next time Johan went into the grocery he slipped Miss Janice a five-dollar bill. She squinted at the bill briefly before it disappeared in her cashier's smock.

~

Imma examined Johan's shaven face as he shifted into gear and navigated the truck down the on-ramp. I guess you haven't joined the church, Imma said as she slipped off her heels and propped them on the dashboard. Her tiny toes reflected on the windshield.

No. Haven't had a need to, I guess.

So you're looking for an *Englische* girl, then?

I guess that's pretty obvious. There isn't much to choose from in Ulysses, Mennonite or otherwise.

Imma laughed. All the pretty ones got married quick, she said.

I guess so.

Nothing more was said until they neared the exit to the pick-up point. You'd better stay in the truck, he said. These guys aren't the most gentrified.

What? And miss all the fun?

Imma slipped her feet back into her heels as Johan backed the truck to the ramp. The cows were shifting their feet nervously. She threw open the door and slid to the ground, her behind taking some dirt and grease with it. She tripped her way towards the fence. Gerald Janzen rounded the fence and pulled off his gloves.

Johan? he asked, glancing at Imma.

Hey. That's my niece. You remember—Nick's girl.

Oh. Huh.

Johan decided to leave it at that. Ready to go? he asked.

Just 'bout. You better get your niece away from there.

Imma was clinging to the metal corral, stroking the head of a rolling-eyed milker. As Johan approached he saw the cow's low dugs, the way the veins seemed ready to burst. Her sides heaved around a thick lump of something solid. He touched her flank lightly. A tumor, probably.

Better get back, he said. They're going to be pushed through soon.

Where are they going? she asked.

He swallowed once. There's a company out in Burlington that makes dog food.

Dog food.

Yeah.

They're going to be turned into dog food? But they're milk cows.

They're too old to milk anymore, or are maimed. Uncle Doyle and me couldn't sell the ones already on the truck; these are from other folks that have the same problem, I guess.

Imma looked at him as if he was the one with the switchblade that would cancel their lives. She walked to Johan's blue cab and sat on the first step. He followed, pulled off his cap and squatted beside her. Her eyes were glued to the final few being chased up the ramp.

I'm sorry you had to see this. I should have kept you from coming.

Some of them know, I think, she said as the last one entered the truck. They're the slow ones. But most are fairly sure of their immortality, you know? They're expecting you to care for them, guide them to that greenest pasture.

They won't feel anything, you know. Men'll slit their throats and that will be that.

You know, she said, looking up at him. I knew it was you in the ad. Your momma sends me the Gazette every now and again. She sent this one with a circle around the ad, and a note asking me to find a nice girl for you to date. I wanted to see you again. I wondered if you'd become the Moses I'd hoped for when we were kids. You were supposed to save me. Protect me from Poppa.

What the hell are you talking about! I tried to.

She stared at him. You tried? Where did you go that day the police took me back to that man!

They woulda gotten us, sooner or later, Imma.

Yeah, you're right. But you didn't try to save me. The first sign of trouble and you were off. All you cared about was yourself.

What am I supposed to say? I was a god-dammed kid, Imma. I was stupid with hormones for you.

Oh, so that's it, then? The only reason you supposedly tried was to get in my pants?

Yes! I mean, no! I loved you! Hell, I liked you, which is saying a lot, but you used that against me. And don't try to deny it, either. He motioned helplessly at her tiny body. A body he wanted even more than ever. Not just physically, but mentally. She had been the only person who softened that pit of anger, yet stiffened it as well. He wondered where this curse came from; how the only girl he'd loved was barred from him because they shared blood, that deep coarse substance that held people together whether they wanted it or not.

What was I supposed to do? No one helped me escape, even though everyone knew what was going on. But I guess that's how it's always been. Even the ancients were men like you.

Men like me?

Just like Moses. He knew what was going on all the time in Egypt. It wasn't till the fucking burning bush that he even had a thought he should return to his people. The problem is, you never had a bush to talk sense into you.

Imma stood up and grabbed the second step. She pulled herself to the first step, then the second, then pushed herself awkwardly into the cab. Johan made no move to help her. Her skin throbbed with life when he'd touched her that first time. He knew he would feel it again, and that he'd melt to her without a fight.

He tucked his lips between his teeth and bit down on them. Johan turned and saw a cow watching him through the slats, her eyes wide and unblinking. She had heard every word and had absorbed it within her doomed flesh. He wondered what she was thinking.

~

Imma shook Johan awake at two in the morning in deep December. Let's go! Her whisper was barely a stage whisper. His parents were away, and Tobias slept through everything, so her rattling around didn't bother anyone.

Let's go where? He sat up and wrapped his quilt around his bare shoulders against the cold. Imma flipped on the light. Johan closed his eyes. When he opened them again, she was rifling through his drawers, yanking out a pair of jeans, long johns and a sweater he'd never worn.

Denver, she said without turning.

Why are we going to Denver?

Because my momma's there. I need a ride.

Several questions floated through Johan's mind, but the only one he could hold onto long enough was: You walked all the way over here?

Imma looked at him as if he'd said something stupid. Of course!

Why do you want to see your momma?

Because she's my momma. Here. Put these on, it's cold out there. I've heard it might snow again.

Johan shook out the long johns and pulled them on under the quilt. Imma laughed at his modesty.

He almost lay down at that. He didn't have to deal with this. He didn't have to follow Imma's bidding at all times, since her orders usually ended badly. But he made his usual mistake and looked at her before he did anything. She stood before him, her arms akimbo; her eyes squinted at him expectantly. Her tiny body was shrouded in a heavy parka, snow boots and a too-large stocking cap. Her glossy black hair fell over her shoulders like a protective cape. He knew she knew how he felt; she knew that he knew what was inside the layers of wool, and that he was addicted to that world beneath.

They first had to sneak gas from his poppa's tank. There was no need for light, because Poppa's unused silo glowed with the Christmas lights he always strung up the ladder each holiday after Thanksgiving. Long after they had left, Johan could see the giant candy cane in the rearview mirror, towering over the fields. Imma fiddled with the radio. The most she could get was an echo of sound beneath the crush of static that annoyed Johan enough to snap: Turn that darn thing off!

Imma laughed. It's *damn*, Johan. You can curse if you want to here. No one's listening but me. As the cab warmed up, she began shedding her winter wear. First her coat, then her shoes. Then her socks. She finally yanked off her sweater. Her stocking cap flew off; her hair stood on end with static. She put her feet up on the dashboard and went to sleep.

He saw the marks on her arm. He could see the print where his older brother's hand had closed around it, twisting her skin. Nick had always been careful not to touch her face. The bruises were always well hidden. As if he'd plotted them out like he once plotted their poppa's fields: soybeans here, milo here, wheat here; this piece would lie fallow this season.

≈

The snow had slacked off by the time the clouds lightened enough to tell Johan it was morning. They were near the Colorado border; every few miles another billboard sprang up, a ridge of plywood mountains above the shouting words: You'll soon be in Colorado! The actual mountains were still hours away.

Johan had driven this part of the country several times, but it was by far his favorite, despite being one of the most barren. The land was completely flat here; no trees except around farmsteads and creeks. Once you got into the high country, even those disappeared. Nothing was all you'd see for miles. All that dotted this wasteland of a place were hundreds of high tension towers, conveying their waves of energy from this desert to the more palatable West. In the summer they shivered in the giant heat. In the winter they stood motionless in the fierce winds that wounded the prairie. At night their lights nested around the highways, pulsing like the beat of a weird and wonderful heart. They were a strange new forest, and Johan imagined it was all his. No one else saw them the way he did. He felt proud to be among them.

Imma finally sat up and rubbed her toes. Shit, she said, looking at Johan's forest. She turned up the heat and pulled on her sweater. Nick's bruises disappeared. Are we anywhere near some civilization? I need to pee and eat.

We're near the border, Johan said gruffly. There's a rest stop there, I think.

They came upon a rest station a few miles into Colorado. A store and a gas pump stood nearby. When Imma broke the seal between them and the cold world, all of Johan's drowsiness dissipated. He struggled into his coat and grabbed his stocking cap.

Imma stood in the frozen air in only her sweater and jeans. Shit! Shit! Shit! she crowed to the spindly fir trees that surrounded the rest stop. She ran around Johan's pickup twice, taking giant leaps as she passed him. Then she headed towards the restroom.

Imma! You'd better put on some shoes! Those floors are disgusting!

The snow will purify me, she called without looking back.

When she returned, her arms were full candy bars. Breakfast is served, she said, dropping her treasure onto the truck's hood. Then she jumped into a pile of snow and squished her feet deep inside. Okay, that's enough, she said to herself. That's enough. She jumped into the cab, while Johan grabbed the food.

Imma started the engine and turned up the heat. They ate in silence, swallowing the waxy chocolate while watching the intermittent traffic. Johan wondered if he should bring up the bruises. They had been there before, the damaged blood vessels pumping purple into her frail arms. He knew his parents knew; identical frowns would crease between their eyes when she wore long sleeves in the summer. Momma would invite Imma to stay at their house for a few days. But she always went back. We are the quiet in the land, she said to Johan once. We will figure out how to solve this in our own way.

As if she sensed his thoughts, Imma said: He's always hit me before. Since I could remember. I'm just tired of it, you know?

She dropped a wrapper on the floor. I need to sleep some, Johan said.

Sounds good.

We should turn off the engine, he said. To save gas—and you can get carbon monoxide poisoning if you idle it too long.

They made a cocoon out of their coats and huddled together. It wouldn't be so bad, you know, Imma said. To fall asleep in warmth and die. I could think of worse ways to go. Her little hands sought Johan's hands. He cupped them, the way you cupped a moth or a butterfly: you don't want to hold it too tight, but you don't want to let it go.

Imma said nothing as she climbed out of the cab onto the pavement in front of the Flying J Diner. Johan watched her walk to a car and get in. She didn't start it, though. She was waiting for him to make the first exit. He honored her wish and raised his hand as he wedged past her.

Johan did not think as he made his way to Burlington. It was only when he stopped to refuel next to a sleeping town he let himself feel the crisp September night. As he passed by the truck's bed, a breath of heated air brushed his face. He turned and looked at the single eye that watched him carefully through the grated wall. Johan waited for the bearer of this eye to speak, to tell him what he needed to do, but nothing came.

He found himself afraid for these trapped souls. For this moment they were alive; they would soon be dead. Not by his hand, but his wheels. They had done nothing to him, but he was pulling them to their end.

Johan knew that Imma didn't need a Moses. She needed an Aaron, who would wear the sins on his head and make a solid God, not a God that raged in bushes and on mountaintops. Moses never made it to the Promised Land because of the sins he committed against God. He only saw it from a long way off.

He wondered if he'd minded it. Minded not living in the land he'd wandered forty years for. Minded not living in the land he'd eaten nothing but bread from the sky for. Maybe he'd been relieved. Relieved of the responsibility of an entire nation, one he'd barely known. He'd grown up as an Egyptian, not a Hebrew. It was Aaron who should have gotten the original glory; the staff that parted the red waters. It was Aaron who led the people into the land. Johan suspected Moses was really just a homebody underneath it all. He had never wanted to cross the sea. Moses had never really been one of them. He had only been their guide.

~

The officer had opened the door and pulled Imma out of the cab before Johan knew what was happening. Her feet slid on the ice. The policeman stopped her fall and held her in his embrace.

Get up, son.

Johan pulled himself up. Another policeman stood at his side. He rolled down the window. What's going on, sir?

This gal here's been reported missing. Her father said she'd left with you. I guess that's the truth, right?

Yes, sir.

Can I see your license?

Johan riffled through his coat and found his license.

This says you're over eighteen, son.

Yes, sir.

You do realize transporting a minor over state lines without parental consent is a felony? That you could see time in prison for this?

No, sir. She's my niece, sir.

That's what I've been told. Sit tight. I'm going to radio this in.

Johan!

The police officer still held Imma in his arms. Johan, get me out of here!

Johan watched the other officer get into his car. He watched himself turn the ignition and hit the gas. He careened past the cruiser and slammed the passenger door shut. He did not look at Imma.

Johan suddenly realized he had to urinate and throw up. But he couldn't stop. The lights of a town blinked on the horizon. The shadow of mountains at the edge of the prairie raced faster than he could drive.

∼

There was a cut-rate shopping center at the edge of Hays, its false lights staining the midnight sky. A few cars littered the giant parking lot.

He left the truck idling. He rounded the back and unlatched the doors. For a little while he stood examining the ramp, chained high at the top of the carrier. He could hear their breath, the expectant shuffle of feet.

Johan climbed to the top, lay down, braced himself and loosened the chains. Nothing happened. Johan gave the ramp a shove. The screech of the hinges on the way down was nothing to the slap of the ramp as it struck the pavement, the beat of the hooves that followed. He thought he might have to coax them out, but merely watched as the line of cattle streamed below his body. The carrier shook and swayed with the power of twelve-hundred pounds each. As if they'd known all along this was Johan's plan. As if they had recognized their guide long ago. None faltered, but flowed between the parked cars like dancers on a stage, their muscles fine-tuned to every pitch the composition gave them.

They headed west, to the mountains yet unseen.

A Careful Dive

1973

Johan asked Ellen to marry him on the high dive above the public swimming pool. The pool was closed for the summer, and Johan had told her that afternoon he knew of a way inside through the maintenance closet. However, when they came to open the door, it had a new lock that gleamed in the late September sunlight. Johan cursed under his breath: Scheisse. Immediately he apologized, but Ellen didn't notice. She was searching through her frayed canvas bag that was always full of bits of everything from her life, muttering to herself until she came upon the paperclip she had been looking for—a large one that had to be tugged straight—she had known it was there because she had opened a teacher's desk and tossed several into her bag on the last day of school before her graduation in May. When she had started high school she found she had an obsession with stationery supplies. The smell of notebooks, the decided snap!of a stapler, the way a pencil chafed against tired fingers comforted her. She slipped these objects from various desks and closets into her bag when the room was empty or the owner had turned away for a moment.

Now she straightened out the paperclip and slipped it into the cavity of the lock. After a few minutes of jiggling and twists, the shank pulled out of the metal's grasp. Ellen grinned at Johan's surprised face. She opened the door and entered the closet, stumbling on brooms and dustpans on the way.

Where is this opening? she asked in a stage whisper.

Just ahead, Johan said, his hand on the small of her back. He was tempted to slide it around her waist and pull her against him, but he didn't. He didn't want to ruin the delicate balance of propriety that Ellen held around her. It had always perplexed him, this strange control and frenzy that was Ellen. She would kiss him with ferocity one minute; the next she would pull her shirt down and look like she'd never kissed anyone in her life.

When they pushed through the door, the indefinable odor that only swimming pools produce swept through their hair and slipped into the darkness behind them. The pool was yet to be drained; the water lapped the edges with a soft popping. Already dead leaves and bits of trash layered its surface. The shadow of the swim house hung near the pool, cooling the air. Without a word, Ellen pulled off her sneakers and socks. She rolled her bare feet on the warm concrete and sighed. She glanced at Johan; he was looking at the high dive that towered over the pool, its tongue forever frozen in place.

I've dived off that board hundreds of times, he said. Maybe thousands.

Yeah, I know, Ellen said evenly.

A lesser person would've poked fun at his boast. A lesser person would have said: *Why don't you show me instead of telling me? Let's see how good you really are.* Ellen always took what was said at face value. Whether she believed him or not didn't matter. She knew the truth would come out sooner or later. Ellen was ready to wait until that time came.

Ellen walked to the edge of the pool and stroked its surface with her left foot. The water smelled stale; the lack of young bodies plunging into it every day had left it motionless, like a bathtub with a stopped up drain. She pulled her right foot out and let it draw itself through the water. Then she let the left foot return. Ellen hopped from one foot to the next, the hops carrying her along the edge of the pool until she'd bounced from the shade of the pool house. She wondered if this was how dancers felt on the stage; their bodies stepping beyond themselves into a sphere of nothing but muscles and joints and flesh that kept it all at bay, kept it all from exploding into the air. She stopped and held her right foot above the water. She searched for Johan in the glare of the falling sun.

Careful, he said. He had come from out of the shadow and leaned against the chain link fence. She couldn't read his face; she knew he was digging into hers.

Certainly, she said, and dove into the water. It was a side dive, an almost-fall that pulled her body into a curve that resembled a leaf about to take flight.

∾

Johan was several years older than Ellen. She had known who he was since one of her neighbors, Huldah, was his sister. She doubted he had known who she was until they met at the county jail in January. She was picking up her father, who'd been arrested for urinating on someone's lawn while high. Johan was leaving his first visit to his probation officer since he'd gotten out of prison. He'd hoped she wouldn't recognize him. His picture had been on the front page of the local paper the day he got out: Cattle Rustler Released, it read. The caption mentioned his past conviction: kidnapping his niece in 1961.

They stood in the entrance together. He was picking up his papers to prove he'd met with the officer; she was signing her father's release form. Neither acknowledged the other. Johan was embarrassed. Ellen was tired. She had stopped being embarrassed about these journeys for quite some time.

When her father came through the door, Johan realized who she was. Momma had talked about her more than once. He wondered if he should say anything, or if she wanted to remain as anonymous as someone could in this county.

Hey, Ellen, Artie Groening said, shuffling his feet as though he'd forgotten how to walk.

Where's your coat? Ellen looked to the corrections officer sitting behind the counter. Where's his coat at?

Didn't have one, as far as I know. Just his sweater.

Where'd you leave your coat at?

I don't remember. Maybe at home.

No, I just was there.

Oh.

The corrections officer expressionlessly gave her the release forms.

You sure he didn't come in without a coat? It's been below zero since Saturday.

I wasn't here when he came in.

Ellen shrugged off her coat and wrapped it around him. He was skinnier than she was, so it could've almost gone around again if you'd pulled tight enough.

Johan couldn't believe a poppa would let his daughter give him her coat. As if the shame of making her come get him wasn't enough. Then Johan thought about how his momma had looked the day she'd come to the jail to bail him out with her savings and money from the church. Her head covering was plastered to her hair, as if she had pinned it with a thousand pins; as if she'd been afraid of it swirling off her head the moment she needed it most.

Hey, Momma, he'd said when he saw her sitting rigidly on the dirty plastic chair beside a dusty plastic fern.

Hello. Do I have to do anything I haven't already done? she said to the corrections officer.

No. Just make sure he comes to court Tuesday.

She looked at Johan. Ready to go?

They never discussed why he had been arrested. What had possessed him when he let an entire truckload of doomed milkers escape into the high plains. When he left to serve his brief time in the prison in Wichita, all she said was: *Behave yourself.*

Ellen and her father were out the door by the time Johan's papers were slid across the corrections officer's desk. He jammed them into his back pocket and hurried towards them. Hey, he called. Ellen turned around.

Lemme give you my coat, he said, pulling his arms out of his jacket. The cold snapped him more awake than he had been in weeks.

That's okay. The truck'll warm up soon.

Here, he said, thrusting it at her like a small boy presenting a gift to his mother at Christmas. He was hopeful, but didn't want it to show, so he tried to sound indifferent.

Put it on, baby, her father said, suddenly appearing again in Johan's field of vision. He looked at Johan with a desperate grin full of yellowed teeth. She never wants to look weak in front of me.

Ellen put it on. The arms hung down over her hands; the hem hung past her knees. She breathed in the air of Johan's body. She could feel every curve it had given the worn lining as if she had run her hands over the inches of his frame. She smiled at him. Thank you.

It was an odd smile; a tired smile, a weak smile, a strong smile. A smile Johan couldn't quite grasp.

∽

When he came home without a coat, Momma demanded to know

where it was. We don't have enough to buy a new one, she said in a huff. I'll have to get one at the thrift store for now. Johan knew his momma would think angry thoughts about him if he kept quiet. He had wanted to be like the poor woman at the temple who gave her two cents and fled, or the plebian who prayed in the corner while the rich man boasted himself to God. But he wanted his momma to approve. He knew she would approve.

As soon as he told her she grinned at him. You'll have to pick it up, I suppose.

I guess so.

I'll go to the thrift store tomorrow and get you something that'll last till spring, but something a bit on the ragged side. Just a bit.

Why's that? I can get it tomorrow.

You can get over there, sure. But she'll see you came to see her, not get the coat, since you have a coat—but you don't want a nicer coat than your other one. You don't want to make her think you gave her your junk coat.

Ellen wondered when he would get it. If he'd make sure she was at school, and ask her father, or if he'd wait till after. She wanted to keep it in her room, since her father might take it when he woke up. But she didn't want him to see her bring it out of her bedroom, either. That night she draped it over her chair by her desk and studied it. She examined the way the lining was patched: they had strong stitches made by capable hands. She noticed the way the pockets hung loose on the front rather than the back, so she figured he held his hands towards the front when he was talking to other farmers, or keeping his fingers warm while he waited for his truck to be filled at the pump.

Johan circled the town several times after he knew that school was out. Sheets of frozen rain had cascaded Ulysses in the early hours. Trees were coated with ice; some power lines were down, the wires stiffly draped on roofs and mailboxes. They had been frozen where they fell. Half the town was without electricity. Johan had wondered if school had been cancelled, but when he passed the high school there was a litter of cars in the parking lot. He remembered the school had a generator. When he pulled in front of Ellen's house, he saw the power must be out there as well. The wires twisted around the stunted oaks in front of the house. Some had crashed on the roof after they had frozen solid, the broken wires reaching out to the sky.

Johan looked at his sister's house. A slim string of smoke rose from her chimney. There was no reason to worry about her. He didn't see any smoke from Ellen's house. Johan realized how it would look if he arrived and demanded the return of his coat when her house would be closed in with cold. He put his hand on the ignition. But then Ellen appeared on the doorstep. She had seen him the moment he stopped in front of her house. Her feet were bare, so she remained where she was and motioned for him to come inside. Ellen turned into the living room without checking whether he would follow.

When she heard him shut the front door, she turned to face him.

Well. This is it. She fluttered her hands like uncomfortable wings.

The house was a receptacle of stacks of many things. Magazines piled around the coffee table and beneath the television table. Books lined the walls on a series of boards supported by cement bricks. The walls were covered with prints of celebrated paintings. No photos but one: a snapshot awkwardly framed and given a place of honor above the bricked up fireplace. The electricity was out; she figured the people within the snapshot would be indiscernible in the fading winter light. He wouldn't see her mother dressed in jeans and a greasy shirt; he wouldn't see how her father's hands were blurred because even back then he could not keep them still when he was clean. As long as his bony fingers worried his sleeves; as long as the palms of his hands were cracked from endless rubbing of his jeans and the stubble of his face, she knew he had escaped for a time.

Electricity's out, she said unnecessarily.

You guys got a little oil stove someplace?

I wouldn't trust my father with it, not when I wasn't here.

Where's he at?

In bed. Getting over. It.

Aren't your toes cold?

Yeah, but it makes the rest of me feel warmer, she said, realizing how ridiculous that sounded. She had once thought everyone did it, until some friends had come over and laughed at her cold-reddened toes. Johan didn't laugh. He looked at her toes. They were small and round, as if her feet hadn't thought to grow into adulthood. The veins skimmed the surface of her skin. Expert swimmers in such a complex habitation.

He realized he was staring. He jerked his head up. You really should get one, he said, as if they had been talking all along about stoves. Have it on at least while you're around.

Johan examined the living room carefully. He saw the blocked up fireplace; wondered whether there was a hearthstone beneath the shag carpet; knelt on the floor and felt around the edges, looking for a corner that would give. Ellen laughed. Johan stopped. Tried to push the anger at being laughed at away. No, he thought. Not with her.

She sat on the floor beside him. I looked once, the last time it went out. I'd considered getting a stove a while back, and thought that it would be a likely spot. Someone'd removed it.

It was gone. He could look at her again. Study her face up close. Freckles. Eyes the color of bluestem grass. Slid her hand across her face to push the strand of hair that had fallen into those eyes. The strand returned. The hand pushed it back, firmly this time. The strand returned. He wondered how many times that occurred in a day, in a decade. The stroke of the hand; the hair too stubborn to pay attention to her wishes.

So, did you come for your coat? Ellen was always straightforward. That was the best way to deal with anyone. She wanted to get it over with. This time of not knowing. She wanted to know if she could breathe in his cold scent and smile.

Yes. He grimaced. No. Johan grinned. Maybe. He wanted to touch her hair. You can keep it for now. He wanted to feel her cheek with his thumb. Just his thumb. I've got a coat that'll work fine right now. He wanted to kiss her. My momma found it in a closet.

Years later she would think about that moment. She would think it even when Johan raged at her or their children. She had known it had come from Ulysses' thrift store because it had that indescribable scent only thrift stores have. She would think of it because that showed the true man he was, not the angry being that prowled within his head, waiting for moments of release. Johan was a man who would paw through dirty shag carpeting for her warmth, lie and wear a coat that was too small and hardly warm enough to last him until spring.

~

Ellen felt she could stay beneath that water forever, as if all her breath in her life was saved for this moment. She shot through the murky turquoise; headed for the deeper blue of the pool. She wondered what Johan was thinking. If he was afraid for her. If he would follow her. She hoped he wouldn't. She needed a moment to swim alone in her thoughts. She needed to decide what she would do when he asked her. She knew it was coming, though she doubted even he knew it.

She finally reached for the surface and bobbed up next to the high dive. Johan was waiting. He had known where she was going all along. Ellen pulled herself up and grabbed his hand. Let's go up, she said, without letting go of him.

Sometimes Ellen wondered if she had made the right decision; what her life would be like if Johan hadn't been there when she surfaced. If she should have swam deeper towards the darkness and bobbed up someplace else. Her decision had been a dive into water without a glance to see if it were shallow or deep. If you looked, you would never let the ground dissolve beneath your feet. You would strand yourself on cement, relentlessly waiting for the arms of the waters to rise to the sky and carry you down in comfort.

Enter Runner

1980

When Johan saw the plume of smoke rise from the southeast, he knew what had happened. He idled the combine for a moment before cutting the engine. He leaped to the ground, pulled off his cap and began to run across the field towards the smoke.

Even though he hadn't run long distances since college, his body seemed to remember its previous calling. As soon as he hit the gravel of the road, Johan slowed. He had to conserve the energy, use that final burst as he entered town. That was why Tobias was always behind Johan at the end of a run. He used his energy up at the beginning. Tobias was the nimbler of the two with lighter bones and longer legs. But Johan was the winner. At the end of a run his churning gait flowed into a charging rush, his eyes focused on the water tower that looked like the mushroom cloud they had always hid against beneath their fragile desks in elementary school. As if the scratched plywood could shelter them from what was in the core of that cloud.

But it wasn't time for that. He had to push his lumbering body into a rhythm first. He began to chant a hymn he and Tobias sang at each other when they camped out in the old silo, their hollowed voices straining for the top:

Praise God from Whom all blessings flow,
Praise Him all creatures here below,
Praise Him all creatures here below.
Praise Him above,
Praise Him above,
Praise—

Johan couldn't keep it up. His body had aged for him; his lungs needed the air he had once used so freely.

He remembered the day the public pool opened the summer after their sophomore year of high school. Johan and Tobias had raced to their yellow-beaten Ford with the cracked vinyl seats. Tobias reached it first and swung into the open driver's side window. He laughed as Johan tried to imitate him, but only managed to arch one leg inside before he fell to the ground.

Too *dikjpanssijch* to get through the window, I see! Maybe you need to go on a diet?

Johan said nothing. He climbed inside and slammed the door. Tobias gunned the motor. When they reached the pool grounds just outside of town, Johan jumped out of the moving truck and began to run with the other boys towards the chain-link fence, pulling off his jeans and t-shirt as he went. He wanted to jump off the new diving board first.

The moment his feet left the board he knew no matter how many times he dove off this board or any other board it would never feel the same way again; this first flight would never return. His arms became a shaft, his fingertips an arrow, ready to pierce the water's skin. He did not remember to breathe—but his body remembered. His body always won, in the end.

When Johan bobbed to the surface he listened for the cheers of the boys who had followed him, but he heard only taunts. His brother was shaking, his narrow body twisted around the topmost rung of the high dive. Tobias hated heights. He needed his feet firm on the earth to think clearly. Yet he sometimes forgot the way you forget the fact that walking or running was always your body attempting to fall. Only your legs remembered to keep moving their muscles towards the horizon.

Johan knew he should stop them. He was the elder brother by twenty minutes. His body had taken more nutrients than Tobias. He was the stronger one, the protector. But as he pulled himself out of the water he felt the shame that had gripped his throat only a few minutes before as he fumbled for the window. Johan stood beneath the high dive and waited for Tobias to look to him for help. He steeled his heart against his brother's face.

Johan felt the power drain from his body. His feet slid in the sunned gravel and stopped. He looked to the southeast. The smoke still stained the sky. The muted yowl of the town fire truck crept in between the pauses in the wind.

He had merely wanted to know first if it did happen, to see the story for himself, to feel the dust that had grown combustible in the grain elevator that once towered the earth like the sail of a ship. To smell the waves of burnt wheat that had been sent to the ignorant sky by the explosion. To taste the grief first if Tobias was dead, as if that could somehow distill it, make it an idea he could package and deliver to their mother. Johan knew Tobias had been gone with the grain truck long enough to be the one under the elevator's shadow; crushed while his feet were properly on the ground.

Johan had never believed in death, but still quietly hoped he would be the first to die. That he would be the first to know if there was anything after, or if it was simple oblivion. To be second meant you spent the rest of your life wondering what the dead one saw the moment he entered the horizon.

Slide

1993

That morning Jeffrey Harder asked Abigail Edwards out with a note slipped into a book. She said no. Actually, he never heard her say anything, because she never appeared for her regular ride to her father's fields after her shift ended. He waited for her in front of Ulysses' only fast food restaurant at nine-o-one, engine running.

Jeffrey held his hope for thirty minutes. At nine-ten, she would come, he thought at nine-o-five. He imagined her washing her hands, running her fingers through her hair, pulling her t-shirt and jeans from her bag and taking off her uniform. He tried to smother that image, but his mind held onto it for quite some time. At nine-twenty, he figured she was talking to some of the other morning staff, maybe trying to get out of a boring conversation with the manager. At nine-twenty-nine his hope slunk to the floorboards. He decided the answer was no, but he couldn't stop himself from getting out of his truck and entering the restaurant.

The old-timers were sitting just inside the doorway, drinking their twenty-five cent morning coffee and talking wheat prices. As usual, the prices weren't good and the yields weren't much better. There had been torrential rain a few weeks before, just as the wheat was turning from sleep. It destroyed some crops and weakened the stalks on many.

My granddaughter—the one who moved last year to Omaha? She tells me it costs five or six dollars for a box of cereal, and then there's only about this much wheat and whatever else they put in that crap, Reuben Willis said, cupping his hand. And they're only giving us two-fifteen a bushel as of yesterday!

He noticed Jeffrey. Hey son, what's your dad up to?

The air conditioning cut out last night. He's trying to fix it before things get going.

Where you cutting? Timothy Carr asked.

By Duke Pearson's.

You're cutting Jim Davis' now, right?

Yeah.

How's his health these days? Jim's?

I heard a few days ago his blood count went down again, Jeffrey said.

The men grunted at that. He's only fifty-five, Timothy said, shaking his head. And here I am, no use to anybody, but chugging along at seventy-nine.

Well, somebody's got to keep Peggy company. No one else wants the job, Reuben said, poking Tim in the arm. They laughed, sipped their coffee, and swept their hands across brittle lips simultaneously, wiping Jim Davis from their minds for now.

See you later, said Jeffrey as he walked to the counter.

The men laughed again as he turned around. He knew they were laughing at his hair. Everyone had ever since Jeffrey had started to grow it out, which was going on four years now. And now he had started his own dreadlocks. This was a place where hair was buzzed on a regular basis. He knew it didn't fit his face or his body, since he'd always been a little chunky, and had a rather conspicuous lump on his forehead. But he loved the feel of it, the texture of each strand, the fact that it made him stand out, even if it was for ridicule. Some of the kids at school called him *Samson*.

Janine was alone up front, cleaning the milk shake dispenser. She barely looked at him when he cleared his throat. He wondered if she knew.

Hey.

She nodded a greeting.

Where's Abigail?

Left.

She left?

Yeah, about twenty minutes ago.

Janine kept wiping the milk dispenser as if it were the most important thing in the world. Jeffrey figured she was trying to wipe him out of existence like Reuben Willis and Timothy Carr had wiped away Jim Davis.

She must have gone out back and crossed the windbreak to her grandmomma's place. He considered driving over there, but he needed to get going. His poppa was expecting him to empty out one of their gravity wagons into the grain bin and bring it to the field by noon.

You can handle at least *this*, his father had said earlier that morning in the round top shed, dust already sunk deep into the lines of his face.

Yes, Poppa, he had answered, almost immune to the disgust in his father's voice.

Jeffrey had never been mechanically inclined. After he burned out the motor of the lawn mower at thirteen, severed the air conditioning hose of the combine at fourteen, and rammed the new pickup into the round top shed at fifteen, his father assigned only the basest of chores for him, and went out searching for a boy that would work properly.

Poppa didn't have to look far. His sister, Gretta, had five sons, two of which she and her husband could easily spare. One drove the truck, and the other followed the combine with a tractor and a gravity wagon so they could unload on the go. Jeffrey's cousins worked like a team of horses: one pulling out the auger of the combine and the other keeping the wagon in line with it, all the while dancing through the waves of wheat.

Jeffrey realized that his father had expected him to come out of his mother's body like a real son, ready to dance with a world of dust and grease. And out he came with a bump on his head, already defeated.

~

Though they'd been in the same grade since kindergarten, Jeffrey only noticed Abigail on the first day of school of their junior year. She walked barefoot between the forests of maroon lockers, the whisper of her feet overpowering all other sounds. That was what initially had called his attention. She constantly wore a pair of ragged cut-offs that sagged on her narrow hips and hung past her knees, even though school regulations banned shorts. She had white blond hair; eyebrows so golden they faded into her forehead. Abigail had high cheekbones that jutted from her face, which she got because her mother was from Bolivia. Her father had lived in Bolivia with the Old Order Mennonites during the war in Vietnam, and returned with a wife.

Jeffrey had been milking for a neighbor since he was fourteen, but he quit because he was tired of wading knee-deep in shit and having to pull himself out of bed at four-thirty in the morning in the middle of January. After a few months with no money, he got a job at the fast-food restaurant. He was surprised to find her among the other crowd of recruits the morning of orientation.

Jeffrey and Abigail were often on the same shifts. Abigail worked the drive-thru; Jeffrey cooked the processed meat products. On weekends during school they opened the restaurant together. The first time they actually had a conversation besides telling each other orders was when Abigail had to strain the fry vats one morning, wearing incredibly huge rubber mittens to protect her from the boiling oil. Jeffrey laughed as she tugged them on.

I feel like an Eskimo, she said, grinning.

An Eskimo who's lost her way. Jeffrey felt rather witty at that comment.

After that, talking wasn't so hard. At least at work. During school they never said a word to each other, though were in many of the same classes.

Jeffrey tried to begin a conversation at school soon after Eskimo exchange, when he saw her with her friends sitting in the gym, waiting for the end of lunch period. He sat down on the bench beside her and smiled.

Abigail was quiet.

How are you doing?

Fine. And you?

Okay. Yeah, I'm okay. Jeffrey wondered what he was doing there. He looked down at his hands that were sweaty and suddenly looked very small against his wide thighs. He took a breath: I was wondering if you're working tonight.

Um, yeah. Her face was pensive. Jeffrey realized she probably thought he was asking her out on a date.

Okay, I just wondered. I'm working till closing time. See you later, then. At work. As he walked away he waited for giggles to erupt behind him. There was only silence. Jeffrey wondered which was worse.

～

Jeffrey took the long way out of town, even though it was past nine-thirty. He didn't go past her grandmomma's house, but stopped for a moment by the street. He scanned the driveway. The car was gone. A woman out watering her flowers eyed him suspiciously. Jeffrey accidentally gunned the motor as he drove away. He felt like a stalker.

He took old 56 instead of the new one. No one used it anymore except for farmers, so he could drive slow and think a little. Think about his stupidity. Out of habit, Jeffrey rubbed the bump on his forehead roughly. It was more of a swell rather than a bump, to the right of his right eye. He had had this bump since birth, and it had been much more pronounced when he was a baby—the bump which should have been Jeffrey's twin brother.

When they had him x-rayed to see the cause of the swelling, they found that it was the leavings of another fetus. Probably the two boys would have been conjoined at the head, but Jeffrey had absorbed all the nutrients. The doctor said that the fetus was harmless, but they could have it removed at any time.

His mother told him this when he asked her about the lump one day as she combed his hair. He was around six at the time, and his deformity had been pointed out to him at recess the day before.

Does it ever hurt? she asked, touching the bump gently.

No.

Do you want to have it taken off?

Jeffrey thought for a few minutes. He looked at his mother carefully. The thought of a little body sitting inside of him was both strange and exhilarating. No, he said with finality.

He barely slept that night. He continually touched the lump. The lump had always been there but he was afraid that now it would disappear. At one point he got out of bed, turned on the light and examined his forehead carefully. It really was a series of several little bumps on one large one. He touched each one, wondering what part of his brother's body was within.

Hello, he whispered to the lump. Hello. I'm Jeffrey. I'm your brother.

Three days after this discovery, as Jeffrey was sitting on the floor and coloring beneath his mother's desk in the library where she worked part time, he asked her what conjoined meant.

It means that your bodies would have been attached.

Like the cord that made my belly button? Jeffrey had gotten hold of a book that explained the pregnancy process through photographs and he had gathered that he once was hooked to his momma through a long rope of skin. It also explained why his mother's belly had begun to grow larger and larger, until he couldn't imagine her growing any farther.

No, not quite. Stay here. His mother disappeared between the stacks for a while. When she came back she had some books in her hand.

He was so taken by the photos of various people attached at the waist, the hips and the head that he asked her to check them out so he could look at them longer. He was fascinated especially by two photos: one of two women attached at the forehead, the way Jeffrey and his brother would have been. The other was a man with a second head.

But one of the heads did not have his own personality. The main head could control some of the muscle movements of the second head, but otherwise it just hung around, saying and being nothing.

He wondered what it would've been like to live like that. To have a body so close at every moment. If he and his twin would have been like the women attached at the head, he imagined their conversations would be the most wonderful of all conversations, since their lives would be together in more than the physical sense. He tried to avoid the idea of the man with two faces. Jeffrey would have wondered if the face that did not speak had any thoughts; he would have wondered if his thoughts were all his own, or if some belonged to that face; he would have worried that he was the speechless face because their thoughts were so mixed.

After a bit of a struggle with the reading, he surmised that with some twins, once one died the other would die as well, because they shared the same organs. Jeffrey didn't really believe in death, but the idea that it was a lonely business had occurred to him. If death ever really happened, he would defy that loneliness, because of the bump that would have been his brother.

Jeffrey was never alone because of that lump's presence. He often felt his brother's soul stirring in that little space on his forehead. Giving him encouragement he needed. A slap on the head when he was being stupid. He was expecting a slap now as he drove east, but nothing came but a flow of warmth.

Jeffrey had confessed this to Abigail one evening during the restaurant's required fifteen-minute break for a four-hour shift. It was the end of March, on one of those days where the weather turns warm as summer for twenty-four hours before plunging back into winter's grasp one last moment. They sat together on the hood of his truck, watching the sun fade into the lap of clouds that settled along the horizon. The few trees that surrounded the commercial development area of the town were still barren, though several birds had returned to rebuild their nests among the yellow lines of the parking lot. This world of concrete was the new, more modern prairie, Jeffrey thought. A new kind of desolation to conquer.

A field of wheat hung on the edge of the parking lot—a constant reminder of what had been. The wheat was beginning to flow in that way that reminded Jeffrey of an ocean, with a constant tide that pulls at a person's feet, demanding a release to her. It was still small and green, but he could sense that the turn from green to gold was coming, that it knew its time on earth was just about spent.

Abigail said nothing after he told her. But it was a thoughtful silence, as if she was thinking about it carefully, considering all the angles before she spoke.

The sun officially set, and they were far enough away from the streetlights to remain cloaked in the warm darkness. When a car or truck passed by the drive-thru window they were bathed in a brief flash of light, which made the darkness that chased the headlights seem that much darker.

When I was a kid, I used to have this obsession with fives, she said abruptly, as if they were continuing a conversation Jeffrey had forgotten. Everything had to be in a multiple of five. Especially words. I had to speak enough syllables to fill out to some multiple of five. I would count them out with my fingers. I was crazy about it. At night I would think of things to say the next day that were in fives. When I turned eleven or so I thought it was stupid, so I made myself stop. It took a long time for me to do it, though.

Jeffrey turned his head to look at her. Abigail was gazing thoughtfully at the last bits of light the sun left among the trees. I never have told anyone about that, she said. I wonder if I should have stopped doing it. I think it made the world make more sense to me.

Abigail jumped off the hood with a little sigh. You have a deep truth there, Jeffrey. In that head of yours.

She tried to touch his forehead, but she was too short. So she tapped his knee instead. I'll-see-you-in-side. She kept beat to her five on his jeans. Then she walked away, dusting off her flat behind.

I don't understand, Jeffrey moaned. He pressed the pedal hard and soon he was well into sixty, then seventy in a fifty-five zone. How had they been able to connect like that on a break at work, but not in any other setting? It was like a bad B-movie plot: a couple who can only communicate in a fast-food restaurant. They get married, move back behind the freezer and have children who eat nothing but hamburgers all day.

Just slide through, Jeff.

Slide through.

It was his brother talking.

He had done this before. His brother had intervened in times of trouble in the past.

When he was twelve, Jeffery had jumped off the high dive in the town's pool, plunging deeper into the water than he ever had in his life. He hadn't taken a very good breath and he knew it the moment his fingers touched the pool's floor ten feet from the surface. As he struggled for the top he felt the darkness pushing in on his eyes, taunting him, telling him he should just give up and breathe in the chlorinated water. But then there was his brother's voice:

Fly, Jeff, fly.

You are lighter than air.

Move with the water, not against it.

Jeffrey stopped thrashing and made his body an arrow, shooting for the surface. Within seconds, he popped up like a buoy. The screeching sounds of children hollering and splashing each other assaulted his ears. He hadn't realized how silent the water could be. After that day he chased silence when he was upset or in trouble. Because then he would hear his brother's wisdom.

Jeffrey let off the gas.

Slide, Jeff. Slide.

What does that mean? Slide through what? he whispered.

Listen.

When the time comes.

Just slide.

Don't think.

Just slide.

And then the voice stopped.

Jeffrey realized he had passed the turn that would take him past Keith Edward's field. He looked at his watch. It was ten-o-five. He had time.

At fourteen, Jeffrey had begun to test his father by growing out his hair. He had returned from a hair appointment nearly in tears, because the barber had cut one side shorter than the other and hadn't noticed. Jeffrey noticed, but because the barber was a family friend and was, of course, a grown up, he said nothing.

It doesn't look so bad, his father said, thumping his shoulder a little too hard.

I'll make you an appointment at Claire's, Momma said, picking up the phone.

Good grief, you don't need to do that! I'll fix it for him.

No, Poppa.

His father ignored him and rummaged through the *everything drawer* in the kitchen for the shears. He grabbed a metal mixing bowl from the dish drainer and plopped it onto Jeffrey's head. No, Poppa, he repeated. His voice echoed up into the bowl.

Johan, this is unnecessary, his momma said.

What, are you afraid? I won't hurt you. My momma used to cut my hair this way. His father's voice sounded far away—a voice he had never heard before. He felt, rather than heard the dull shears sever the hair from his head. A hand rested heavily on his shoulder.

No! A rage Jeffrey had never experienced shot into his arm and shook that weight from his shoulder. The bowl crashed to the floor and bounced once on the cracked linoleum floor.

Scheisse! He heard his father curse. *Ekj hab en Äakjel fonn di.* The voice was louder than Jeffrey thought was possible. *Hast dü kjeene Schaund?* It was his father's language of fury. *Dü best Drakj.* The Low German was buried deep inside like a hidden wound. It was a language Jeffrey did not know, but felt. He knew the meaning of those words within his flesh. He did not move. He knew by the sounds of his father's breath he was sucking blood from his hand as he finished: *Ekj wenschte dü weascht nie jebuare.*

Johan! Do not say those words to my son! Jeffrey felt his momma's hands slip around his shoulders and pull him away.

He heard the screen door slam.

Two days passed. Jeffrey and his father avoided each other as much as possible. Three days passed; Poppa called him into the tool shed. Look at this, his father laughed, holding a wrinkled photograph. I found this in a box in here.

It was a photo of a much younger Jeffrey perched on the ladder of the giant combine. Utter terror gripped his face. His father, thinner and happier, stood beside the beast, his arm stretched up around Jeffrey's legs. He did not know what to say.

It's a good picture, don't you think? I remember that day.

Jeffrey realized this was an attempt at peace, an attempt to apologize. He strained a smile. It is a good picture, he said.

You should do what you want, Jeff. His father signaled to Jeffrey's hair. Hair doesn't matter. It's the soul that counts.

Jeffrey wanted to believe him. So he decided to never cut his hair again, and see what his father would do.

∾

The chauffeuring of Abigail Edwards to her father's fields had started soon after harvest had gone into full-swing. Her car had bit the dust, and since her father—or anyone else's for that matter—had no time to try and urge it into life, it sat where it had died in the restaurant's parking lot. After that, her mother would drive her to work in the mornings and Jeffrey took her to wherever her father was cutting when she got off her shift at nine a.m.

Jeffrey had been on that shift the day her car died, since all the farm kids had to be out by nine or ten to help their parents. He immediately offered her a ride.

She stood before her car considering his offer, smelling of grease and stale bread. He poked around the engine, but he knew nothing of engines besides changing the oil.

As she clambered into his pickup that day, a book fell out of her tote bag and thumped on the floor. Abigail quickly picked it up and shoved it back in.

Wait, let me see. Jeffrey reached for the book. *In Cold Blood*.

Have you read it? she asked.

No, but I heard it was made into a movie.

Maybe he could rent it, he thought. They could curl up on the couch and watch. Maybe that'd be his in.

She grimaced. I saw it. It was horrible.

Jeffrey started the engine and pulled out of the parking lot. Isn't it about some people out in Holcomb who were murdered?

Yeah. I've been reading it while I'm waiting for Poppa to unload, she said. I probably shouldn't be. It's kind of spooky, being out on the field while Poppa's far away and there's no one around and reading about it.

The next day, the book slipped out of her bag again, but this time neither of them noticed. It was only when he was bringing lunch out to his father that he saw it peeking out beneath the seat. He read the book in one night. After he finished, he couldn't stop thinking about how isolated each farm was. Death and life could be going or coming, and no one driving past on the highway four miles east would ever know. Even though he was nearly eighteen, Jeffrey crept downstairs to lock the doors. None of the locks worked. Death could enter, unobstructed, anytime.

He couldn't sleep, so he turned the lamp on and tried to read something else, but he was too distracted. His eyes kept wandering to the book on his desk. He realized this would be his chance. He wasn't working the next day, but he could write a note and put it in her book. Then he'd give the book to her.

It took nearly an hour to write a four sentence note. At first it was a page, but by the end he kept it simple. He liked her, it read. Would she mind going out for a movie maybe once things settled down. If she didn't want to, that was okay. He just wanted her to know.

Jeffrey decided he'd give her the book and the note right before her shift ended, so she could see it in private first.

At twenty-to-nine he pulled up in the drive-thru window. When Abigail pushed open the sliding glass, a burst of canned cold air struck him full force. It was already eighty degrees and it was a dry heat, so cutting could start early. What was left of the wheat would be dried out from the night's dew before noon.

I'm not off till nine, she said.

Yeah. I have to go grab something before you're done, and I might not be here on the dot. You left this in my truck. Jeffrey handed her the book.

Thanks. I thought I'd dropped it in the field.

She was about to close the window, but Jeffrey stopped her. Hey, I read it yesterday.

The whole thing?

Yeah. I couldn't sleep at all.

She grinned. I know what you mean.

Hey, there's a note in there. You—you can read it now, or later. Whatever.

The car behind Jeffrey honked impatiently. He drove off, circled the town a few times, and then parked near the front at nine-o-one.

Over a week before the note was written, Jeffrey, Momma, Poppa, Grandmomma, Jeffrey's sister Minerva and his two cousins had a picnic in the south pasture. Minerva was going to summer camp the next day, and this was her farewell party. Poppa kept calling it a *Bon Voyage*

party with an exaggerated French accent, which infuriated Minerva. A thunderhead started forming at about three in the afternoon, just as they were finishing up and stretching out.

The thunderheads morphed into mountains and moved gracefully, like glaciers across the open sky. But Jeffrey knew they were faster than any glacier, and can be ungraceful as far as anything on the ground was concerned. As the height and width of the cloud increased, so did Poppa's irritability.

The wind picked up. Dry lightning flashed beneath the cloud. His momma, Minerva and grandmomma started to gather everything up and put it in the cooler.

That was when Momma found her camera and cried out: Pictures! We need pictures!

The thunderhead served as a backdrop.

Family without Grandmomma, his momma ordered. *Family with Grandmomma minus me.* His momma took that one. *Now, a photo of the harvest crew.* Ellen, Minerva and Grandmomma stepped back. His father draped his arms around Jeffrey's cousins, his gut hanging between them. Jeffrey stood to one side, trying to smile and ignore.

Smile, honey. Smile, his momma urged, scrunching down like a real photographer.

The picture taken, everyone breathed a sigh and went on getting ready to run before the rain came. But Jeffrey's father grabbed the camera before his momma put it away. Let's get one of the ladies! he shouted, a note of desperation in his voice. Jeffrey saw the visions of hailstones and cyclones ripping apart a year of work swirling in his head. His father was laughing, but it was dangerous and made Jeffrey's mind prickle.

Momma, Minerva and Grandmomma formed a little triangle. Jeffrey's father waited. Everyone else waited. Come on, son! he called over the increasing wind. What're you waiting for? You got long hair like the rest of them!

Johan, his momma said.

He ignored her. Come on, kid! Get with the women. My arms are getting tired.

Jeffrey slung his beefy arm around Momma's neck. I would be glad to stand with these ladies, he said.

As the camera flashed, the first boom came from the sky. As the camera flashed, Jeffrey heard himself say: I don't think it's a shame to be considered one of them.

What did you say?

You know.

Are you disrespecting my wife, my mother, my daughter?

No, you are.

I think you are. You're saying my wife is a shame.

No. You said that when you wanted me to stand with them. Instead of being with you men.

I was only kidding, Jeff. Kidding. And here you are, taking it so Goddamned seriously.

I don't like your jokes.

There're things about you I don't like, but you don't hear those things.

You don't say them. But I hear them.

I don't like your hair. See? See how that feels when somebody says that to you. I don't like your hair!

Maybe I don't like it either, but I keep it anyway.

What? That don't make no sense.

So you only have fake reasons to hate me, and don't think about the real ones.

What did you just say?

You know.

His father strode up and shoved his face into Jeffrey's. What did you just say? He grabbed Jeffrey's forearm and began pulling him closer: What did you just say? What did you just say? What did you just say?

His father's other arm circled his neck in a strange embrace. Jeffrey's face pressed against his father's shirt. He smelled Grandmomma's potato salad on his father's breath; felt it entering his eardrum. His father's arm bore down on his windpipe.

Ekj hab en Äakjel fonn di, his father whispered. *Dü best ne Schaund fer onsere Famielje.*

Why do you hate me, Poppa? he gasped, feeling the darkness hovering on the horizon. I'm your son.

Something in his father changed. Jeffrey felt the body of his father stiffen, then relax. He pushed Jeffrey away. Stared at the mark Jeffrey felt grow on his throat. Jeffrey saw his eyes widen with a fear he had never seen. As though someone else had left that mark. As though his father had just walked into the violence that ebbed from that moment.

The storm never came. It stayed west, blocking the sun until nightfall.

∽

When Jeffrey reached Keith Edwards' field at ten-forty, he saw the combine was heading west to the summit of a small swell in the prairie. Jeffrey watched the machine prowling the horizon; he figured they had done a test cut and found the grain dry enough. Which meant his father would be expecting that wagon soon; he wanted to be done with Davis' field by evening so they could move equipment to their own land that night. He noticed how jaggedly the combine had cruised through. Which meant that Abigail was driving.

Jeffrey turned off the engine, climbed out and strode through the stubble to her father's jalopy of a wheat truck. Abigail's bag containing her greasy work clothes was on the passenger seat. He kept an eye on the combine, expecting it to turn soon.

They had always frightened him as a kid; those combine monsters that devoured wheat, corn and milo with abandon. When he was still small enough to squeeze in the cab behind his father's seat, Jeffrey would sometimes ride all day, transfixed by the way the passing wheat was mowed down with such speed. He felt that his father was God; destroying life because he could.

Later, he learned that the wheat was already dead by the time it was cut. Nothing was being taken from them. They had already made that choice. And his father was reduced to a mere human being.

Jeffrey opened the cab door. He pulled her tote bag on his lap and rummaged through until her book appeared. He opened the cover, where he had placed the note. It wasn't there. He searched her bag again, until he found torn up bits littering the bottom of her bag.

He knew Abigail would be turning east soon. She would see his truck. Thought about writing her a note, but there wasn't enough time. He looked at his watch. Ten forty-seven. He needed to hurry.

No one was around when Jeffrey's truck skidded onto the yard. His mother was at her new job at Dr. Diener's office, Minerva was still at camp in Colorado. Even the cats had disappeared. They had probably retreated to the coolness of the windbreak of hedge apple trees north of the barn.

He got a quick gulp of water from the pump beside the house and walked to the grain bins. As payment for his father's service, Jim Davis had given some of his prime seed wheat. His father had tried to say no the Sunday a gaunt-looking Jim made the offer of this exchange.

Nothing needs to be paid. My boys and I can get it done in two days, he said.

He meant Jeffrey's cousins, of course. Jeffrey stood behind his father, wishing he was somewhere else.

In the end, his father had to accept. He planned to put it in a small field south of Ulysses, and grow it for more seed. The evening before, Jeffrey had brought the wagon in and placed the auger at the spout of the wagon, but it was too dark to put in the bin.

He combed his hands through his hair and tied it up in the bun he created when no one else was around. He stood awhile in the shade of the gleaming white-hot bins, the wind cooling his neck. Maybe he needed a change. Maybe he should cut his hair. He loved his hair, but it would always grow back. Maybe the absence of the hair would be an opening between him and his father. It wasn't so much of a sacrifice.

The auger was ready to go, so he climbed up on the wagon with a shovel and stripped off the tarp. The wheat shimmered in the sun, a light tan turning to yellow turning to gold. He scooped a handful and stood on top of the grain that moved like quicksand, grasping his feet. Chewing the grain into a mouthful of pulp, he looked at the sky that had become pale in the heat. Jeffrey hoped this dry spell would last, so they could be done soon. He shoveled a small depression above the wagon's chute, to help the flow of the grain.

He looked at his watch. Eleven twenty-four.

Jeffrey hurried down and turned on the auger. The engine rattled a bit before exploding full-throttle. He unlocked the chute at the navel of the wagon and cranked the door open a sliver. His father had just greased the chains that morning, so it opened easily. A small river of grain poured into the auger's basin, and began to trundle up the tube into the open bin. Jeffrey remembered he had left the shovel on top of the wagon; he needed it to pull the grain closer to the tube. He climbed up the ladder and tried to reach it without getting in, but it was too far away. So he hopped up, careful to hang on to the wall and stay away from the little funnel that was forming to his left as the wheat coursed downward. He crept towards it, keeping an eye on the funnel. The shovel had fallen sideways. Once he was near enough to grab it quick, he let go and reached for the handle.

Jeffrey heard the shutter of the chute spring wide open.

The shovel immediately disappeared from sight as the entire wagon became a funnel, the wheat crashing down, pulling at Jeffrey's feet, then legs, then torso. He flailed, attempted to grab the side of the wagon nearest, but his fingers couldn't quite reach. He took a frantic breath as he was covered by the cascading flow.

His ears were completely stopped up. He could feel each kernel searching for some kind of crevice. Jeffrey felt them seal up his nose, pound at his mouth, demanding entrance. His arms tried to move, but they were paralyzed by the weight pushing him down.

Slide, Jeff, slide.

Everything seemed to slow in his mind. He realized he'd never asked Abigail about her feet. Why had she been barefoot in the fall? Jeffrey imagined her above this pile of wheat, wading in the grain like an ocean. He waited for her to see him. But she never did.

Slide. Slide.

Jeff, you must slide.

Don't fight it.

Let go and slide.

Jeffrey imagined himself as an arrow and headed for the door.

Slide.

Jeffrey felt a bump at his feet.

He'd hit a wall. The door shut in his mind.

He saw Timothy Carr talking to Reuben Willis the next day: He was only seventeen. And here I am, seventy-nine, healthy as can be.

He took a sip of coffee, and wiped Jeffrey Harder from thought.

He saw the cars rushing past on the highway, ignorant of what was taking place at this moment. His story was ending. Theirs was moving on without him.

Before he opened his mouth to let the wheat take their place inside, he envisioned himself as a furrow in the ground, ready to swallow what will die in the winter but will be resurrected come spring.

Ellen Harder, Annual Physical

1993

Ellen encountered Huldah in the dairy section of Deb Duerkson's IGA the morning Jeffrey died. Ellen was preoccupied; she'd forgotten her list of groceries on the kitchen table when she left for work, and though her cart was full, she was sure she'd missed something, and wandered the aisles distractedly.

She was preoccupied because she had realized that morning that she was attracted to her boss, Dr. Harold Diener. Ellen became conscious of this when she opened the office calendar to enter in an appointment, and saw that she was scheduled for her annual physical in two weeks' time. The thought of him touching her in even the most professional manner made her blush like she hadn't in years. The fact that he would note her weight, height and age embarrassed her—and usually none of those things disturbed her until now.

Fortunately, she always wrote appointments in the office calendar in pencil, so she immediately scrubbed out the date with her eraser. It bothered her that she could still see her name and reason for the visit imbedded in the soft paper: *Ellen Harder, annual physical,* the ghosted print whispered. She rubbed the space again, but she could still see her name.

This is ridiculous, she muttered, and glanced at the clock: ten fifty-five. Harold was in his office with Francine Kreutzinger, who always demanded a double slot so she would have plenty of time to air her troubles. He didn't have another appointment until after lunch. She told the nurse's assistant that she had a quick errand to run. She almost added that if anyone called for an appointment during the first week of July, there was one that had opened up, but then she realized the nurse's assistant would see the strangled writing on that one-by-one-inch square: *Ellen Harder, annual physical.*

Ellen had known Harold long before she became his receptionist. They had lived on the same block as children. They attended the same church and sang in the community choir together. His daughter was the same age as Jeffrey, so they saw each other at school concerts and parent-teacher conferences. Harold was always pleasant, though he had a distracted air about him, as if he were unsure of the appropriateness of his presence.

The first time they talked beyond the weather, children and spouses was when Ellen interviewed for the receptionist position. She had never been a receptionist—her only past professional experience was working part time at the public library—but she felt it was something she could master.

Harold seemed more nervous than Ellen when she arrived. He avoided eye contact and stumbled through the random questions scribbled on a yellow tablet:

How many words per minute do you type?

Seventy.

Impressive. Do you smoke?

No.

Good for you. Have you used a computer before?

Yes. At the library.

Of course. Will you work weekends?

I guess I can. Are you considering being open on weekends?

Ah, no. I just read somewhere that you should check and see how flexible a person is. Harold glanced up and smiled nervously.

Ellen smiled back, thinking that she would never have thought Harold Diener handsome if he hadn't smiled at just that moment.

∾

Ellen rounded Ulysses twice before she finally parked in front of Deb's IGA at eleven-twenty. When she saw Huldah in the dairy section, she nearly turned away. Ellen knew everyone in that store, but somehow she felt that maybe Huldah would see something that no one else could spy out of rosy cheeks and frustrated breathing.

But Huldah had seen her; she stared at Ellen as though she had just made a somersault down the aisle. Huldah was poised above the rows of milk jugs, her fingers reaching to make their final choice. Ellen waited for her to choose. The two women watched one another for a few seconds before Ellen realized what her missing item was. She moved closer to Huldah and reached out to grab a gallon of whole milk. When Ellen had chosen, Huldah followed suit and placed her jug into her low wooden wagon. They regarded each other carefully, nodded, and moved on.

Ellen returned to the office at twelve-thirty. She brought in the milk to put into the employees' refrigerator, but before she made it to the kitchen, the phone rang.

Ellen? Ellen, come home, Agnes said. I just got home now. Ellen, there's been an accident.

What happened? What happened to Johan? Ellen found herself in a long moment where she envisioned the funeral, the burial, the nights of an empty space in bed. For a moment, Harold Diener filled that space, but she shook that vision away.

It's not Johan. It's Jeffrey. He must've fallen in the grain cart when he was unloading the wheat into the bin. He got caught in the wheat coming out of the chute.

How is he? How is he?

Ellen, Jeffrey's dead.

Ellen held the phone and watched the condensation build and drop from the gallon of milk she had purchased as her son died. She wondered what it would feel like to drown in a landslide of grain, what the sounds would be as your breath was siphoned away. She wondered if you could drown in a flood of milk sweat. She wondered which death would be worse.

$\sim$

When she had finally returned to work at the clinic after the accident, a month had passed. One of Harold's nephews had come and installed a new computer and recorded all the appointments on it. She found the appointment book stashed in a corner with other files he had entered into the computer, and looked at the page where her name had been. Violet Vogt had taken her place—a case of watery bowels and sick stomach. The entry had been made with a felt-tip pen. When Ellen turned the page and felt the backside of that week, she could still feel her name beneath the bright purple tinge: Ellen Harder, annual physical.

She wondered if she had not erased her name if she would have decided to run home and get her list. She wondered if she would have remembered that Jeffrey would be at home around noon, and she should be there to make sure he had some lunch before he unloaded the grain wagon for Johan. He wouldn't have been alone on the farmyard with no one to protect him. She wondered if there would have been some way to stop that moment when she reached for that unnecessary gallon of milk and her son fell into that chorus of wheat that gave way to no voice but its own.

Drinking Water

1994

The summer after Jeffrey died, the Harder family took a vacation. Or at least that's what Momma called this rare event. But it wasn't a vacation. It disguised a visit to a special doctor. Poppa was sick, and this doctor was said to be the best. Minerva understood this, but she let her parents think she didn't know.

It had been a long time since their last family vacation. Poppa was always too busy and Momma had to help him. In an effort to make it up to her children, Momma saved enough money to send one of them to camp each summer. Neither of them enjoyed the camps she sent them to; they were Midwestern and boring. Jeffrey and Minerva figured they may as well camp out in the west pasture with Poppa's old camping gear. At least then they'd have each other's backs, since they both had a knack for attracting bullies. It never occurred to them to complain about it. Instinctively they knew Momma couldn't afford to send both of them to camp at the same time and that she sacrificed a lot for that week of supposed enjoyment. So Jeffrey and Minerva had taken turns going to camp after miserable camp for several years.

Minerva thought she had finally found a camp to embrace when she went to one in the Rockies the previous summer. On the second day, she climbed a little ridge called Inspiration Point. She was a bit on the heavy side, so it was more of a struggle for her than for most of the kids. She had to crawl over boulders on her hands and knees, while other campers pranced past. But once she reached the top she decided it was worth the trouble. Mountain after mountain pushed through the horizon like frozen waves, the clouds wrestling with each other over each peak. It made Minerva want to believe in God.

A camp counselor had seen her crawl up to the summit. With a joyful bounce during the evening Share, Prayer and Dare time, he said to the gathered campers: An inspiring thing happened today. Minerva Harder, in spite of her affliction, climbed Inspiration Point! God was with her today!

The doctor visit would be on Monday. They went on a Saturday. They were going to spend two nights with a family Minerva had never met. She constantly forgot their names and their relationship to her parents. They were people unlike any she had ever known. Their house was large and cool, and had a basement with a pool table. Fluffy towels were curled neatly in a large basket in the bathroom. Little white soaps sat primly by the sink in the bathroom without a bathtub off the main hall. Minerva was convinced they never washed their hands because none of them wasted down with use the entire weekend.

What really set them apart was the fact that they owned a sailboat. And they were going to take Minerva and her parents sailing on a large lake. Though Jeffrey and Minerva had taken out a patched canoe many times before he died, she'd never been on a real sailboat. Jeffrey and Minerva had always felt superior as they bumped along the creek-like canals that wound through low-hanging cottonwoods and fields of corn. They felt superior because this lake was really a man-made reservoir that fed Ulysses' water supply. Their house, like all the farms in the township, was fed by an aquifer that lay cool and dark beneath the fields and pastures. It was more pure, they had decided, than the dirty drinking water they wandered through without life vests.

When they arrived at the dock that Sunday, the lake was filled with gleaming white boats. For some reason they did not have their sails open to the breeze. This mysterious friend of the family had no trouble picking his out from the dozens that bobbed with the lap of the water. The name of the boat was *Caroline*, after their newborn baby with the sweaty dark curls.

Her family stood uneasily on the deck and watched this man and his wife dash around, shouting odd words to each other, pulling snake-like ropes and pulleys. Momma held the baby. The baby wore nothing but a diaper and a sun hat. Her pale skin reflected the light like the lake, and glowed against Momma's black shirt. Minerva wondered if she had ever looked that way; Caroline was so calm and sure of this stranger's care, as if it were an expected gift.

The man revved up the engine that would take them out of the docks. Poppa sat next to him, and they navigated the boat together, laughing at unheard words. They passed the other boats smoothly. Most of them were not nearly as nice as theirs—Minerva claimed it for the Harder family immediately—as if the man and his wife were the guests. She saw rust dotting hulls, badly coiled ropes, men and women stripped to their swimsuits, their stomachs drooping. A two-tiered houseboat bobbed next to them for a moment; it was painted a bright red with yellow trim. An older woman sat on the very top, reading a magazine and drinking out of a silver can. Minerva waved at her in a burst of sea-bound camaraderie, but the woman didn't respond. Then they were out of the mess of boats, and came into the main part of the lake. Wind blew against Minerva's face, wiping the smell of rotten wood and dead fish from her nose. The man and his wife began to scurry around again, pulling out the sails and shutting off the engine, leaving a water-filled silence. Once they were up, the wind took over, taking its cargo to wherever it wanted them to go.

You can walk around if you want to, the wife said. She had reclaimed her baby and was heading to the cabin. And you can pull your shorts off your swimsuit. No one will see you but us, if you're self-conscious. She looked at Minerva as though to say: You certainly should be self-conscious, with hips that wide.

Minerva stared at her, visualizing herself throwing the wife's waif-like body overboard with meaty hands, or stealing her baby and raising it on hot dogs and candy bars. The woman gave Minerva a weak smile and disappeared. Momma must have heard, because she came and put a hand on Minerva's shoulder. Her hand was strangely cold.

Isn't this fun? Momma said. I feel like we're like our ancestors on the Atlantic.

Minerva sighed. Yeah, kind of. Is it okay if I look around?

Sure. But wear a life vest.

Momma!

Momma lifted one out of a box with the words *Life Vests* painted in bright red letters. Come on, humor me.

Though she smiled, her body tensed and she bit her lips which muffled the false laughter. Minerva knew she was thinking about Jeffrey. Momma always got that way whenever his death became fresh to her. As if it had just happened.

Minerva was at the camp in the Rockies the week Jeffrey died. Two days before the last day, the camp director found her and said, You need to go home. There's been an accident.

She sighed with relief. The experience was over. But a second breath later, that feeling vanished. Minerva was old enough to know that having to go home because of an accident meant someone was dead. She had heard over and over about cars careening into other cars, balers ripping arms and faces from the bodies of men, falls from the tops of grain elevators, children tumbling off tractors and crushed by tires or mauled by a soil ripper.

Accidents happen, her momma had said more than once before and after Jeffrey died. Death happens.

Minerva put on the vest. Its buckles strained against her large chest.

She headed to the front of the boat and inhaled the spray of the water as it skimmed over the billions of molecules that supported the world. She clung to a rope, and slowly inched towards the very tip. Minerva grew braver as she moved closer. She let her eyes wander from her feet to the horizon. Dozens of other boats slipped alongside, white and glowing in the sun. Flashes of glass reflected the lake, and dotted her eyes. Minerva blinked. Each time she closed her eyes she saw the echoes of the images she'd seen, like ghosts of boats and water.

Still clinging to the rope, she took another step closer to the bow, but found nothing but air beneath her right foot. She hovered over an open square in the deck. A square that would have fit into that space lay to one side. She hovered over the hole, squinting to see what was inside.

The wife and her baby were sleeping, facing each other on a narrow bed. The wife must have been nursing her baby, because the top of her one-piece was pulled down to the waist, exposing her breasts to the sun. The baby lay centimeters from her mother's breasts, her sides pushing in and out with her tiny chest. Her left hand scratched at the tip of her mother's right breast with each breath.

She couldn't stop looking. Although Minerva knew the wife thought she was alone, it seemed a little unnatural to leave the skylight open to the world. It made what should have been a tender, necessary act somehow disgusting. She couldn't stop looking. Minerva's hand crept to her chest, unloosened the straps of the vest and came to her own overgrown breasts. She wondered what it was like, to have another life touch that part of your body—a part that was considered forbidden. Momma had once said that the Amish were so conscious of their women's breasts they sewed their dresses with a special cape on the front in order to disguise that cleft between them.

Minerva pushed her fingers into the top of the swimsuit; crossed the bulge of flesh of her right breast and found the nipple. It grew hard at the touch. Her fingers circled the nipple, pressing it into her body. Minerva wondered how it felt to have a baby pull the milk from your nipple, the lips like a water pump high above an aquifer that lay so dark beneath the earth.

A shadow fell across the woman and her child. Minerva ripped her hand from her breast and looked up at Poppa. If he had seen what she was doing, he said nothing about it. He took her hand and pulled her upright.

Leave them in peace, he said.

Okay.

Poppa led Minerva to the bow of the boat. They leaned carefully against the high metal fence. Look at the water, he said. There's so much water.

Minerva nodded. But she could only think of that pressure on her breast, the heat between her legs, the gasp she had to stifle before Poppa arrived.

An Invitation

It was a Tuesday when he received the invitation to Cora's wedding. He knew what it was before he even opened it. With his right stump he held the envelope down, and slit it open with a penknife.

Black tie, it read. *Feel free to bring a guest.*

Harold threw the invitation away.

Five-thirty was his last appointment. He waited for the noise in the waiting area to die down, then went to a little room just off the main hall and turned on his computer. Harold had never really gotten used to writing with his left hand, so he kept a micro-recorder in his pocket, and made notes that way. At the end of the day he would henpeck them in. He had gotten into the habit of making side comments to his recorder about patients, what was going on outside his window, random thoughts.

Mrs. Carr was wearing a sweat suit colored rust orange—why does she attack her figure like that? There's John Wiebe racing by on his motorcycle without a helmet again. I can't remember if I bought eggs yesterday. I think so. Maybe. When is Melanie Hiebert going to tell her parents she's pregnant? They can't be that blind. Ellen is wearing a new blouse. It's egg-shell blue.

He enjoyed it. He always erased the tape once the medical information was in the computer. There was never anything of importance to keep.

The light tap on his doorframe was the first sign he didn't have the office to himself. Harold snapped off the recorder. Ellen stood in the doorway, holding something. Doctor, I found this in the garbage. I figured you didn't mean to throw it away.

For the rest of the week the invitation lay on Harold's desk, and for the rest of the week he argued with the micro-recorder: *Good God, Harold, why are you even considering? She's your ex-wife. Why do you even ask? She sent a goddamn invitation! It's probably from her future mother-in-law. She probably sent all of the invitations, and wanted to see if the horrible wreck of a crippled ex-husband would show up!*

The following Tuesday evening he found Ellen emptying the trash, a smile playing about her lips. Harold cleared his throat. She looked up and grinned. Did you need something, Doctor?

Harold always felt that Ellen was secretly thinking of an inside joke. He wondered if it was about him, but the way she was smiling now while emptying a trash bin told him it was something else entirely. Ellen's humor hid the fact that she was plain. They'd been neighbors as kids, but he was older by nearly ten years, so they had hardly known each other until she showed up to interview for the receptionist position at his clinic. She was in her late thirties and wore her age nicely. Her fat had settled, but didn't sag, and she wore flattering skirts and dresses instead of elastic-waist pants and oversize blouses. Unlike most of the women in the area, she wore little makeup and her hair was unfrosted. More than once he found himself describing her to the recorder: *Ellen's hair fascinates me. It isn't overly long, but just crosses her shoulder line. When she laughs at my jokes, thank the Lord, her hair sweeps her shoulders as she shakes her head. There is one piece of hair that keeps falling into her face. She tries to fix it, sliding her hand across her face to move it where it belongs, but it always comes back. Always.*

During the summer she wore her hair up and he couldn't stop looking at it; it was piled on her head like a twisted serpent; little tongues of curls slipped out upon her neck. It was an unconscious serpent, Harold knew. Ellen had an essence of Grace that never meant to cause discomfort. She loved everyone without expectation of reciprocation. He had seen it with grumpy patients who thought she should drop everything to serve them and impatient nurses that groaned when she held them up with a medical question. Harold wondered how she had come to possess such Grace. Her father had been a junkie and a suspected abuser. He figured she would've grown a hard shell rather than a porous one.

Harold cleared his throat again, which made him cough this time.

231

He turned away to cough into his elbow. Too late he realized he was coughing into his right elbow, making his amputated arm open to her. He straightened up, expecting her to have turned away, embarrassed, but she was still watching him, her smile swaying on her mouth as if nothing uncomfortable had happened.

Heartened, he said, Ellen, I was wondering if you'd accompany me to that wedding. My ex-wife's wedding, actually.

Ellen looked surprised, but she covered it nicely. You know I'm married, Doctor.

Harold had never understood why such a woman would marry Johan, the well-known bully when they all were young. Johan, the one who could run the fastest, played the best in every sport, won every fight. Johan, a man who raged like a tiger at any imagined insult or injury. He realized now that perhaps it was the fact that the nonjudgmental attitude she brought with her into the clinic extended even to a man like Johan Harder.

I know. I wanted to invite you because then you wouldn't—expect anything, he said.

Yes, most married women don't expect anything.

I'm sorry—I didn't mean to imply—

Oh, good grief, Doctor, Ellen laughed. I know what you meant.

If you'd like, I'll talk to Johan.

What, and ask permission? I've never asked Johan for permission for anything. Yes, I'll go, whether he likes it or not.

Um, excellent. It is a black tie affair and if you need—

No. Don't worry. I won't embarrass you.

Harold began backing out of the room. Well, I'll see you later.

One thing, Doctor, she said with a grin. I'm curious: why take me, of all people? I assume you're going to prove something by going, but how much can you prove anything by my presence—you should bring someone mysterious, not me. Cora surely remembers me.

No. No. He attempted a laugh. I'll just feel—more of a man with a woman on my arm.

That night Harold thought of the ways she may have taken such a statement: *One: that I had to show off a woman to show my testosterone's power. Two: I was trying to make an off-handed joke at my missing fourth of an arm. Three: that she was the only woman I could think of because she happened to be in my sights. Four: that she is the only woman I talk to anymore; she couldn't possibly say no.*

$\sim$

Harold kicked the gravel in his driveway while Johan heaved his sagging stomach around the engine. He noticed Harold's skin looked yellow; he wondered if he had seen his oncologist in Kansas City lately.

I think it's the alternator, Johan said, emerging from the hood. I can fix it, but not today. It's too late to go and buy a new one.

Ellen emerged from Harold's front door.

Gretta's going to lend us her car. She says Nate will be here in five minutes.

She wore a gown of deep lavender, with a black velvet shawl to ward off the early spring chill. Harold understood why Johan had married Ellen. As always, he wondered what had been her motivation to marry Johan. He examined the man before him carefully, wondering how he'd done it.

They had already merged onto the interstate when it occurred to Harold that he ought to make conversation. You look quite nice this evening, he said.

Ellen was busy passing a tractor-trailer, so she did not reply right away. Thanks. You look pretty nice there too, Dr. Diener.

He winced. Please, feel free to call me 'Harold' for the evening. He winced again, realizing how pompous that sounded. In fact, if you'd call me 'doctor' less often, I'd like that a lot, too. Harold sighed. He was practically ordering her to call him by his first name now. You can call me whatever you want, really. Don't mind me.

She laughed. You know why I call you 'doctor,' now don't you? It keeps us separate, professional. As we should be.

They arrived at the church in Salina at five-fifty. It took them fifteen minutes to find a parking space five blocks away. The ceremony was already underway when they entered the sanctuary.

Cora stood at the alter with a pride and assurance that had always floored him, even years into their marriage. He wondered what she was thinking. He wondered what sort of man she was marrying. The groom's nondescript back faced Harold.

After the ceremony, Ellen and Harold sat in the back of the church, watching the wedding party take photographs.

I brought my camera, you know, she whispered. You should go up and get your picture taken.

I don't think she would like that. We haven't spoken in years.

Why are you here, then? She invited you, didn't she? How can you come all this way without a word to her?

During the ceremony, Harold wished he could've worked this question out with his micro-recorder: *What the hell are you doing here, anyway? She just wanted to see if I'd have the guts to come. To throw me into the same disorientation that I always threw at her when Hannah died. To shove your face into her happiness and watch you squirm.*

I imagine she didn't think I'd actually come, he said.

Ellen pulled a camera out of her purse and began to stand. Harold, this is your only chance to prove to her that you've continued on with your life—

No! he hissed, grabbing Ellen's hand. A few people glanced at them. Harold kept his hand closed on hers and made for the door. As soon as the swinging doors shuffled closed behind them, he realized what he had done. He dropped Ellen's hand.

I'm sorry. I'm sorry. That was horrible of me. He kept his eyes glued to the exit sign above the entrance. Did I hurt you?

No. Surprised me more than anything else. I never saw you with that amount of spirit before, she said, laying a hand on his right shoulder and smoothing out the wrinkles of his jacket.

That was the first time Ellen had deliberately touched him. There had always been incidental moments with fingertips, but nothing else. Though he was careful and exact in the clinic, outside that cocoon of glaring lights and scentless skin, Harold was a fumbler, tripping into people and brushing up against others as he walked. He hadn't been able to rule his body like he ruled his actions. But Ellen had always kept their bodies apart, in defiance to his clumsy gravity. He wanted to know her secret, to ask her how she did such a thing.

You know, he said, I never apologized to her.

Apologized for what?

For Hannah's death.

It was an accident.

But that doesn't matter, Ellen. Hannah was our daughter. I was driving. It doesn't matter at all.

Accidents happen, Harold, Ellen said evenly. Death happens.

Harold remembered when Ellen's son, Jeffrey, had died in a freak farming accident a few summers before. He drowned in a gravity wagon full of seed wheat. Some of the neighbors had emptied the wagon and placed his body beneath a tree next to the water pump when Harold arrived. Ellen knelt beside her son, dusting off his face, his shoulders and his hands with a bandanna. Her body rocked with each moaning breath that poured out of her body. When she finished dusting him off, she opened his mouth and began to remove the kernels of wheat that had stopped up his lungs, dropping each grain gently to the ground until his body was surrounded with a dull shade of gold. Harold saw the Grace in her grief. Like those foreigners he had seen on television keening over their dead, she acknowledged her grief, gave herself the Grace to feel the wrench of her heart just as she had the love of those around her.

Done with its work, Ellen's hand slipped off Harold's shoulder.

I think I need some air, he said.

∼

Almost three weeks passed before Hannah's funeral. Harold had been in and out of consciousness for a week, and when he finally woke up, he was too weak to stand for long periods of time. On a hot July day he got out of bed, let Cora dress him and pin his sleeve loosely around the remnants of his arm, and got into the waiting car that took them to the church.

An urn shaped like a scalloped vase sat in from of the simply draped lectern. Cora had Hannah cremated without consulting Harold. When she had told him what she had done, he snarled at her and sat up. Roger, Cora's brother, had been with her when she told Harold. He took Harold's shoulders and gently maneuvered him back to the center of the bed. Harold glared at Roger. Cora began to cry.

Why are you crying? Harold demanded. You got to see her face; you were able to touch her hair; you got to see her whole.

She did not see her whole, Roger said, putting his torso between them. Her body was too damaged to see Hannah as she really was. I identified her body. Not Cora. Neither of you should have seen her like that.

He had only wanted to look at her; see her body to prove to himself she was dead. Even if she was nothing but pulp, Harold would have felt better. It would have comforted him to see that the Hannah he knew was not housed in that shell; that her body had turned into mere flesh. He had seen dead bodies before; bodies that were damaged in a hundred different ways. Harold had thrown up the first time he cut open a cadaver, but he didn't ever again. He was amazed at how easily he grew callous towards physical death. He had needed to see the grossness of her body to accept the end of Hannah.

While the preacher intoned Hannah's spirit to heaven that day in July, all Harold could hear was Hannah's crow of laughter, see her mouth that formed a pout when things didn't go her way, feel the crinkle of her forehead beneath his lips as he kissed her goodbye the day she left for college. Harold didn't believe in heaven. He knew Hannah was gone. All that remained of Hannah was in that ugly urn.

He hadn't believed it when Cora told him Hannah had died. He could not see how he and Cora had survived but she had not. He remembered reaching his hand out to stop her. Though they had removed his right hand and half of his forearm, he could still sense his fingers catching her t-shirt, his nails gripping the unraveled hem. Even years later he would find himself searching for those fingers at night; when his left hand found nothing, it would climb up his stubbed arm and caress the scar that shrank with age.

But I caught her, he had protested when he first learned of her death. I caught her in time.

≈

A few weeks before Hannah was born, Cora decided they needed a fence around their backyard. She didn't want a chain-link one, either, but a tough sturdy one that would hold their child safe from harm.

I want one like that, she said, pointing at Huldah Harder's fence across the alley. I heard some kids talking about her yard a few years ago; that the fence holds a tiger. Knowing Huldah, I wouldn't be surprised.

That's just kids talking, Harold said.

Anyways, I want a fence to keep our tiger in.

So he began to build a fence for the being they did not know yet. On the days when he wasn't at the hospital, he was putting in fence posts and nailing boards. Their yard was huge, so even after what Harold felt was long enough, he had only fenced in a quarter of it. Neighbors would watch from their houses. Boys would help for a few minutes before slinking away. Only Huldah came out and helped. When he was done for the day, he usually dropped his tools wherever he was and went into the house for supper. Invariably, he would find his tools neatly piled by their back door and the scrap lumber bundled by the shed the following afternoon.

Harold never finished the fence. He had it wound around one side and half way around another when Cora's contractions came. After that, they were both too busy to think about fences. Hannah's cries for food or rest or cuddling drowned out all thoughts for months. Each season that passed brought up a discussion about the unfinished fence. A few years later, when they sat in their backyard and watched Hannah scoop up dead leaves and toss them at a neighbor's patient dog, Cora said: You know, I'm glad you never finished it. The fence.

Yeah?

Yeah. I guess I figured I had to protect her from everything. That's what a mother does, right? But then, she laughed. I remembered how I howled at my mother for doing this kind of thing. And I certainly don't want her to howl at me!

As she laughed, Harold looked at Cora's profile. In the past five years, her youthful glow had been replaced by a subtler finish. Though they'd tried to give Hannah a sibling, only three miscarriages had followed her glorious birth. The night before, Cora had given Harold a condom for the first time.

I don't want to do this anymore, she said simply.

Harold felt freed by the condom, instead of emasculated. It seemed slightly devious, to only have sex for the experience, but it was just that that made him want her even more. She was an independent being now, instead of a woman hampered by those children who didn't come. Cora had bumped against a fence and wanted out, he realized.

The day after Cora left, Harold sat on an over-turned bucket in his backyard and studied the fence. It had snowed a few days before, and a dirty crusting laced the teeth of the palings.

Why didn't I finish the fence? he asked the micro-recorder. *Maybe that would have stopped this. Maybe we would still be as we were. She would have howled and howled at us, but she would be alive to howl at us. And that's what matters.*

~

After the funeral, Harold tried to remember the accident. He began to question Cora about her memories. Had he been going too fast, or had the truck ahead of them stopped short? Was she awake the entire time? How soon did the ambulance arrive? Who were the EMTs? Was Otto Funk one of them? He never trusted Otto. Was Hubert Fleming one of them? That guy could work miracles. If Hubert had been there, things would have been better. Maybe he would have managed to save Hannah.

At first, Cora answered his questions with terse shrugs, nods or shakes of her head. But when he repeated the same questions over and over, she began to walk out of the room in the middle of his interrogation. That was the name she called his series of questions. When she had left the room, the house, or once, the car, Harold would come to himself and wonder why he was berating her every answer. The day she had stopped the car, handed him the keys, gotten out and began to walk back home, Harold went to his clinic and retrieved his micro-recorder. He began to ask these same questions to the recorder. He recovered the police documents, the hospital documents and even the mechanic's report of their totaled car, and began filling out the blanks for himself. He knew people were talking about him and his obsession. Although he felt he kept his fixations out of the clinic when he returned to full-time, he sensed his patients' discomfort as he clumsily examined them with one arm.

One morning, he sat for some time in his back office, trying to transcribe his notes from the day before, when he realized it was ten-thirty and Ellen hadn't brought any files for him to review. He went up to her desk and stared at the empty waiting area.

No patients this morning?

No, Doctor.

When's the first one coming this afternoon?

There are no appointments today.

I'm one of three doctors in town. How can I not have a single patient in a day?

Ellen looked at him calmly. Because you have frightened people away.

That evening he looked at the reports for what he hoped would be the last time, and asked the same questions of his micro-recorder. He listened to his questions, anticipated answers already given twice before adding one more comment: *The one question I've avoided for so long is why she wasn't wearing a seatbelt that day. Cora had always told Hannah to fasten her seatbelt. Why hadn't she told her that day? What kept that one comment from slipping through her lips?*

Even as he said it, he felt ashamed. How could he think this of his wife?

Out of habit, he hit the rewind button and dropped the micro-recorder in his pants' pocket as it whirred to the beginning. As he walked home in the stillness of February darkness, a small load crept down his shoulders to the cement of the sidewalk. As he walked home, he found himself crying for his daughter whose ashes were now circled around the trunk of a small elm on a swell of prairie. On the Christmas Eve after the accident, he and Cora had sat next to that struggling tree and laid the gifts Cora had purchased the spring before without knowing the recipient would never receive them: a small necklace of bright red stones and a jangle of bracelets like the kind that Hannah loved to wear. Harold always knew his daughter was approaching when he heard the soft rattle of the hoops encircling her wrists and sliding up her forearms.

~

The conversation just before the accident had been ridiculous, easily avoided, had Harold not taken the reason so seriously. Hannah had declared that morning, with that assuredness only the young possess, that she wasn't going back to college.

It's just a phase, Cora said. After she's worked a few months at a fast food chain, she'll change her mind. Cora grinned at the combine churning up dust a hundred feet from the highway.

Momma! Hannah said, leaning forward from the back seat. I'm not going to work at a fast food place!

Where then? Cora countered, cocking her head and looking at her daughter in the rear-view mirror. You aren't just going to slum around the house. You've got to earn your keep, since you won't be working on that brain of yours.

No, no, no. Harold pounded his right hand against the steering wheel. It's too easy to fall into the abyss of Ulysses. She needs to go and see other places, other things while she's young.

Are you listening to yourself? Where did you go when you were young? And here you are, back in Ulysses.

That's different.

How?

I came back because of you.

Excuse me? Because of me? You're saying the only reason you returned to the abyss was to marry an uneducated country gal?

I didn't mean it that way!

Then what way did you mean it?

Yeah, Poppa, Hannah said, leaning even farther into the front seat. What did you mean?

Listen here, young lady, we were talking about you, not us!

Don't speak that way to her!

She's trying to make us fight between ourselves, he said, breathing deep and focusing on the road.

You didn't answer my question, Harold.

There were more reasons than that. Than you. I wanted to come back—it wasn't a forced issue.

What were these other reasons?

Harold looked sideways at her dark hair. A few gray hairs sprouted from the part. He could smell her. She smelled of the air conditioning that flowed through the vents. He wanted to kiss those gray hairs, smooth this unexpected riff.

I figured you wouldn't want to be anywhere else.

So. I was just clean and simple and ignorant—is that it? Did you think I'd embarrass you?

No!

She looked again at the combine a hundred feet away as it made its giant turn to the north, spewing straw onto the highway so the air was filled with a sparkled rain. Harold closed his eyes. Took a breath, and prepared to say what he hadn't had time to say.

Stop the car, Harold, Cora gasped.

Cora, it's not true.

Stop the car now.

Cora, please.

Stop the car, Harold!

Hannah grabbed his shoulder. Poppa, stop the car.

Hannah, be quiet!

That night in February, Harold let himself remember what happened next: he pressed the gas first and opened his eyes second. The car struck the back of a pickup. Hannah flew through the air. Harold saw his arm stretch towards her.

I caught her, he whispered in the dark. I thought I'd caught her in time.

∾

Harold thought he had erased the tape before he took his pants off that night in February. The next day was Saturday, so he didn't go to work. Instead of khakis, he wore jeans. Cora rushed around the house, picking up shirts, towels, skirts and pants. Their washer was broken, so she was taking the laundry to their neighbor's house. Harold offered to help, but she had that need to be alone the way she always needed the day after they had sex, and she refused with a grin.

He wasn't sure how long it took her to find the recorder. He wasn't sure what moved her to play the tape; he'd left it lying around before, and she never touched it. But the moment she came through the door, the wisps of hair standing straight up in the static of winter, he knew what had happened.

She didn't say anything. Harold stepped forward. I want to tell you something, he started.

Cora flung the recorder at his face. Harold ducked. The recorder struck the wall and fell to the floor in pieces.

~

Harold stood in the back of the church, watching the few stars that could be seen in the city's glare come out. A damp wind was blowing, smelling like garbage and greenery at the same time. He wished he had brought his coat. He pulled out the cigarette a busboy at the reception hall had given him. He hadn't smoked since medical school, but this day made him hunger for nicotine like it had in those days of cramming for exams. Clamping the cigarette between his lips, he felt in his pockets for the book of matches the busboy had also given him, but only came up with his micro-recorder and lint.

The sound of heels on the gravel made him turn. Cora rounded the corner and halted. Her fitted floor-length gown with a long side slit was hiked up past her knees and wrapped around her arm; her hair, coiled at the base of her neck, was loose and beginning to unwind. A pair of car keys fell out of her hand onto the ground.

He quickly dropped the recorder and lint back into his pocket and pulled out the cigarette. Are you running away already, Cora? He picked up the keys and held them out to her.

She dropped her dress back into place and uncoiled her hair. He could see her mentally gathering everything back into place as she shook her hair free. And what are you doing here? she asked.

Getting some fresh air.

Cora saw the cigarette in his hand, and grinned.

Do you have a match?

No. But my car's over here—I think the lighter still works. She walked to a Honda and unlocked the door. Here, hand it over.

Harold obeyed, and stepped back as she stuffed herself and the dress into the car. The length of her bare leg seemed a being separate from Cora. He turned away. He felt the micro-recorder bump against his leg. He put his hand in his pocket and hit the record button.

She pulled herself out, smoking. I hope you don't mind, she said, handing it back to Harold. A smear of dark lipstick tinted the cigarette. She held an empty pack and waved it at him. This was why I came out in the first place.

They walked back to the wall and traded the cigarette between them. Harold searched for something to say.

Thank you for inviting me, he said to the darkness.

I wasn't sure you would come.

Neither was I.

She held the cigarette out to him. So, you won Ellen's heart, I see.

Harold inhaled the smoke deep into his lungs. He was unsure if he could actually speak. She's not with me in that sense.

So, Ellen's still married to that jerk?

Yes, but it's not what you'd think. She came—to humor me, I suppose. So I could convince myself I'm not an ineligible old bachelor. He handed the cigarette back to her and smiled.

She laughed. It bounced and echoed on the stone, up into the glow of the night.

Is he from Salina? Harold asked.

Yes. *His* name is Greg, by the way.

Why didn't you have it in Ulysses? Most of your family's still there.

I needed a wedding where no one knew I used to be Mrs. Dr. Harold Diener.

The wind changed and blew stiffly, bringing a sharp acrid scent of tires and asphalt with it. Cora sighed before dropping the cigarette. She shook her hair loose and then began to recoil her hair. Even in the dingy light of an alley-way, the curve of her arm as she pinned it was beautiful.

Harold knew he had to say something real this time—to fit his words well within his thoughts.

Cora.

She stopped. Her arm remained above her head, holding down her hair and shading her face from him. He thought he could see her eyes in the recesses, gleaming.

Cora, it was me who killed her. I pressed on the gas.

Cora finished coiling her hair before she spoke: You know, I didn't remind her that day because I had decided she was an adult and could make her own choices in life. She had always said I treated her like a child. And I didn't want to do that to her. Treat her like a child. But I should have. I should have made her angry.

Cora smiled sadly. Harold realized he saw a Cora he would never know, a Cora with hours and years ahead of her that he wouldn't be a part of.

Do you think we'd be together still, if you hadn't listened to that tape?

I won't answer that. Because it won't change anything. There's no use in it.

∾

Ellen dropped him off at the end of the street behind the grain elevator. She wasn't sure she should be seen bringing the doctor home at three in the morning.

Ulysses has eyes even when they're closed, she whispered.

It had rained briefly while they were gone. Harold picked his way to his house through alleys and backyards, and entered through the unlocked sliding glass patio door.

Standing in the mute darkness, he remembered the micro-recorder. He pulled it out, pressed rewind and then play. His voice filled the silence, bounced off the tiles and cupboards, tiredly repeating medications needed, supplies missing.

The clicking of the machine prompted Harold to stop. He must have hit something other than record. The voices were gone, without measure or memory.

He hung his tuxedo neatly in the closet, put on his pajamas and sat on the bed, waiting for morning.

Tornado Slide

1997

Ellen was sitting in the shade of the grain wagon, waiting for Johan to make a final pass with the combine when her mother-in-law announced that she was going to die.

Agnes said it in such a matter-of-fact way that Ellen caught herself acknowledging it with a nod. She had been twisting her hair into a knot in order to give her neck a brush of air; her hair was of the sort that was neither curly nor straight, but a strange in-between that ignored any hair products and fashioned itself at its own will. Getting it into a simple bun took concentration that Agnes' statement very nearly stripped away. Ellen held on to her remnant of a knot with her left hand, took the bobby pin from her mouth with her right and turned her head calmly towards Agnes, who sat on a camping stool, hands folded, ankles crossed.

When harvest's over, of course, Agnes said. Which is a good thing. I don't want to ruin this dry spell by dying and gumming things up.

How do you know this? Ellen gently asked. She had never planned on Agnes declining like everyone else—she had seemed too sensible for that sort of thing. But perhaps she had been wrong to depend on Agnes' lucidity.

Huldah told me yesterday, during my visit in town.

How does Huldah know this?

She's often predicted the deaths of our family in one way or an-other, for as long as I can remember, Agnes said. The day before my Poppa died, she gave him a stocking cap for his bald head and told him to have a good, warm journey to Heaven. We all laughed about it because Poppa was stronger than most—but he died of a stroke the next day.

Ellen returned the bobby pin to her mouth and focused again on her hair, but it wasn't in the mood for a bun anymore. It was past noon, and the sky looked almost white, as though the sun had bleached each molecule of air on the earth. Johan's combine slipped behind a rise in the field; only a cloud of dust marked his progress.

Ellen wondered what her husband thought during these hours as dust, grease and sweat filled out each wrinkle to reveal the face he must have owned when he was young. When they first were married, she would ride along with him, perched on the arm of the seat until her buttocks lost all feeling. They rarely talked; the noise in the cab was too loud. Then she got pregnant and had children to hold back from giant tires and exhaust pipes that spouted dirty heat.

When Jeffrey was very young, she heard him half humming, half singing a song she didn't recognize. She asked him where he had learned that song.

He looked at her in surprise. Poppa sings it, of course.

When did Poppa sing this for you?

In there, he said, motioning out the window. The combine stood there, quietly brooding, for harvest was over for that summer. Jeffrey was terrified of it, and refused to speak its name.

He sings to you?

Yeah.

Always?

Yeah. He sings because he knows I'm scared. He likes the engine roaring and the music together. Jeffrey said all of this slowly, as if everyone had been privy to Johan's concerts with his machinery. Ellen wondered why Johan had never sung for her in the cab of the combine.

Ellen wondered if Huldah had known that Jeffrey was going to die right before his eighteenth birthday.

Does she know how you're going to die? She heard the slight bitterness in her voice and wished it back. The combine was crawling towards them, the air thickening with chaff.

No one can know that. The moment of death surprises everyone—even the most prepared. I think even God is surprised by it. Every time. Every single time.

~

The summer Jeffrey was six, Ellen took him to the community pool nearly every day. She didn't really want to do it; she was very pregnant and felt like a giant balloon amid the twisted bikinis and firm thighs of the teenage babysitters. But it was hot and they didn't have air conditioning at home. This was the only place where Ellen stopped sweating. She found that if she sat just right in the kiddie pool, she could sink her whole belly into water and imagine that her stomach was flat again.

She was tired the day Jeffrey disappeared. She usually never took an eye off of him as he splashed around, but that day she must've dozed. When she opened her eyes, he was gone. Ellen began to scream, which made the other mothers scream, which made their children scream. Lifeguards flocked to her, their lanyards and whistles swinging between youthful breasts. She began to run around the pool, panting his name under her breath: *Jeffrey Jeffrey Jeffrey Jeffrey*. She stopped at the gate between the pool and the surrounding park—it was unlatched.

Of course, she muttered. Of course. Her son was smart; too smart to drown. He probably went to the park to play—to his favorite slide that twisted like a corkscrew. The children called it the tornado slide. Ellen opened the gate and ran barefoot across the graveled parking lot of the playground. She did not feel the rocks; she was not ashamed of her waddled run; she did not hear the shouts of the lifeguards; she only heard her voice: *Jeffrey Jeffrey Jeffrey Jeffrey*.

When she reached the tornado slide she did not see him, but there was a little hut at the top of the slide that teenagers sometimes used for a make-out spot. She awkwardly climbed the ladder of the slide. Jeffrey was there, a grin on his face. She knew he'd been watching her all along.

I hided, Jeffrey said. Momma, I hided.

Jeffrey seemed surprised by the tears on her face. He reached out and touched her cheek with a gesture so courtly it made Ellen laugh as she squeezed him to her: I know, I know, I know, I know. Just don't do that again, okay? You can't go out by yourself just yet. Soon, but not yet.

I wasn't by myself.

You weren't?

Nope. She was with me. He pointed to the bench near the slide.

It was then that Ellen noticed Huldah. Huldah stood up and walked to the ladder, smiling.

I told him to stay and wait for you.

Jeffrey nodded his head vigorously. She stood here while I climbed, he said proudly. He smiled at Huldah and reached out his hands to her. Huldah laughed and stretched her arms to him.

Jealousy nagged at Ellen. That was the look Jeffrey gave her when they shared a joke or she tickled his stomach. That was supposed to be for her alone. Ellen wanted to hold him back from Huldah, but she knew it would be rude. Jeffrey leaned into Huldah and she took him into her arms. Huldah and Jeffrey laughed as if no one had laughed before—like it was their own private invention.

∽

Huldah's prediction of Agnes' death proved itself a few weeks after harvest was finished. During the funeral, Ellen saw Huldah hunched in a corner, examining each person that entered the church with a fascinated stare that would end with a blink and a shake of her head. She couldn't concentrate on the service, she was so curious about Huldah's thoughts at that moment. As soon as the service was over and people began to leave, Ellen looked to see if Huldah was still there. She carefully walked towards her, examining every word she would speak.

Huldah waited until Ellen spoke her name. Then she turned and smiled.

I wonder what Momma would have said about that preacher who's going to bury the dead and wear such a shiny *knaul'root* tie at the same time.

Ellen laughed. She gathered up her courage. Huldah, did you know Jeffrey was going to die that day you saw me in the IGA?

Huldah looked at her evenly. Yes.

Why didn't you tell me? Why did you wait until it was too late? Ellen wanted to throw something at this lump of a woman who had kept back a secret that had taken a chunk out of her life. Huldah looked at her in surprise, as Jeffrey had the day she asked him about Johan's singing. As if her answer was the only answer anyone with any sense in the world would consider.

I didn't wait. I didn't know until the moment I saw you that day—I don't know people are dying because a spirit tells me. You had a smell of death about you—it didn't come from you, but it had tagged along somehow. That's why I didn't say anything. It was too late. He was already gone.

Ellen leaned her back against the wall. Too late, she repeated.

Look! Huldah whispered, grabbing Ellen's hand and pulling her into the crouch position. Come watch the spirits dance.

It was then that Ellen saw what Huldah had been thinking about during Agnes' funeral. One of the long, high windows' shades had not been pulled against the heat of the day, and as people passed before it Ellen saw the motes of dust swirl around them and cavort to the ceiling.

When I was a girl, Huldah said, I got the idea that those were people's souls riding into Heaven. That the souls needed our help to get where they were going. We had to pass through them to give them enough speed to get on their journey. And we could keep on with ours.

Ellen remembered the day that Jeffrey leaned out of her arms into Huldah's arms with such heartbreaking ease—as if he recognized the one who would carry him to his destination with joy. Ellen leaned into Huldah's embrace and laughed as each soul whipped its way towards the sky and the possibility of Heaven.

Shaken in the Water, Part 5

1918

Elder Wiebe did not die right away; it was after the Armistice, in November, before the remaining elders of the church gathered up twenty Bibles and placed a slip of paper into the front cover of one. Agnes watched the twenty men walk to the front; some strode with confidence, others shuffled reluctantly. Peter was among them. He neither strode nor shuffled. He merely walked as though he was in a herd of milkers—gently moving past without a touch or a gesture meant to harm.

Five young boys were handed the stacks of Bibles. No one knew but God where the slip of paper was. The five boys gave each man a

Bible. No one opened his. All the Bibles were different shapes and sizes, from large ones with broken bindings and faded German words, to small, nearly pocket-sized versions that were so new they looked hardly read.

Elder Janzen prayed for a long time, asking God to choose a man who would honor His glory, hearten His people and serve Him at all costs.

People began to tire of Elder Janzen's prayer. It started softly: a cough, then the lift of one foot to relieve the other—for the congregation was standing this entire time—until finally someone audibly sighed. Elder Janzen stopped his prayer and looked around at the culprit, but every head was bowed, revealing nothing.

Amen, he said abruptly.

Amen, the congregation echoed.

He nodded to another of the elders, who began to open each Bible. When the Bible revealed nothing, it was taken from the man's hands, showing dismissal. Some of the rejected breathed a quiet thanks to God, others stood, unable to move beyond this moment.

There were five more Bibles left. Agnes was tall; she could see Peter clearly: jaw set, eyes straight. Unreadable.

No one breathed. The elder seemed to slow down, as though he were a showman, rather than a servant of the Lord. Two left. Joel Siebert and Peter Harder. Joel was next. The elder opened his Bible. A pale yellow slip of paper lay beneath the cover.

Bless you, Elder Siebert! the other elder exclaimed. Everyone let out a breath of stale air. They would have clapped, had it been allowed.

Instead, Elder Janzen and the others embraced him and exchanged the Brotherly Kiss before returning to their seats. Elder Janzen opened the bright red hymnal and was about to call a number when he saw Peter Harder still standing to one side, holding his unopened Bible.

Brother Harder, he said gently. God has made His choice.

No one has opened my Bible, Peter said, his voice almost a whisper.

No one needs to, brother. Elder Siebert's Bible held the paper.

Peter looked at Elder Janzen warily. That means nothing!

There was only one paper. The elder said edgily.

How do you know that? If God wished to have another paper appear in this Bible, He would do so, correct?

Brother Harder. We are not Catholics. We do not believe in those kinds of miracles! An elder's position is only one of many in our community. God obviously has other plans for you! Now, please take your seat.

I will sit when an elder opens my Bible.

One of the older elders began to rise, but Elder Janzen held out his hand. No. Our elders are not playthings. Open it yourself if you like.

An elder should open it, not me!

Well, then, you may stand here for as long as you'd like. Now—

For the Lord shall smite Israel, Peter said softly.

Now we shall sing five-hundred-fifty-four, Elder Janzen pronounced.

As a reed is shaken in the water, Peter continued.

Elder Janzen motioned to the pianist.

And he shall root up Israel out of this good land—
The piano began a heartless tinkle.
Which he gave to their fathers—
Ein' feste Burg ist unser Gott, Elder Janzen boomed.
And shall scatter them beyond the river—
Ein gute Wehr und Waffen, the congregation barely lifted their voices.
Because they have made their groves—
Er hilft uns frei aus aller Not.
No one would look at the spare figure that stood before them, slightly hunched over; a blade of grass under bitter ice.
Provoking the Lord to anger.
Die uns jetzt hat betroffen.
Agnes would remember that stance, years later, when *Englische* men surrounded their home with tar and feathers all because of Peter's stubbornness. A mixture of absurd pride and shame filtered through her. She wondered how long he would stand like that; what blow would finally bring him down.

That spring, a photographer wandered the county. He was said to be from New York, and was working on a story about the disappearing West. Alma wondered aloud what had disappeared that needed to be photographed, but the Saturday noon when the photographer appeared on their yard, she was gracious and acquiesced to his desire to take pictures of her family and farmyard. She'd heard that the man promised a copy to everyone who stood for a photograph. Alma was a shrewd woman, and was always looking for a bargain. Abram and Peter were called in early from the field, the boys were forced into clean shirts, the girls twisted their hair a little fancier than usual into head coverings.

Agnes watched from the porch as the photographer set up his camera before his impatient subjects. He looked her way at one point, and motioned her forward.

No, she said. I'm not family.

Ah! He looked intrigued. So, who are you, exactly?

Good grief, Agnes, Alma snapped. She's a neighbor. Come join us, for heaven's sake. We're all related, one way or another, she explained to the photographer. We all come from the same village in Russia, at least.

Agnes was on her way home when the photographer overtook her in his carriage and offered her a ride. She regarded him for a while and breathed in the air around him. She smelled horse, leather, and a heavy smell she assumed came from his equipment. He was a man, but unlike Peter, he did not smell dangerous, so Agnes accepted.

Are you really here to look at the disappearing West? she asked.

The photographer laughed. Is that what people are saying?

It's what I've heard. I don't understand what it means.

Well, what it means is I'm being paid to cross the Mississippi and take photographs of a West people actually live in, not the one folks believe in. Does that make it any clearer?

Maybe.

He grinned at her. So, what kind of West do you live in?

Without thinking, Agnes touched his sleeve and pointed at the rise in the land that hid the barn and creek from sight. There, she said. There's my West.

Agnes had not been to her circle of earth for several months. The barn looked more dejected than ever, the trees seemed to have lost weight and height. Despite the spring rains, the grass looked withered and dull. She wondered if it had always looked like this—she wondered if she had imagined her West after all.

Do you—live here?

No, sir. It's where I used to go to be alone. It's where I met—Agnes stopped. She wondered if it was possible that she had imagined Nora as well. If there had never been a Nora. Her birthmark stung her like the whip of thin rope. Agnes bit her lips to keep from crying out.

You met someone here.

She nodded.

Is that her? the photographer asked, pointing behind her.

Nora stood in the shadow of the barn, her hair spread over her shoulders. She wore a loose red dress that exploded from the shade—knaul'root. She watched Nora walk towards them, smiling, swaying her hips slightly beneath the weight of her unborn child.

You can see her?

I most certainly can.

Could you take a photograph of her—of us?

I was hoping you'd say that.

Soon they were standing in front of the barn, the sunlight dappling their faces. The photographer took ten pictures. On the last one, the one he would give Agnes a year later with a sad smile, they stood close together, Nora's head tilted to one side. As the camera flashed, she felt Nora's hand encircle her waist. The day the photographer returned to Ulysses and found her, she was studying a bright red bolt of cloth in the window of the variety store on Main Street. She waited until he walked away to pull the photograph out of the large brown envelope. The thing that she was looking for, the thing that she remembered the most was that moment before the touch. The light had caught Nora's hand just as it was about to rest on Agnes' hip. She had felt the breath of air, the buff of cloth meeting cloth as Nora's arm traced itself around the small of Agnes' back. It was the anticipation of the touch Agnes favored the most, because once it happened it would be gone for good.

1918

The photographer packed his equipment and drove away; Agnes and Nora stood several feet apart, each one frankly examining the other. Pregnancy suited Nora. Agnes had seen nearly every grown woman in her church pregnant. Some glowed with contentment and expectation—their faces would flush as though they were in a constant state of gentle embarrassment, their hips would sway in a manner that cleared the path of men that surrounded them like insects headed for damnation via fire. Most looked like Agnes' momma—tired already of the life within them, their skin either draping over the bones or puffing and stretching, enlarging pores that glistened with constant sweat. No men moved for these women—they had to push themselves past them. The men would merely turn away just enough to let them through, already back to their interrupted conversation.

A brush of wind threw itself against Nora's skirt as if to prove any doubt about her condition. Agnes signed to her: How are you pregnant?

Nora spoke: Talk to me. Her accent was thick, as if she held a pillow against her mouth. But Agnes understood each word clearly, as if every syllable crossed the air and entered her eyes.

I am.

No, talk to me! Why are you so stubborn after all this time?

Agnes stepped closer, until only a small space allowed her hands to converse with their silent partner. How are you pregnant? she repeated.

Put those hands down! I want you to hear me!

I hear you! Why do you shun this now? Why is it dirty to you?

It is not dirty! It is for darkness now. For when you cannot see each other, but you need silence. You can say things then that you hold shut during the day.

Who do you speak into the darkness with? How are you pregnant?

Nora's hand sought Agnes' hand and pulled it until it rested on her belly. She moved it around in circles, as though she were searching for something yet unknown. Her body smelled like newly washed sheets mixed with a deeper, stronger scent that reminded Agnes of the way the soil smelled when you first dig it up after winter had gone.

Ah! Nora breathed. There, she said. Right there. Agnes felt the bump of tiny feet. Agnes had felt many babies kick before they were born, but this touch seemed like the first. She pressed gently, imagining the warmth and darkness within Nora's body. She wished she could remember what it was like: that life before she was pushed into the cold world. She wondered if anyone had welcomed the sight of light and air, or if that first cry had been the cry of mourning, not of joy.

She realized her hand had remained too long on Nora's belly. She began to pull it away, mumbling apologies, but Nora pressed against her until only their hands stopped the melding of flesh. Nora's fingers were warm and sweaty. Agnes breathed and leaned against Nora's right cheek. Eyes half open, she watched how her breath sent the strands of her hair on the nape of her neck back and forth.

1924

A coil of pain wound itself up inside Agnes when she went into labor. It wasn't a sharp pain, as she expected, but more a grazing pain that slowly inched itself tighter each time she took a breath. Agnes knew it had to end sometime—but she had seen how a coil of barbed wire untangled itself, so she knew that the end would be worse than any twisting and tightening.

When Huldah pushed her way outside, and Agnes saw her writhing in the gnarled hands of the same *Poppemutta* who had delivered her own body into the world, she found herself saying: Is there a mark on her back?

Midwife Hiebert was quiet. She examined the girl carefully, as though she were a cabbage at a market. Huldah was large for a baby, but that didn't worry the midwife; she simply gave off a strange vibration that disturbed her more than any other newborn had. Mrs. Hiebert had seen every kind of birth defect imaginable, from *Hoseschoa* to *Schwamfeet*, and she had never once held her tongue when a new mother asked the question, but now she knew she could say nothing that Agnes would understand. It had nothing to do with her body, she decided; nothing to do with her mind. It was the soul of the child. It seemed so large and so impressionable. Like a tiger's daughter, not the daughter of a human being. She remembered the words she'd spoken to her sister the day Agnes was born: *Tieja Kjoaw* — Tiger Scar. Perhaps this was what Agnes was born for—perhaps her birthmark had merely been a serenade that crashed into a cacophony without end.

No, she said after a few beats. She's healthy and strong—like a little barrel full of sand.

Agnes reached for Huldah's wrinkled red body. Huldah squirmed and yowled as though she held the tears and torture of generations before. It was as if Nora had reappeared in Huldah's lungs. As if she'd never been away at all.

When Peter shuffled into their bedroom, Agnes wanted to push him right back out. He didn't belong with them—this was a world that she and Huldah owned—they needed no one else. But she stayed still as he leaned over their daughter who continued to wail. He leaned over her contorted face and kissed her softly on the forehead.

Agnes was shocked. All their kisses were awkward. Even in the darkness she could feel the muscles of his lips cringe against hers. But here he was, eyes half closed with a look of shy but utter pleasure, his beard pulsing against Huldah's screams. Then he quickly straightened and backed out of the room.

Men, the *Poppemutta* laughed. They don't know what to do with themselves when this happens. She leaned in and guided Huldah to Agnes' breast. But they still keep at it!

The pull of Agnes' daughter's lips and tongue made her gasp aloud—it was an aching pain, as if it had always been there, waiting for her remembrance.

Knaul'root

2004

Johan waited for Ellen to fall asleep before he pulled his arm out from under her head and got up. He knew once she fell asleep there would be no chance of waking her, for she was a weighty sleeper.

He remembered one night when a thunderstorm pounded the roof and the children screamed at each thrust of lightning, so he let them come into their bed. By four in the morning the thunder had subsided and his sweaty children lay draped like cats on the end of the bed. Johan was exhausted but wide awake. He examined his brood: Minerva took up twice as much room as Jeffrey, even though she was half his size. Jeffrey was nearly off the bed, his tawny hair sticking up like wheat stubble. Ellen lay on her stomach, her nightshirt pulled to her armpits as though she was struggling to release herself from its grasp.

When she finally woke she was furious. Why didn't you wake me up? she demanded, pulling her shirt over her breasts. We should have been in the cellar! There could have been a tornado!

That's alright, Ellen. You know us Harders; we are picked up by the beast every now and again and always live, Johan laughed. Ellen did not laugh.

Even in grief Ellen seemed able to push it aside long enough for sleep. The night after Jeffrey died, she wept as Johan's momma steered her to bed. Within five minutes she was unconscious. Johan, however, didn't sleep a night through for months afterward, and wandered the house, the yard or the fields until morning.

He was grateful for her heavy sleep tonight, when the expensive doctor had said the chemotherapy was no longer viable. That Johan would die with or without it. The doctor recommended stopping the treatment.

It's about quality of life, the doctor said. More of this will incapacitate you more and possibly sooner than if you stop now.

Johan struggled into his jeans and cinched the belt to the tightest notch. Even though it was dark he grabbed a cap from a shelf in the mud room before he left the house. The only day of the week he left his head uncovered was on Sunday. He wasn't sure where he was going; he listened to his boots scrape through the grass and then the gravel; he smelled that scent only the prairie has at night at the beginning of fall: a damp odor filled with decaying dust from forgotten harvests. When Johan found himself inside his truck he wasn't surprised. He released the clutch and coasted to the edge of the yard.

When the truck bumped onto the smooth highway surface he sighed almost with pleasure. He loved to drive. No matter how tired he was, he was always ready to drive anywhere. The road knew him better than anyone; it would lead him somewhere new, even if he was heading towards old places.

Johan had been driving since he was a child. He would sit on his poppa's lap and steer the giant wheel with a seriousness that made the entire family laugh. As he grew older and longer he followed Poppa around the yard, hoping he would mount the tractor, the car, the harvester. Johan and his twin, Tobias, had been the children of his parents' old age. He doubted such behavior would have been tolerated had they been born ten years—maybe even five years earlier. The family would have been hungrier then; his father desperate to finish as much as he could without a child following him at every step. Johan's older siblings had been worked harder than him, he knew. The notion of childhood—even among the backward Mennonites—had changed with the end of the war.

The moon glided west, leaving the sky a tinge of purple that announced the coming of morning. Old 56 gleamed as though it was littered with shattered glass. Johan opened the windows wider; breathed the crisp air that he had always figured would be his. Even after Jeffrey died, he felt death would never come for him. He had reasoned then Jeffrey had died because of some inner weakness. Johan was too strong, too rough for that final end. He now knew it had nothing to do with his son's flaws.

Johan hadn't physically seen his son that last morning because Jeffrey's back was to the early sun, so Johan had to squint at the dark figure that appeared in the doorway of the round-top shed.

When you've picked up Edwards' gal, unload that wagon of grain into the south bin. That shouldn't be so hard for even *you*, he had said.

His mind had been elsewhere, thinking of the acres left to cut, which fields he would disc first, whether he could be sneaky and cut Orel Kaufman's piece tomorrow, even though that particular landlord forbade any work on his land on Sundays. He had not thought that would be the last words he had with his son, or that the next time he would see Jeffrey would be at the bottom of a gravity wagon in a pile of grain that had suffocated him.

It was only when he hit Main Street that he knew his destination. He let his pickup slide past the church, the coffee shop, Dr. Diener's office, until he was parked in front of a small gray house with a wrap-around porch and a high wooden fence that cloaked the backyard. It was only then that he realized how tired he was. He stumbled onto he porch and settled himself on the swing. There would have been a time that it wouldn't have stood Johan's weight without a groan of rusty chain. Now it barely moved.

When he opened his eyes he saw Huldah perched on her porch steps, her white bronze hair spread in the sun like a glorious cut of silk.

Morning, she said, handing him a cup of coffee as though it had not been years since they last spoke.

∽

Huldah was nearly twenty years Johan's senior, and had left the community before he ever registered that one of the places at the table in his parents' house stood empty every morning. One by one the occupants of the table disappeared into their own houses, and after each wedding Momma would set that person's dish in a separate cupboard, waiting for their return visits. But one place remained even after only Tobias and Johan were left: a yellow plate and a chipped glass always sat empty on a little table at the end of the family table. Johan had no memory of the person who sat at this place.

He was about eight when he noticed his momma sometimes disappeared for hours at a time. When he realized this he combed the yard and the pasture where the single tree stood alone amongst the cattle. He climbed the tree and clung to its battered arms, calling her name over and over.

Tobias heard his voice and found Johan with snot and tears running down his face. Tobias laughed. Ah, *Kjleendümkje*, he said, crooning the nickname Johan hated, what are you crying for?

Momma! Where's Momma?

Tobias was skinny and weak, but he could make the sturdy Johan feel small inside. You don't know? She's at our sister's house in town.

None of their sisters lived in town. Which sister? Johan demanded.

The sister that's been shunned. Momma goes in secret. We're not supposed to talk to her or say her name. We are supposed to pretend she's dead.

How do you know this? Why pretend she's dead?

Tobias shrugged. Nobody tells me anything. I just heard Gretta say something to Momma once. That's all I know.

For two days Johan followed Momma everywhere, waiting for her to disappear. The afternoon of the second day Momma made bread. Johan watched her from beneath the kitchen table. What are you doing? she finally asked. You're too big to hang on me.

Momma, why do we pretend my sister's dead?

Who told you? Her voice was hard.

He thought about giving up Tobias, but he couldn't say the words. He scuffled with his twin in private, he even mocked him among other kids, but they always were back to back when it came to adults. I heard something, he said weakly.

Momma let go of the dough and settled on the floor, flour dusting the air as she sat. Tobias, I'm sure, she said to herself. Johan wanted to run, but he sensed she was going to tell him something, so he stayed still.

You have a sister, named Huldah. She lives in Ulysses.

By herself?

Yes.

Johan had never heard of a woman who lived alone. Why doesn't she live here?

Because of the *Meidung*—the shunning. She broke a rule with the church, and the church says we cannot talk to her until she changes her mind.

Did she do something really bad?

Some people think so. She wouldn't wear this anymore. Momma pointed to the small cap on her head.

Johan laughed. That's silly.

Momma grabbed both ears and pulled him to her face. *Das Herz der Weisen ist dort, wo man trauert, aber das Herz der Toren dort, wo man sich freut*, Momma said. That means 'The heart of the wise is in the house of mourning; but the heart of fools is in the house of mirth.' Watch what you laugh at, Johan. A life was ruined by what you just laughed at.

He tried to fathom the logic of the church they went to at least three times a week. Why would the people he saw, the kind *Grossmuttern* and *Grossvatern* and elders and neighbors want to throw this sister away for something so unimportant? What if he did something they did not like? His throat tightened at the thought. Would he be forced to live in town alone? Would Tobias never speak to him again, even in anger or derision? How far would they let him go in sin before they would throw him away, too? Would his empty plate and cup remain on the table long after everyone had gone?

But Momma, he persisted, why would you pretend your daughter was dead? Why would you do it even if the church said so? You're supposed to protect us kids, not kill us.

Momma let go of his ears; she eyed Johan as though he were a stranger who had just said hello. She got up, her knees cracking beneath her. Johan watched her face as it curled with pain. His momma was old, he decided. The lines on her face were deeper than those on the faces of the mommas of his friends at school.

His momma seemed to avoid him after that, as if he had seen a part of her he wasn't supposed to see. But Johan was determined to keep himself in her sights as much as possible. He followed her around the house on the weekend. She banned him from the house. He helped her in the garden. She banned him from the hateful chore of weeding and made Tobias do both twins' share. He tried to sin, tried to see if he could equal his missing sister's transgression.

As he grew older his sins grew along with him. Every time Tobias baited him, every time his momma or poppa punished him, he added to his pile of sins that were yet to throw him out of the church. He would fight any boy who taunted him about his size, he would shout at Tobias when he showed weakness in front of others. When he was seventeen he overturned the family table when his poppa said he could not date an *Englische* girl. One summer day he whispered words of hate to his only son. All of it only pressed anger closer to his heart.

When he was young, he poured this anger through himself by running. When he was older he would go to the tree in the pasture and strike the trunk until his knuckles bled. He wondered how the tree stood his strength. It never bent to his violence, but remained still and silent.

∾

Huldah sat in silence as Johan finished his coffee. When he was done she took the cup. Do you want to go in? she asked, her eyes darting around the street.

Johan laughed. Huldah, the only ones who care about those

things anymore are either asleep in their graves or belong to our family. Nobody cares about that anymore. Most of the ladies don't wear coverings—Ellen never even wore one when we got married, and no one in church said a thing.

I guess you're right. But I still feel it, inside, she said, tapping her chest.

I can see that, he said, wondering what it would be like to be ostracized most of your life, only to realize one day everyone had forgotten the reason why.

I guess Momma visited you in secret up until she died.

Every Friday.

Not so secret when you could see that monster of a car in the alley.

Huldah laughed. Johan loved her laugh. It was light and musical; it was hard to believe it came from a woman twice his size even when he was young and well.

I'm going to die, he said.

She nodded. I know.

How?

She reached for his cap and pulled it off. His threadbare head felt the breath of the morning. I've felt it every time our family goes. Before Momma died I knew. So I told her.

What did she say?

Huldah smiled. She said: *Well, it's about time.*

They both laughed. I can see her saying that—like it was about time for me to get up when I was a kid, Johan said.

Johan stretched his legs out into the sun. He studied his boots: the leather was worn paper thin, the heels down to the nails. Ellen kept trying to convince him to get new ones, but he resisted. These were the boots he had worn when he was well. Letting go of them would mean something was over for good. And now it was true.

He felt more relaxed. Huldah acted like death was the most normal thing in the world. And it was, he decided. He had been ridiculous, thinking otherwise.

∾

Though Johan looked for a woman in plain dress without a head covering nearly every time he went into Ulysses, he never saw her until he was twenty.

It was on one of those nights in August when sleep was impossible. The act of lying down onto sheets that were blanketed by that day's humidity and letting the head fall into a pillow that still held the sweat from the night before was too much. Johan undressed completely and sat by his bedroom window. He could feel each individual strand of sweat travel down his neck to pool briefly in that hollow above the buttocks before it dripped onto the rough carpet.

It was the first time in his life that he found himself alone at night. He and Tobias had always shared a room even when they were the only ones left at home. When they'd gone to college they stayed at home and drove together to school. But Tobias was gone. He had decided to leave Ulysses. He had applied to the state college in secret, and only told the family three days before he left.

Johan decided he would go for a run. He found a t-shirt and shorts and tiptoed out of the house. Even outside, he could hear Poppa's deep snores while he tied his sneakers. Once his feet struck the gravel, Johan could feel the loneliness lift. Movement, whether it was on foot or vehicle, seemed to understand his soul.

Before long, the gravel gave way to pavement, and he was running down Main Street, past the darkened windows of the few stores that still survived, past the houses that were blank. Sometimes he saw a tiny light within the wide picture windows of the ranch-style homes that people seemed to want. He went through the community park, where the heat still clung to the branches above his head. He came to the county's only stoplight that turned to a steady beat after ten o'clock. Johan jogged in place before the pulsing light, waiting for his feet to guide him. They headed left.

He found himself in one of the older neighborhoods. No treeless yards and split-level houses in this bit of Ulysses. Old, chaste homes settled behind the trees that lined the cracked sidewalks. Johan slowed his gait, looking for life. A dog barked at him; a cat scurried across the street.

That was when he heard it: a throaty growl. He looked for the cat; doubting such a scrawny animal could produce what he had heard. The cat sat primly near the curb, eyes glittering in the streetlight. Then he heard it again. Johan slowed to a jog and tried to decide where the growl had come from. He found himself holding his breath in anticipation.

As he neared the end of the street, he heard a Voice. *Herein.*

The fear in him vanished. It must be one of his friends who saw him run by. Someone wanting to scare him. He laughed, his voice pushing against the humid air. All right then, he crowed, come out and show yourselves!

The leaves in a newfound wind answered with a *swish!* and the crickets raised their voices to match Johan's.

Nein. Herein.

It came from a tiny house with a high backyard fence. A single window was lit with shifting light. Johan crept towards the house until he came to an elm near the window. The window was barely curtained by a set of lace panels. An army of bookcases lined the walls. Johan felt his breath stop, for every book that stood in those bookshelves was red—a glaring red that assaulted the eyes. *Knaul'root*, his momma would have called them.

The scrape of a screen door pulled his eyes from the books. A large woman in plain dress stood on the threshold. A cape of hair hung down her back. The shifting light behind her painted it a fire red.

Herein, the Voice ordered. Johan obeyed.

The inside of the house was plain, and reminded him of his childhood. A sturdy couch and lightly upholstered chairs stood in one corner. A square table filled the other. Four chairs sat at the table. They looked unused. Though he had always lived in the same farmhouse, Momma had slowly made it into an *Englische* house: soft carpet, thick sofas, and a bright yellow refrigerator that hummed and rattled at night. He did not mind the changes—he had barely noticed them. But as he stood before the plainness of this house, he sensed the presence of something lost forever to the people that stood beyond this door.

Huldah was barefoot: her naked feet seemed small for her huge frame. Johan wondered how she even stood on such tiny feet. He realized he was staring, and looked away. Huldah laughed. He looked into her face. Though he guessed she was somewhere near forty, her face was without a single wrinkle. Time had stopped for her.

Do you want some coffee, or tea? she asked, shuffling into the kitchen.

Johan stood immobilized before this alter of red. Close up, he saw that the individual books weren't *knaul'root*. Each of them had faded into a different shade of red: some were a husky maroon; others had a pink tint to the spine that bled from the red they all had once been. It was only when you stood out in the street, far from each individual book, that you saw the reds congeal into that magnificent artery. He wondered if this was how God saw the people of the earth. To God they were all *knaul'root*; their individuality wiped out at a distance. A knot of anger at a God who chose to blur everyone together tightened in his belly. He wanted to pull each book from its shelf, rip each page from its spine, and spread everything out so that God wouldn't be able to see them as one.

He curled his fingers around a short, fat text and pulled it out, ready to begin. The title was in harsh German script: *Analyse der Phobie eines fünfjährigen Knaben*. He closed his eyes, took a breath, and looked at the title again: *Analyse der Phobie eines fünfjährigen Knaben*.

Johan remembered the day he had ripped *The Secret Garden* from Tobias' hands next to the water tower. It had felt so good to tear each page, to spread the spine until it cracked like a bone. It frightened him a little, to feel such power, such ecstasy.

The cover of that book was red. He realized where Tobias had found the novel: *It's not mine!* he'd shouted. *I borrowed it! I borrowed it!*

Tobias had met Huldah years before, then. Another secret that Tobias had kept from his twin. He returned the book to the shelf and tapped the spine.

Another time, he whispered. I'll get you later.

He entered the kitchen. A white refrigerator and a gleaming sink commanded the room. Small scraps of paper littered the front of the refrigerator. There were pictures of food on them, with awkward German and English beneath. A round kitchen table with mismatched chairs that had cushions tied to the seats were beneath a lamp hanging from the ceiling. A tall fan stood in one corner, filling the dense air with a breath of coolness.

Sit, sit. You've been running, I see. You must be tired.

Johan felt naked as the fan's air touched his bare legs. He hurried to one of the chairs to hide them.

Huldah filled a decanter with water and poured it into the percolator. I'm out of tea, actually, she said. I hope you don't mind.

No. That's fine.

The percolator burped as the coffee trickled into the pot. Huldah pulled a plastic bag from a cupboard and poured tiny hard cookies into a bowl. She set them on the table and settled down. Can you believe I still have *Pepanät* from Christmas? I don't know why I made so much. It's really the only thing I've baked since the war. I eat *Englische* food now. She smiled. They get better with age, anyhow.

That's true, he said. Johan remembered when Momma and his sisters would spend days making *Pepanät* for Christmas, the house filling with anise. For months afterward, when visitors came for Sunday *faspa*, Momma would bring them out and they would drink coffee and spoon *Pepanät* into their cups. The grownups would talk in Low German, thinking the children wouldn't understand. Momma still made them at Christmas, she still brought them out for *faspa*, but the quantity had ebbed, since her daughters left and made new lives without baking.

They sat in silence. Johan heard the hiss of the percolator in its last breath; a hidden clock ticked. He had always been a person who hated silence. He filled the air with his voice, afraid of what others were thinking in that silence. For the first time he didn't feel the need to speak. Being there with Huldah was enough.

Huldah rose and poured the coffee into thick brown mugs. Milk? she asked.

No, I like it black.

She handed him a spoon and he sunk it into the mound of cookies and carefully released them into the dark liquid. They disappeared, but soon resurfaced.

Do you run a lot at night? she asked, once he had sipped half the cup and spooned a few *Pepanät* into his mouth.

Sometimes. I like it because no one's up, and I can have the roads and the streets to myself.

Momma says you are on some kind of team?

I run track for the college.

I see you run around town sometimes.

Really? Johan looked into her eyes. I never see you. I've wanted to meet you my whole life.

I'm dead, remember? You can't see the dead. She said this without bitterness. Johan was surprised. If he was shunned by his community, his family, he would have raged against it, he would have torn the church and the house to shreds. He would not have stayed in Ulysses.

How can you say that so calmly? he asked.

It used to make me sad, make me angry, but not anymore.

Why not?

I defied the church. I made the choice, she said, looking past Johan. But God told me I could do it—who's going to argue with that?

Johan finished his coffee and let the remaining *Pepanät* rest at the bottom of his mug. Some preferred the cookies to be larger, softer. They disintegrated in the coffee quickly. Huldah's were still hard at the core. It would take more than liquid—it would only disappear with the cut of the teeth.

I heard a growl of an animal before I saw you. Do you have a dog somewhere?

No, she's a tiger.

A tiger, Johan said. In Ulysses.

He eyed her carefully, unsure whether this was a joke or, like the collection of books, a symptom of craziness.

Huldah's eyes twinkled. Yes. You do not believe me.

He tried to believe it. He wanted to.

It's alright. She lives without the need of belief.

Can I see the tiger?

Did you see her before you saw me?

No.

Then she doesn't wish to see you. You would have met her otherwise.

Why doesn't she want to see me? Johan was insulted, even though he'd been rebuffed from an imaginary tiger.

You've been tainted by anger. More than anger. Rage. I can see that. She can see that.

Huldah's words struck Johan firmly in his gut. He shoved his chair back. How do you know how I feel? What I am? We've met just tonight.

I see you in other ways. Through Momma, through your races against yourself. There's nothing magical about what I've seen. I just see you when you think no one else's looking, that's all.

Johan knocked over the chair as he rose. Huldah remained in her seat. Out of some strange habit he set the chair back on its feet, the way he had righted the table after Poppa had said he could not date an *Englische* girl.

I'm sorry. I'm sorry, he muttered as he left the room, passed the red books, pushed open the screen door and began to run back into the dark that was becoming light.

◞

Johan didn't know the warmth of the sun had lulled him back to sleep until he woke in its glare. Huldah was on her knees in her flower bed, clawing and reshaping the earth around each blossoming plant. Johan got up and stretched. His knees and hips whispered beneath his jeans. He was dying, he decided. His body had given up on him long ago. He tried to lower himself onto the swing gracefully, but he fell back awkwardly instead.

Momma once told me a story about a girl she knew who was an expert tailor, Huldah said without looking at Johan. There was nothing that she could not create or mend beautifully. You would never know it—the clothes they wore back then were of the old country: black and brown and muddy blue. Then one day she got a small bolt of red cloth. *Knaul'root*, Momma said. Huldah stopped and gave the mounds a final pat. Momma said this girl sewed a set of curtains and hung them in her bedroom. The window was tiny—barely three feet wide. The girl figured that no one would ever notice. Her parents begged her to remove them. She refused. Her father pulled them down and ripped them—she merely mended the tears and hung them up again.

Then one day one of the elders stopped by for *faspa*. As he was leaving, he saw the curtains through the girl's window. But he said nothing about it to the community. Time passed. The girl's parents forgot about the curtains. When she turned sixteen she decided it was time to join the church; she went to the elders to apply for membership and baptism. She began to prepare for membership. Two nights before she was to be baptized, the same elder who had seen the curtains came to the house.

Sister, he said, the church will receive you with open arms in two days. I will receive you with open arms as well—but only if you do one thing: remove those curtains from your window. If you do not do this, I will tell the community of this childish act of pride. I will tell them how you disobeyed your parents and wished to flout yourself. I will ask for you to be shunned.

Huldah rose and dusted off her bare knees, her soiled dress.

What did she decide?

She decided to take them down, of course. She was young; she knew nothing of the world. The community was her world. She knew this elder was not a bad man. He was not trying to show power. He said this in love. He knew the community would find out someday about the curtains. He was saving her from future pain. A *Meidung* that would force her future children to see nothing of her, that would make her lie somewhere away from her future husband.

Huldah held out her hands and smiled at them. Of course you know, she told the hands, this girl was Momma.

Johan thought about his momma. When he and Tobias were very young, and everyone else was away, she would force them out of the house and tied their wrists with a long string to the chute of the gutter. Johan and Tobias would howl and cry, but Momma wouldn't come to them. He once heard her sing the Doxology over and over until her voice had rubbed itself raw. One summer day, they had fallen asleep in the grass, their hands reaching for the gutter. When they woke up, they found themselves a bright shade of pink. Poppa came home, saw them, put them in a salt bath, set them on their bed, gave them a strong-tasting medicine and went downstairs. Johan remembered him shouting at her at the top of his lungs in Low German. He remembered when they found her naked body in that little copse of dying trees. Her skin was burned borderline fuchsia; the birthmark he had never seen crossed her back like the sigil of an unknown army in a forgotten war.

Though her daughters always visited her until the end, it was out of duty rather than love. They would arrive with their painted faces and their puffed up hair and bring her gifts of electronics and shiny clothing. They became more *Englische* in defiance to everything Momma had denied them. His brothers, including Johan, had become indifferent to Momma, especially after Poppa died.

How do you know?

She never admitted it. She only told me the story once, when I was young—before I was shunned. She only said when she had heard the story she had decided to defy any order to shun anyone. She thought it was ridiculous to shun a soul for curtains. So I wasn't surprised when she began to talk to me late at night when Poppa was asleep; when she drove to my house in Ulysses. She'd decided to keep her promise, in her own way. I knew it was her when I cleaned out the granny house before I moved here. I found a small box in the closet. In it was a set of red curtains. Curtains that once were *knaul'root*.

The sun shifted a centimeter west, thrusting Johan's eyes into shade. He blinked sunspots out of his eyes. He was somehow glad he had not known this while Momma lived. She had probably needed a secret for her life.

Huldah was going into the house, heading for the back door. Johan did not follow. Instead, he called out: Huldah, where's that tiger of yours? Am I still too angry?

But she had already disappeared.

Johan smiled. When the light had shifted and Johan could finally see again, he had seen a depression in the earth Huldah had not touched. The depression was deep; the weight behind the step that created it was more than a human foot. Around the top of the depression were five deep cuts—a person could imagine the cuts were from the claws of a tiger.

Silage

2004

The metal burned with frost when Tobias grabbed the first rung. He pulled away his hand, knocked it on the second rung and cursed softly: *Scheisse*. He dropped the Christmas lights and fumbled in his coveralls for his gloves, then shouldered the lights again and squinted up at the grain silo.

The sun glinted off the metal darkly, since a large amount of the ladder was iced with rust older than Tobias. Walls no heavier than corrugated cardboard were circled with bands of metal every five feet or so, and rose up to a hundred feet. Tobias tapped the timber wall gently, then hit it harder and finished with a punch that glanced off the side and echoed in the emptiness within. When he and Johan were small, they would poke their heads through the silo door and shout at the circle above that drifted like an enchanted land. Their voices chased each other to the top and down again, until nothing but a hum rang out at them.

Tobias knew he was stalling. Stepping forward, he took hold of the rung with his right gloved hand and began to climb. The first few feet were easy, especially once the guard rail that encircled the ladder brushed his back. He knew the terror would come later. Tobias hummed to himself, whispered music, searched for the German of hymns that once sucked his voice dry. They were words that only came to him when he returned home; they scattered as soon as he pulled out of the lane and headed east for the interstate forty-two miles away.

The terrors were coming. Tobias could feel them itching up his legs and to the arch of his back. He sang out loud:

Ermuntest euch, ihr frommen,
Zeight eurer Lampen Schein!

His voice trembled against the aging wood and clung to it.

Die Abend ist gekommen,
Die finstre Nacht bringt ein.

Hunting for breath, he stopped, and the wounding terror grabbed hold, winnowing Tobias like chaff to be destroyed.

He remembered the day the public pool opened the summer after they turned sixteen. Tobias and Johan had a truck by then and didn't need the bus to carry them home. They raced Johan's friends to the pool just outside of town, climbed the fence, and headed for the new high dive, pulling off t-shirts and struggling out of jeans as they ran. They both clambered up the ladder, Johan first. He took off running once his feet hit the heavy rubber-plastic; he executed a beautiful dive as if he'd done it all his life.

When his brother bounced off the diving board, Tobias froze. He hated heights. He'd never scaled the silo all the way. Too many times his father had to carry him down, leaning against the guard rail, Tobias keeping his face against Poppa's chest. He figured as long as he followed Johan's lead that afternoon, he would make it, as if he could breathe in his brother's courage like the scent of fermented silage drawn through his bedroom window. But Johan had left him.

By this time a crowd of boys were climbing to the top, shouting at Tobias to get going or get off. He tried to move, but his fingers had created a film of sweat, and he suddenly imagined his fall onto the concrete, brains scattered everywhere.

The boys began to jeer at him. The *Englischejungen* called him dirty English words, the Mennonites sang dirty words in High German, their accents harsh and Midwestern. Tobias looked for Johan in the crowd. And then he heard him. He spoke in Low German, his voice lower than all the rest. Few children knew Low German anymore—Johan and Tobias had learned it so they could understand what their parents said when they argued.

Dü best Drakj. Ekj hab en Äakjel fonn di. Hast dü kjeene Schaund?

Dü best ne Schaund fer onsere Famielje. Ekj wenschte dü weascht nie jebuare. The words were harsh, rasping.

It was then that the pool director arrived. The boys scattered. The pool director climbed the ladder and gently led him down. He wrapped him in a towel and drove Tobias home. Johan had left with the truck.

Without a word, he was gone. Johan was gone even now, when Tobias needed him again. It had been Johan who withered away in a dank little hospital overlooking the town water tower, without the rambunctious cheer that had surrounded him that day by the pool. It had been Johan whose visitors were only his sisters and Johan's wife, since Tobias could not find the time to leave his veterinary practice. Johan was the one who had scrambled up the silo each Christmas to twist the lights down the guard rail, so that in the dark the lights resembled a giant candy cane. It would tower over the plains, silent among the dispersed carols.

Tobias wanted to continue. He wanted a pair of arms to guide him to the top. He wanted to hear Johan, even if he ruthlessly cursed in a language Tobias no longer knew.

Tobias decided to sing. He knew which song he would belt out like the graybeards at church; their voices deaf and out of tune and now turned to dust. He gasped for a bit of air, that unnecessary breath anyone takes before a dive, for the mind has already jumped, its fingers brushing the surface of the water. The body just needs to follow.

Drown

2005

The tires on Tobias' Toyota jostled and threatened to turn off the washboard road into the deep ditches that lined Medora's driveway. The gnarled trees that attempted to protect her farmyard from the gusts of the South Dakota winds bowed under the weight of the ice piled upon ice; broken branches littered the ground. The yard seemed ravished and deserted, with field equipment parked haphazardly and piles of tools scattered like abandoned islands.

A thin line of smoke trailed from the stovepipe. Tobias pulled out his veterinarian kit, headed for the back door and knocked. A faint *come in* echoed somewhere within, and he stepped inside, pulling off his boots. Tobias left his boots on the rug in the mudroom, set his bag on a chair and padded into the kitchen. Too late he realized one of his socks had a hole in the toe—Medora would certainly notice.

Tobias found Medora folding laundry in the living room. He was struck by the room's emptiness. Enoch's family photographs that had once cluttered the walls, the pillows and blankets on the couch were gone. Only the fire in the woodstove and the mounds of wood around it suggested any human warmth. But she looked up at him and smiled that slip of a smile he had seen so often; he couldn't imagine that she was lonely.

Toby, she said, her eyes returning to the sheet she was carefully folding.

He disliked being called *Toby*. Though everyone but Johan had called him *Tobias* since childhood, and though he always introduced himself as *Tobias Harder* with an inflection on *Tobias*, Medora insisted on belittling him with two syllables instead of three. Poppa had told him once that his name came from a hero in a forbidden Biblical text that fought a demon. Tobias wasn't a religious man, but he always felt pride that his name proclaimed something so important. When he was young, it made him feel he would do something great in the world.

Tobias walked farther into the living room and promptly stubbed his toe on a leg of the coffee table. He winced and examined his foot. The ingrown toenail that stuck through his sock needed trimming. It had begun bothering him again, as it had for years, and the cutting was always painful. So painful he avoided it until he could no longer stand the throbbing.

Medora looked up, followed his gaze and laughed. You want me to take care of that?

I don't know if I really have time for that, today. I need to get home soon. Alice doesn't know I'm here.

Ah. At least let me get a fresh pair for you. I still have Enoch's somewhere around here. Those things look ready for the garbage, anyway.

Before he could protest she ran upstairs, her bare feet slapping against the hardwood. Tobias knew that Enoch had removed the moldy carpet and cracked linoleum and put wood floors in every room of their house not long before he died. Tobias noticed that even her rugs, like the photographs, had disappeared. Each grain of wood shimmered through the hours Enoch had spent polishing them.

She returned with several pairs. Here. Have them all. I honestly don't know why I've kept them this long. They're too big for me.

Are you sure?

God, yes. What do you think I am? One of those widows who cherishes every item her husband ever touched?

Tobias sat on the sofa, pulled off his old socks and put on Enoch's. They were stiff and had sculpted to feet that were gone. He looked up at Medora.

Thanks, he said. For the socks, I mean.

Medora grinned. He would never wear these socks again. He would tuck them in the back of his drawer. Unable to throw them out, unable to confess this exchange with Alice. She would certainly laugh at him.

Well, let's take a look at Bossie, he said.

The previous winter, he had just birthed a calf with a large set of tongs when Alice called. When the phone rang in the Wiebe's barn, he figured it was for Donny or Davy, but while he was washing his hands and watching the red calf clumsily haul itself to its feet, Davy handed the receiver to Tobias.

He's gone, Alice said matter-of-factly. She had never been one to dress up even the worst news.

Who? Tobias said stupidly.

Johan. Johan's gone.

When?

About a half hour ago. Gretta called just now.

Tobias wondered what he had been doing the moment his twin died. Had he been grasping the head of the calf with the tongs, or had he been reaching into the mother's womb to try to extricate it with his bare hands? He should've felt something was wrong in the world at that pinnacle of time. He had heard that when one Siamese twin dies, the other soon follows, and that there were stories about normal twins feeling a twinge of pain when their siblings passed—even if they were thousands of miles apart. But Tobias had felt nothing. It was as if his body no more sensed his brother's death than it sensed its sheath of skin cells dusting off each day.

Tobias?

Tobias leaned his head back and studied the abandoned yellow jackets' nest in the rafters. Yeah?

We need to be heading down there.

Yeah. I'll be home soon.

Tobias?

Yeah?

I'm sorry.

Had this been anyone but Alice, it would seem a cold understatement. But he knew she meant it. It had been this inane habit of meaning something whole-heartedly even if it was clichéd or obvious or cold that had drawn him to her in the beginning.

A few weeks into their marriage, she said: Do you want me to give you a blow job tonight?

Her intonation of *blow job* sounded like it was a word she'd never heard before and was trying to hide that fact.

Yeah, he said, keeping his face as serious as hers. Yeah, I'd like that.

∽

Enoch died a rather quiet death only a month after Johan. One minute he was at the town's donut shop, refilling his coffee at the counter, laughing at something someone said. The next he crumpled to the floor, cradling the paper cup as though it needed protection.

Tobias had been there. He dropped the dozen he always bought each morning for his staff and people waiting in the reception room for their pets to be castrated or get their shots. He crouched over Enoch's body helplessly. For the first time in his life he wished he had become a doctor for humans. Tobias confessed this once to a local doctor when he returned to Ulysses for a weekend sometime after. Dr. Diener told him that Enoch was dead before hitting the floor.

That's the way brain aneurysms work, he said.

It took nearly ten minutes for anyone to say, Where's Dora? Enoch and Medora had been married just three years, and few people in Pilsen knew anything about her, since her family was from Sioux City. The question of who was to go to tell her drifted among the crowd. The police had arrived with the EMTs, and one of the deputies volunteered to do it. Tobias made a move to stop him, to go instead, but the deputy was out the door. Tobias figured he knew Medora better than anyone. He knew people through their animals; saw how they treated these voiceless beings. Kyle Plenert, a Mennonite deacon, let his sows wallow in their own shit for days. *Englische* Enoch and Medora treated their pregnant cows like precious vessels of life. He felt himself privy to the owners' souls, in a way that no minister of God could ever know.

Und der König wird antworten und zu ihnen sagen: Wahrlich, ich sage euch: Was ihr getan habt einem von diesen meinen geringsten Brüdern, das habt ihr mir getan, Poppa had once told him. Though he wasn't a religious man anymore, Tobias hung those words in English in his office next to a montage of snapshots of his patients and their owners:

> *And the King will answer them,*
> *I assure you: Whatever you did*
> *for one of the least*

of these brothers of Mine,
you did for Me.

Some thought he was a little sacrilegious to compare animals to humans, but they were of the *Englische* Mennonites. The graybeards smiled and tapped the wooden plaque reverently.

He had to be out of town the day of the funeral, so the next time he saw Medora was at the bi-monthly auction, where he was examining cattle and making sure they were fit for sale. Tobias managed to catch her by the coffee line and tapped her shoulder. When she turned around, he was shocked to see her face. Instead of being older and more subdued from her husband's death, she seemed younger, more cherubic. It was May, and the breeze that came up from Nebraska already bore the scent of summer heat. Her hair lifted and rose like a resurrected being. She wore her hair long and flowing down her capable back. It was a silver-blond, and seemed to Tobias like aged wheat in June.

So, you're selling the stock then, he said.

No, I'm looking for a bull, she said, surprised. Didn't Mike tell you? Chevy gave up the ghost yesterday.

No, he said, surprised that his partner at the clinic hadn't said anything about this. I've been out of town a lot lately. Have you ever— bought a bull before?

Ah, no.

Did you ever come here before—with Enoch?

Ah, no.

He couldn't hide his grin. Do you know what to look for?

Besides his balls?

Yeah. Besides that.

Ah, not really. Could you help?

Over the next few months, Tobias often found himself driving in the direction of Medora's place. At first it was to show her how to tell when a cow was in heat, how to prod a shyer cow into the pen with the bull, now named Julius Caesar, how to do all the hundreds of things he had purposely forgotten from his youth. Sometimes before he left, they would sit on her porch and watch the sun stretch itself towards the horizon. Or they sat on her rusty swing set and saw the green leaving the fields beneath the heat; the fresh cut bales squatting, sprouting shadows. They would sip iced tea at the edge of her garden and eye thunderheads that skimmed the west; at times these clouds reached the farmyard, cracked dry lightning and moved on. Other times Tobias and Medora would have to scramble through pea-sized hail onto the screen porch, clutching hands and stumbling.

When Julius Caesar finished breeding his harem for the first time, they celebrated with a bottle of wine, followed by cheap beer and a finger of whiskey. Alice was visiting her sister in Fargo, so he stayed on past sunset. Tobias wasn't much of a drinker. He usually hated the way he felt when he'd taken more than what caused a pleasant buzz somewhere deep in his brain. But this time he felt at ease with the world. He didn't care about the amount of debt he still had on his new clinic, the way his eyelids drooped with age, the fact that he was again attracted to a woman other than his wife.

They faced one another, balanced on a shaky porch swing. Parts of her faded jeans were worn into gaping holes. Her unshaven knees poked out, the skin red and dry. Her armpits gave an unwashed scent. In a wild wave of her right arm she accidentally splashed her whisky on Tobias's face. Swiping a grease rag from her pocket, she leaned towards him, laughing apologies. As her face loomed closer, he closed his eyes, smelled her freshly dirty skin, and felt the coarseness of the rag she dragged across his face. As soon as the cloth left his mouth, he caught her lips in an awkward kiss, his teeth scraping the inside flesh as she pulled away. For a moment he remained as if they were still locked together, unsure of what he should do.

He felt the pressure of the humid sky about to hammer down on him, its drum about to echo through the night. Tobias waited for the crash to come, to strike at his stooping back, for his beaten body to swell up to the cottonwood that sprang up beside Medora's porch and strain among the branches. He hoped the moment would pass quickly. When he looked up she was standing, biting her lower lip.

I am not a lonely widow, Toby, she said.

I'm sorry. I should go.

The earth moved as he got up from the swing, and he leaned forward, catching himself on the porch's handrail.

No. Don't. You should sleep here. You're too soused. Sleep on the hammock. It's a nice night.

She went inside, brought out a pillow and a blanket and shut the door. Tobias heard her flip the lock. The living room light snapped off, leaving him alone in the bulbed porch light. The insects crawled upon the screen door, hissing.

～

Johan's funeral was blessedly bland, but the viewing the night before was horrible. People Tobias hadn't seen in more than a decade were there: distant cousins from Texas wearing brass belt buckles with their suits; a great-aunt that he had assumed long dead wheeled over his foot; Tobias' older brother, Nick, slunk around in the background in patched jeans and shit-kickers; Nick's daughter Imma came for five minutes to look at the body before rushing out. There were dozens of others who were there just to find out what Ellen was going to do with the farm.

When Tobias' son was married the spring before, none of these people had felt it was important enough for them to haul themselves up to South Dakota, but they came from Texas, Arkansas and California for a funeral in Kansas. Huldah, at least, behaved with decorum and had no agenda; she stood by the body, rearranged what was left of Johan's hair then sat in a corner, staring at the obituary with amazing concentration. The rest of his sisters annoyed him. They wept and carried on as if Johan had been their dearest brother, even though they had little to say about him that was positive while he was alive. They constantly embraced Ellen and blew their noses in balled-up tissues.

He noticed it was Ellen who was the calmest of them all, though she had every right to be the one in tears. Her daughter was yet to show her face. Her son was dead. Her parents were dead. She had to know everyone was wondering who would get the land and the ramshackle house. She'd been a town girl before she married Johan, and had little to do with the daily operation. No one expected her to rent it out, much less farm it herself. Farmers from Johan and Ellen's church had voluntarily taken over the fields once it was clear that Johan was unable to keep up with the work. Any questions about the farm had gone to him, not her, even when he was in the hospital for the last time.

She circulated the room, calmly listening to everyone's stilted condolences, straightening tablecloths, accepting drooping flowers from Tobias' thought-dead-great-aunt. Tobias couldn't keep his eyes off her. Though they had rarely spoken to each other in private before now, he wanted to say something or do something that would matter—something that would make her smile years later, when the pain of Johan's death was a mere throb. He sat on a low bench in a corner, crushing and smoothing out his plastic cup from the table of beverages in the lobby, trying to come up with the right comment.

Tobias wondered if a meaningful story about Johan would do it; he tried to think of something she wouldn't know, but he couldn't break into his past life and grab anything. It was as if every moment he had spent with his twin never occurred. Gretta had told him that he and Johan had been born on the coldest day in ten years; Poppa had dragged a kerosene heater into the bedroom to stave off the cold, but Momma had refused to let it be lit. When Johan had entered the world, he was full of screams and the heat from his body enveloped him in a cloud of mist, but when the cold hit Tobias, he couldn't breathe because of the frigid air.

It was as if only Tobias had entered the world that day. That he had refused to breathe because of the realization that he would always be alone in the world the moment the umbilical cord was cut.

Tobias caught Ellen's eye. She crossed the room. From his vantage point, he saw her legs like he'd never seen them before. They were short and plump, shaped like sails on a ship. Her brown skirt fluttered over them, as if the fabric was thinking other thoughts than death and eternity and tablecloths. Tobias straightened his back, his lips ready to throw something, anything out into the air that would shimmer between them. But then something blocked his view. A man in a blue suit had stepped in: Dr. Harold Diener. Tobias saw her change her trajectory—saw her sad smile settle on someone other than himself. Harold didn't touch her; he didn't need to. But that was when Tobias knew what possibly neither of them realized. And he found himself enraged with jealousy. Tobias wasn't a violent person, but he wanted to throw Harold into the street and kick him in the stomach, the ribs, the head.

He mentioned this to Alice as they drove home. She laughed.

Why are you laughing?

I noticed you were staring at her the whole time.

I was not.

Yes, you were! Don't worry, I'm not jealous. You just feel the need to fall for the damsel in distress if she comes your way.

You're joking.

Come on, she's a widow with a dead son and an ungrateful daughter, her momma died when she was a kid and her daddy was a junkie.

She totally needs your arm of support, right?

Well, maybe—

Or, my other conjecture is that you always fall for the damsels whose dead husbands are the kind of men you wish you were, she said, tapping his knee. Though I can't fathom why you'd think Johan was better than you. You are far better-looking than Johan was—even before he got sick.

You do know how awful that sounds.

I suppose so. It's a good thing only you hear these things without judgment.

~

The calf had only partially turned. Tobias could feel its head butting its mother's flanks, trying to find a new breach in her overused body. Pushing his arm deeper into her womb, he felt a large lump. He felt it gingerly, glancing at Medora stroking the mother's nose as it jerked about in the holding pen. It was a solid growth, partially pinning the calf to one side.

It's a tumor, he said.

Medora came to his side. Is that why it hasn't turned?

Probably.

Tobias pulled his gloved arm out of the cow's womb with a popping sound and headed for the giant tin sink in the corner of the barn. Medora opened the stall gate and let the mothering cow leap into the corral.

So, what are you going to do?

I don't know if I can turn it, with that lump there, without killing it.

It will die anyway if we don't do something, won't it?

When's the gestation period over? Tobias opened the spigot and waited for the water to come with open hands. His fingers felt warm from the womb; for the moment the aches of his approaching age disappeared.

It ends this coming week.

Well, I'd recommend just sitting tight for now. When Mike gets back, get him out here and tell him what I've told you. Maybe the calf will still turn at least partway, then he could move it easier. You'll have to use a chain, you know. To pull it out.

When the boiling water rushed out he snapped back his hands and yelled. Medora stood, biting her lower lip. The skin around her chapped lips grew white; the teeth digging deep into the flesh.

Tobias wiped his burning hands on his jeans and took a step forward. The steaming water continued flowing, pausing for a moment before gushing out again, kissing the cold.

You have to know you should probably destroy her, the mother, after the birth, he said. She's very ill, I think. That tumor is causing pain, I'd say.

Medora stayed planted where she was, her eyes wild on him. She was so small and square, Enoch's coveralls slouching over her like a weakening outer skin. Her ski cap was shoved down on her head, her hair flowing out of the bottom—a frazzled lightning. Tobias was about to open his mouth, to say something to force away her expression, when it disappeared.

She dropped her eyes, nodded once and smiled to herself.

You're right, she said.

She adjusted her cap and smiled again. She had come to some decision that Tobias would never know.

She stopped at the tiny door that was encapsulated by the larger barn door. My mother once told me that in ancient times women birthed in private—that they went into the fields alone to have their children, even in winter. It was an intimate act, reserved for the woman and the gods. That the cold brought the spirit.

Medora smiled like a sprite and gave the door frame a little tap, as if her fingers had other things on their mind.

Two days later, Tobias drove past Medora's. He thought he caught a glimpse of Mike's giant SUV as his little Toyota slithered by, but he knew her drive was too long to tell for sure. He had spent the weekend wondering if she would call; ask him to come pull the calf out with chains that would rub its legs raw and tear open its mother's vagina. He knew from experience how the blood and placenta would nearly drown this awkward life. That it would only breathe if it sincerely wanted to begin, on the outside, in the cold.

Missed

2007

Jasper didn't notice the cat's absence until five days had passed. The office assistant had noticed, but she didn't bother telling him. He didn't care at first, really. More important issues had arisen.

He had found a small suitcase in his wife's closet, for one. He hadn't opened the suitcase, but the closet was empty enough to tell him where the clothes were. The heat in the church was gone, for another. The boiler in the basement had expired without warning. It was ancient, more than likely as old as the church itself. It had used coal and had been converted to use steam whenever such things had been done. The boiler was huge, and would have to be taken out in pieces, or so the contractor had told Jasper.

It was the beginning of November. The building was poorly insulated and after a few days the chill of the basement had reached the church office.

Jasper would have refused a coat, had anyone offered him one, and sat in denial of the cold. He only allowed himself one cup of coffee in the morning to warm his hands. His mug emitted a damp sensation in solidarity with the unused radiators and the cans of beans in the kitchen pantry. Jasper imagined the entire church did this on purpose, as a quiet rebellion against him. Though why the church would rebel against him was a mystery.

The first Sunday following the boiler's demise had the small but usual number of congregants. The second Sunday only half showed up. By the third Sunday only the hardy souls who ran the soup kitchen arrived. He ushered them into the church office, turned on the space heater his assistant had brought from home, and began to speak.

He found himself ranting against the disciples, the men who wished to disperse the people and their hunger on the day of the feeding of thousands with loaves and fishes.

It was not a mysterious feat by Christ! he sputtered. That day the people gathered on the hillside had taken his message of love and sacrifice to heart, and put it into action by sharing their loaves with one another, not keeping it all to themselves! *That* was the miracle! The ones, the ones who had a *front seat* to the peaceable kingdom hadn't grasped the simple message understood by everyone else!

Jasper was gesturing so violently, he nearly pounded his own Bible, amazed that his audience, this remnant population of seven, held such stoic faces at this heresy, this offering of a choice between the magic Jesus and the human one.

He decided the rest of his absent congregation was merely there for the social church, not the spiritual. They were only there when they knew there would be heat, coffee and bagels. They were the chaff, surely. They followed the disciples, not the discipler.

Later, he wondered if he would have done the same, were he not the pastor. He doubted he would have rolled out of his warm bed to tramp through rain to listen to one of his stuttering homilies in that huge, frigid sanctuary.

$\sim$

Minerva spent most of that afternoon at the farmer's market. The dusty feel of the potatoes and carrots, the dark scent of compost gave her a stirring below, deeper than any orgasm. Minerva secretly smelled the musk of soil on her hands after she combed through the soybeans for the plumpest ones. Felt wicked satisfaction when her feet crunched the castaways into the pavement beneath the table. Quietly handled her kind of harvest. There was a primeval feeling to her soul as she wandered away, like she had been paying homage to an ancient deity.

She wasn't fooled by the romantic picture of living on the land these organic growers painted for their city-bound customers. She knew the reality. After her brother, Jeffrey, died, Minerva spent years of her life chasing loose hogs and taking her poppa's Ford to various far-flung places, fiercely on the hunt for engine parts for a small army of tractors that were practically antique showpieces. She had spent sweaty summers delivering hundreds of bologna sandwiches, chips and iced tea to her cousins cutting wheat. She came to pick them up at that last moment of sunlight before the moisture would weigh down the grain. Stood on the verge of the field, listening to the distant, lion-growl of the combine as it made its last pass. Waiting in darkness for the men to arrive.

It was the first afternoon she hadn't been in pursuit of a job, cleaning the abominable sacristy, painting the bedroom walls yellow, or any of the other hundreds of things that had swallowed the last six weeks since they had left Ulysses. She now had a part-time position as a cafeteria card-checker at one of the public schools and had an interview on Tuesday for another part-time job as a librarian. The church closets were mostly immaculate, though cold, and their bedroom walls glowed.

She decided that was the extent of her invisible role as The Pastor's Wife. She would do no more. She had done her Martha duty far enough.

Minerva had secretly somersaulted in their overgrown backyard after Jasper told her that the Mennonite church in East St. Louis had accepted his candidacy. The town of Ulysses left her in that moment en masse. In a city, so Minerva believed, one became anonymous. No one would recognize her as The Pastor's Wife unless she wanted them to. She only went to church that first Sunday, to let herself be greeted by the retired women in the congregation, made plans to join them in the soup kitchen once things were straightened out with the new apartment. She never came to church again.

Jasper took her behavior calmly. Which surprised her. Perhaps he had known she would do it. Perhaps he was relieved that she wouldn't embarrass him with her off-key voice, her ill-fitting dresses from thrift stores, the way she stood aloof after services instead of greeting the people. Perhaps he'd even been surprised that she'd done anything at all. That second Sunday he woke her with a single kiss before he left for the service. She looked at him through sleep-matted eyelashes, waiting for a fight that wasn't there.

Something akin to shame flooded her stomach and nearly crossed her lips. She opened her mouth. Minerva said: *I'm sorry.*

Jasper leaned closer, his aftershave pushing all other thoughts from her mind. He gently knocked his forehead against hers: *Liar*, he mouthed.

≈

A week before the cat vanished, one of the hardy souls was missing from soup kitchen duty, and Jasper, unable to think of an excuse, picked up the slack. He secretly hated this part of the job, even though he knew how shameful such a feeling was. The volunteers probably guessed it, at least somewhat, for he was given the most innocuous jobs: peeling carrots, carrying trays up to the fellowship hall, mopping spills. But the preparation wasn't what Jasper hated. He enjoyed being around the women of the kitchen; listening to their small talk and gossip. The way they took him as seriously as a child. He felt the least responsibility around them. Perhaps their theology was flawed or ignorant, but they would continue on with this Martha service with or without him.

Jasper had always felt that the Martha of the Gospel had gotten a raw deal—it was she who made the food that was eaten that day that would not have been there had she followed Mary's example. He wondered what Christ would have done for the Communion had someone failed to make the bread or buy the wine because they were pious at His feet, like Mary. But he couldn't help being a Mary. He was too lazy to be a Martha.

Sensing the fact that he was being lowered in some way, some of the homeless men treated him with a contempt he never experienced when he said a prayer and drifted among them, his imaginary clerical robes flowing. They demanded more of the main course, extra jam, tried to bully him into unlocking the restroom that Jasper had declared off-limits after he found a bloody syringe in the toilet.

Jasper hoped Hannah would show up, but she didn't.

Only when Hannah was present did the taunting stop when he served in the kitchen. Hannah was built like a carrier, and smelled like urine. She wore three sweaters at once, even in summer.

No one crossed Hannah. Everyone stood in silence while Jasper prayed. Everyone said *thank you* to the people who served the food. Jasper knew her behavior wasn't entirely altruistic. Each time they met on the street, Hannah asked for money in payment what she called *her services as a soup kitchen referee*—Jasper said no; when she was near the church she would always ask to use the restroom—Jasper or the office assistant said no.

But Hannah wasn't there. He wondered where she was.

You do know the cat's missing, the office assistant announced when he returned from the kitchen, wiping his hands on his pants. Jasper looked at the half-eaten cat food in the dish, the unused litter.

For five days, in fact.

Oh.

Well, what are you going to do about it?

You do know I've other things to worry about.

She wiggled her gloved hands with the fingertips snipped off. Her nails were painted fuchsia, but he could see an underlying blue of cold.

Yeah, I'm aware.

When did you see him last?

Four days ago. I'm the one who feeds him, among other things.

This was a sore point. He knew she hadn't expected to feed a cat and change his litter box when she'd taken the job.

Do you think someone let him out?

Impossible. Five days ago I fed him and locked him in the kitchen. Hannah and I left together. There was no one else.

Did you look around the church?

My domain is the office. Beyond that, it's yours.

Jasper couldn't argue with that.

Okay. I'll look around.

He thought the disappearance was weird, but a boon in disguise. There was no love lost between them. When he was frustrated about anything, the church, his marriage, his life, he focused it on the cat. The cat knew this, Jasper was sure, but it continued to wash itself calmly in his presence and sprawl on the parts of the floor where he wanted to walk. He'd wanted the cat out upon his arrival. But the cat was some kind of an icon to his congregation, and had apparently been in the church for a decade or more.

Jasper suspected this little piece of life would be there long after he was gone.

He got up reluctantly, found a flashlight and went down to the box-filled basement. There was a rotting smell, but after a few turns he found a box of vegetables covered by a blanket, apparently forgotten by the volunteers. Jasper reached the defunct boiler and stood before this, the god of heat. The one thing that kept his congregation coming back. Not Jasper or the Presence of God.

Fucking piece of shit, he said, almost reverently.

He returned to the first floor, looked at the cat's dish, glanced at his coat, and went into the sanctuary.

It was beautiful, the sanctuary, if you ignored the scuffed floor, mismatched pews and their smelly cushions. It was the one place Jasper felt the Presence. Something about the vaulted ceiling covered in fading frescos, the way the sunlight filtered through the dirty stained glass, the tarnished organ pipes for an organ long gone—this was where it lived. Not the one that walked among the lepers and beggars. That Presence was too dirtied by life. Too real for worship. That Gospel stank of human flesh.

The face of this Presence was pure, virginal amid the dust.

～

Minerva entered the apartment a few seconds before Jasper. They struggled in the tiny vestibule together, pulling off hats, coats and sticking gloves into their respective pockets. Nothing was said. She knew he had seen the farmer's market produce; he'd learned long ago to leave Minerva alone after she had re-tasted the agricultural life, just as she had learned not to mention the church until he did. From their three years of marriage they had learned this: to avoid the topics of their obsessions and torments as though they had no existence in their world. To ignore the fact that the other was even in the room at times.

Jasper tested the waters sooner than she expected. After he changed clothes he sat on the counter. So, what's for supper, goddess? I'm hungry.

Minerva laughed. And laughed again as a smirk crossed his face after his triumph.

Depends on how quick you want your supper, Minerva said, shoving potatoes in a paper bag and placing them in the cupboard nearest the sink.

Very quick.

Pasta?

Didn't we just have pasta?

Soup?

What kind?

Any.

Borscht!

That won't be quick.

True. But it'll feel good to chop things up and throw them in the pot.

She knew what would happen later. The way their bodies moved in the tiny kitchen, never touching. It was almost tangible—the sensation. Minerva had long ago learned to recognize it, even on days when they barely spoke.

Like everything else in their relationship, they only shared their bodies when the lamp went out. Minerva reached for the memory of the soybeans as her fingers plowed through Jasper's back, felt the dust of his flesh like caked soil beneath her fingers.

Later, Jasper mentioned the missing cat.

I suppose it got outside, she said.

Maybe. But I've seen it sitting at the open door, never stirring a foot outside.

I thought you hated this cat.

I do. But I miss the object of my hatred. I actually miss tripping over him.

Perhaps the boiler will do.

Minerva heard her mistake even as she said it. She had hit on the reality of his failures with the church, both physically and spiritually. She felt him stiffen in the darkness.

She rumpled around the bed sheets and managed to pull on her pajamas without leaving the bed. They both lay there, motionless. Long ago she had learned to compartmentalize her relationship with Jasper. To put his negatives away from his positives—his tempers away from his gentleness. She viewed Jasper's compartments like a huge dresser, some large, others narrow.

Minerva woke early. She rolled over and examined the man sprawled next to her and knew that the destructive drawers were overflowing, had begun to seep quietly into his smiles, his affection, the way he carefully caressed her thighs, as though they were a comfortable yet sacred gift they shared.

Minerva slid out from beneath the covers and stumbled to her closet. When she opened it, the breath of a frozen dragon swept her face. She looked at the small blue suitcase she had begun to fill. As if she was only a visitor to this place. As if she was an uncomfortable tourist in a city that carried an infinite sadness under the embrace of the Arch.

∽

Jasper and Minerva met while he was drunk by the lake a few miles out of Ulysses. He asked her if she knew she had the name of a Roman goddess. Minerva was angry-tipsy and would have walked away in offense at his suggestion that she didn't have the intelligence for such knowledge had he not smiled a sleepy smile and added, You know, the Romans killed Jesus. They killed him, not the Jews.

So I've heard, she said dryly.

I wonder what would have happened, if Pilate had freed Jesus. If we'd all be worshipping you right now instead. You're beautiful enough. He reached for her hair which hung loose to the waist.

You're drunk, you know. That line only works if you're sober and in the library.

When Jasper drove up their driveway the following Saturday, she was rinsing off her boots outside the house with a hose. He skidded to a halt with a flourish and stepped out amid a cloud of dust.

What on earth are you doing here? Minerva saw herself as he probably saw her: braless with an oversized t-shirt brushing the nipples of her oversized breasts.

I'm here for a date. He smiled that smile at her again, at the rickety farmstead surrounding them as if he quite approved.

You're not serious.

I came quite a-ways for a joke. Let's go.

I'm not dressed for a date. I just got out of a barn. I smell like shit.

I don't care. We'll go to the lake or a cow pond or something, if you want to wash. I could baptize you myself.

To both of their surprise, Minerva dropped the still-running hose and her boots and climbed into his car barefooted, in the driver's seat. Jasper got in on the passenger side. I've been baptized before, you know. We'll see if you'll do it, she said.

Do what?

Baptize me. Again.

I will if you want me to.

∾

When Hannah appeared the evening before the cat disappeared for her usual requests, Jasper had just gotten off the phone with one of the area trustees, who seemed to disbelieve the estimate amount the contractor had given.

No, he said to Hannah preemptively.

Pastor, you don't even know what I'm asking.

Yes, I do. No.

Can I use the toilet?

You know the answer.

I have my period, Pastor. I need a little privacy. I need to change my underwear. I can't afford tampons.

Jasper felt his face turn red with an image of Hannah's blood seeping through the crotch of her underwear.

We all have it, Pastor—even your wife. She motioned to the ring on his hand.

Yes, I'm quite aware.

The only way he knew Minerva was menstruating was when the box of tampons sat on the tank of the toilet instead of under the sink. Once he happened to see one of her used tampons in the trashcan, and all the romantic visions about the blood of Christ flowing down like a river left him once he saw reality. True blood was clotted and dark; discarded cells that were shunted out of the body in spite of its life.

Even the Virgin bled before she had her baby, Hannah said, almost piously.

All right, all right—let me unlock the door. He pulled the kitchen and bathroom keys out of his pocket. But don't use this excuse again. And don't tell anyone else.

Thank you, Pastor. Hannah shouldered her backpack. She followed him to the restroom door. Your wife is sitting on the steps of the church, by the way.

She is? He looked at her sharply. How do you know she's my wife? I don't think you've met her. She's never at the soup kitchen. She doesn't even come to church.

Pastor, I've been in this neighborhood for twenty years. I don't do drugs and I only drink a little. I know everyone. I know who's sleeping with who and what gets thrown away by who.

When he went out the side door, he looked towards the stoop. Minerva sat on the topmost step, wrapped in her old barn jacket and a hat shoved over her ears. Jasper realized he wouldn't have even glanced her way, had Hannah not told him she was there. Minerva looked homeless, in that ragged, oversize coat and pilled stocking cap. She was looking up at the winter-darkened sky, as if she could actually see the stars through the city glare.

He knew he should go over to her, wrap his crisp, city-black coat around her. Tuck his scarf around her neck. Kiss her chapped lips.

Jasper wondered when he had stopped loving Minerva.

He had loved her quickly. She had the most beautiful eyes—a pale blue that seemed to leap out from her sun-darkened face, her long black hair. She carried her weight with a grace he had never witnessed in heavy-set people, as if she was merely draped in flesh she could step from at any given moment. Minerva had been silly in a sadly profound way, which Jasper had always loved the most. When he had pulled into her father's farmyard that first time, she had dropped her shit-covered boots and the garden hose away the way a queen would spread largess to the people. Jasper was dry and breathless, covered in dust. Minerva was moist and grinning, covered in soil. They had careened out of the yard, billowing exhaust. Jasper looked back once, and imagined he saw the hose still running, making a small pool among the gravel.

That silliness had disappeared since her father died, he realized, leaving only sadness that was beautiful in a strange way. But the part he loved was gone. He marveled at the weakness of his initial love as he drew his coat collar to his throat and walked away.

∾

I think I want to go to seminary, Jasper announced during harvest. They had just dropped her cousins off for the night. Their wedding was three weeks away.

What?

Seminary. I need to go, I think.

They were sitting far apart in her dad's yellowing Ford, tufts of foam leaping out between them. Minerva kept her hands and eyes on the steering wheel.

Why?

I don't know. I think I'll know once I get there.

You've got to be kidding.

The night was hot and close, multiplying the face of the moon into a giant, drifting ring. A combination scent of grain and diesel fuel saturated the air. Minerva straightened her back, peeling her bare shoulders from the faux-leather cushion.

No. I'm not.

Why haven't you said anything about this?

Because of your reaction. Like this. Right now.

Do you realize what a commitment this would be? For not just you?

I think I need a commitment like this.

Different from the one we have?

No. The same. She heard him take a deep breath. Only more pure.

Minerva felt her throat close. The moon edged a little higher, diminishing its size.

I need an object for my hate. An object for my love. Something that will not change over time. Ours won't be like that. Ours will only be altered with time. It's mortal.

Minerva laughed. He sounded so formal. She'd always teased him about it—this need to sound official at ridiculous times.

When she had proposed to him as they were swimming in the lake, he didn't answer. Instead he rose and grabbed her hand. Pulled her to the rocky beach. Let go of her hand and clasped his arms behind him. They stood just inside the lap of the reservoir, her t-shirt clinging to her thighs.

Now, he had said carefully. What was the question?

The truck's cab bounced the vibrations of her laugh before escaping through the window. She heard its echo briefly, before the heat of the moonrise swallowed it whole. It would always be like this. Standing in the darkness, waiting for the men to make the decision for the last turn, let the machines idle before shutting them down to let the crickets rasp be heard. Waiting for the men to arrive.

You don't have to go through with this. The wedding. I'll understand. That's why I'm telling you now. He inched towards her, despite the heat, despite the foam that rose up between them.

She felt his breath, humid and close. You know I love you, she said, However impurely.

He laughed. Minerva waited for his voice to be consumed into the darkness, but she heard it bounce against the barn.

There are different kinds of love you know, he said, touching her hair lightly. Agape and Eros are not in competition.

She let herself be convinced by this lie. Minerva now knew Jasper had been true to his name: like his namesake, one of the searching kings of the desert, attempting to reach the birth of the Christ, he had offered her the magi-gift of freedom. And when she refused it, he took it and walked away to his mythical land without her.

When the first drops of rain began to fall Minerva got up from the church steps and retreated to the coffee shop across the street. She stared at the place she had sat a hundred times. She could see the outline of her body's heat, still seated, before it evaporated into the misty rain. When the homeless woman and the office assistant left the building, she took the spare church keys she'd found in Jasper's desk in the apartment and slipped inside. She found the cat curled up by the refrigerator. It didn't even wake as she took its heavy body into her arms and unhooked its collar. Its entire body began to purr. She stroked his matted fur. The purr intensified. Minerva leaned against the humming refrigerator and closed her eyes.

She wondered if she could do it—if it would make any difference at all between her and Jasper. He complained about the cat, but the cat held his wrath instead of the people—the cat kept him from failing in front of this congregation. Maybe this was what he needed. A slaughter of what kept him sane. He might stumble too much; he might lose the church; he might return to her.

Herein, said a Voice.

Minerva opened her eyes and looked around the kitchen. Who's there?

Here, the Voice repeated. I'm right here. *Herein!*

The cat stretched one of its paws and nicked her chin. Minerva yelled and flung the cat out of her lap. Who are you?

The cat had landed on its feet and sat in the shadow of an overhanging counter. Minerva only saw its white paws that flashed up and down as it licked them.

Where are you? Minerva stared at the cat, willing it to speak.

The cat continued to clean itself calmly. The Voice laughed somewhere that Minerva could not place. It was an odd laugh, as though it had never heard anyone laugh before. Why do you people always wonder where I am? You're all so blind. Except for Huldah—Huldah always knew—always accepted the truth right away. And you all think she's slow.

You know my aunt? Minerva couldn't believe she was talking to thin air.

Good grief, the Voice growled. I know all of you. Of course, the

Voice amended, I probably know you least of all.

Why's that?

You're probably the toughest of the bunch. There was no need to bother with you. You're like your grandmomma. If something needed to be done, she did it, no matter how hard.

What do I need to do that's so hard?

You need to end your family's dependence on me. I'm tired of waiting.

For what?

I'm tired of waiting to fill your needs. I'm just tired of everything. I need to be set free. Go where I need to go.

Where do you want to go?

The Voice chuckled off-key. That's my business.

How do I set you free?

You know. That's why you're here.

The cat stopped licking itself and stretched, keeping its eyes on Minerva the whole time.

She opened the first drawer next to the refrigerator and pulled out the knife. She picked up the cat's purring body, blessed it with a little prayer and slit its throat.

As she gathered up the remnants, she realized that the world had again accepted the mortality of another creature, swallowing it with ease. The event was so commonplace. The refrigerator still hummed. Her body kept breathing. Her knees made a soft *crack!* as she stood. Everything stayed the same. There had been no schism in the universe, no thunder of anger from above.

I hope that was what you wanted, she said to the Voice. I hope it does what I want. The Voice did not reply.

She rose and cleaned her mess. Minerva thought some blood might sneak on without her notice, so beforehand she'd gone to leave her clothes in a pile in the bathroom only to find someone had left a used tampon on the floor. Instead, she deposited her jeans, socks and underwear at the office door.

Still naked, Minerva wandered towards the sanctuary. It was eerie, being alone and exposed in the presence of God, the spitting rain smearing the broken stained glass. Her body sprouted hairy goose pimples, her nipples hardening against the cold. She felt it twisting around her, draping her body in drafts that wrapped around her neck and wriggled up and down her spine. The hand of God Itself was combing the air, testing her value for harvest. Even though the sanctuary's ceiling disappeared into the shadows of the streetlamp darkness, Minerva sensed the trapped feeling it must have, this God who had been named and forgotten. It was begging for relief. Begging for one breath of fresh air. Hoping to be let go like the Voice. Such an ordinary request, for a deity.

It had always been Minerva standing like this, waiting for the men. Ignorant of her own power. Ignorant of the fact that she could drive away at any moment without them. They would be stranded, because these men needed her for their return home.

She almost gave in. She nearly yielded to that desire to smash every piece of stained glass, to dance in the ensuing rain of slivered sand. To see God breathe, move out of Jasper's vaulted cage into the streets.

But she knew God wanted freedom too badly. It had climbed off the combine with assuredness and was waiting for her to take it home. God did not want to be left alone in the fields, among its dead harvest.

The fingers of God paused in their search, then combed anxiously for that kernel of escape.

Enough! she whispered.

When she locked the door of the church behind her, plastic bag in hand, Minerva felt the rain pelting down her back, smoothing out the kinks, blessing her triumph. She realized only the Divinity of potatoes and wheat and the soul of a cat deserved attention: stark, dirty and gorgeous all at once.

∽

Jasper was among his books and papers on the floor when Minerva entered, soaking wet. He stood and made movements to touch her, but he was surrounded by concordances and texts, so he stayed where he was.

Where were you?

She was pulling off her sweater. Waiting for you. Minerva's voice sounded trapped beneath the wet stitching.

Where?

Where else?

When did you get there?

Seven.

I left before that. Six-thirty, I think. Jasper sat down as she pulled off her jeans. Leaving them on the floor, Minerva made for the bathroom in her oversized, soaked t-shirt, its tail slapping at her bare buttocks.

Before she could close the door, Jasper spoke up. I'm sorry.

For what?

That I missed you.

She nearly spoke then, nearly said what they both knew to be true. He knew she wanted to say the word. He longed for her to say the word. Instead she closed the door. So he said it himself: *Liar*.

A week after the cat's disappearance, Minerva was gone, and the office assistant had found the cat's collar on the rectory steps. She also found a pair of women's underwear scrunched behind one of the file cabinets next to the office door, but she didn't tell Jasper. Jasper imagined the cat, in opting for paradise rather than persistent damnation, had unloaded its burden and headed for the wilderness. Perhaps it had followed Minerva.

He had stayed at home the day Minerva walked out the door with her suitcase and a potted geranium. Jasper had just emerged from the bathroom in time to see her putting on her ragged coat. She hadn't even looked in his direction as she closed the door behind her, wrestling with her spoils from their marriage. As though they had never met in their lives. As though Jasper had never driven towards her in a cloud of dust, his heart pounding.

He put off entering the sanctuary until just before his tiny congregation of four or five arrived for Wednesday night prayer. Jasper wondered if the Presence would still be there, or if that, too, would have absconded with his wife and the cat. He needed it to be there. Still his. He wanted to bare his feet in thanks as he strode in, in spite of the cold.

He wanted to encamp himself, wrap himself in all of it. He wished he could send the beggars, lepers, Marthas, Marys away for good, to allow him this. This one thing that would sustain him: the relief the three desert kings had felt when they found the Christ.

Shaken in the Water, Part 6

1919

Nora's belly had dropped by late August. Agnes had seen her momma's do exactly the same thing weeks before she gave birth. She told Nora to stay at home, but Nora refused. She continued to wait for Agnes every day, sitting beneath the cottonwoods when it was sunny or inside the barn if it rained. Most of the straw was moldy, so one night Agnes surreptitiously took several wheelbarrows full to the barn so that Nora would have something comfortable to sit on. Now every day Agnes was torn as she raced to the barn. She wanted Nora to be there, but she wanted the baby to let loose of her mother's skin into the capable hands of Mrs. Hiebert, not hers.

Agnes was the oldest of seven children. She had seen her momma's face contort like an animal's; she had smelled the blood on the sheets she scrubbed afterwards. She didn't want to be a part of that. She wondered if she would see Nora in a different way, like she had seen her momma the first time she witnessed every second of one of her siblings' birth. Agnes found herself loathing her momma after that. Her momma, who was so strong every other moment of every other day, squealed like a hog before the slaughter on those days. She wanted Nora to disappear and return to the barn with a baby with skin like corn silk; hair that waved like the soft prairie grasses that had just woken up from winter.

On the last day in August, a thunderhead roiled in the west, drawing itself closer to Agnes' piece of earth. Agnes watched the clouds as she hurried her brothers and sisters to pull the damp laundry off the line and chase the hens into the hutch. She knew Nora would be there, waiting. Momma was visiting a sick neighbor; Poppa was in town. With a firm hand, she told her siblings to get into the cellar and stay there—she would be back in a little bit. When the youngest tried to follow, Agnes slapped him and shut the door. She took two heavy bricks and laid them on top of the cellar door.

She found Nora prostrate on a mound of straw; her hands clutching her belly, the heat of her body swimming into the dust of the coming storm.

Wie geht es Ihnen? she said needlessly in High German. This moment seemed to call for reverence, like High German at a Sunday service. Agnes hoped if she kept this moment holy, her disgust for Nora would be held at bay.

Agnes paced back and forth as Nora groaned. It was too late to get a wagon to take her home. The storm was nearly on them, flattening the grass to its roots, racing clouds low to the earth, as if they might sweep Agnes and Nora into another world.

Nora's eyes rested on Agnes' face. She smiled, and then winced. I shouldn't be surprised, you know? I always knew it would come, but I never believed until now.

Agnes knelt beside Nora. I need to get Ruby Hiebert. She lives only a quarter mile away. She will help us.

Agnes leaned over Nora's head. She had knelt at the top of Nora's head, so instead of being eye to eye, she felt her heated breath on her forehead. It spread and cooled Agnes' sweaty face, like a blessing she would never understand.

I know.

You must wait. *Aufpausse.*

I will try, Nora said, a touch of her old crashing laughter escaping her lips. I will tell her to wait for her momma a little longer.

How do you know it's a girl?

I don't know, I guess. I just feel like it is.

Do you have a name?

Huldah.

Why Huldah? Agnes had never liked that name; it sounded so harsh on the tongue.

It's the name of a prophetess in the Bible. I like the idea of being the mother of a prophet.

Agnes knew she needed to leave, but the thought of running away from Nora, from this place could not yet be imagined.

What did she prophesy?

She prophesied about the wrath of God. She was a person who told men they were wrong. Peter never told me about her—I suspect he didn't think I could handle a woman who told men what they didn't want to hear.

Agnes laughed. The name sounded like the prophet's message: harsh and somehow beautiful. She liked it a bit more.

Agnes rested her head on Nora's chin. Nora's neck lifted. Agnes felt the brush of her lips against Nora's. She froze for a second before brushing her lips in kind against lips that tasted like blood. Then, without meeting Nora's eyes, she ran to the door, slammed the other shuddering barn door and heaped two stones in front of it to prevent the flimsy latch from breaking.

Agnes found the *Poppemutta* and her family in the root cellar, but the midwife gathered her equipment and left immediately, deaf to the cries of her children and anger of her husband. Agnes had expected her to be slow; Ruby Hiebert had broken her leg badly as a child, and it hadn't healed straight. But the midwife sprang out like a newborn calf, unsteady but fast.

The storm rolled above their heads, alternating between blue and green and orange with flecks of oddly-tinted red. No rain or hail had come yet. Agnes felt something odd within this storm, as though it were filled with something other than nails of water. She never saw the flash.

She felt it pierce her skin like a thin shank of metal that was yet to cool into permanence. When she opened her eyes, she was on her back. Something burned in Agnes' throat and nose. She smelled smoke.

Agnes raced towards the fire that was reflected against the contorted clouds. When she got to the barn, the heat pushed her back as she tried to move the rocks that had trapped Nora inside. She tried to hear Nora's voice, but she could only hear the roar of the flames. She called to her again and again, but the only answer was the heat that pressed against her face. It searched and found her nostrils, her ears, her lips, and fought to find a way inside. It caressed her forehead, swept her hair from her eyes, penetrated her skin, parted her lips, a growl surrounded her and lay like a garment over her body.

Herein, said the Voice.

Agnes would have stepped forward into the tempting glow had Ruby Hiebert not jerked her away, shouting words she could not understand. She tried to break from her grasp, but Ruby's arms steeled themselves against her desire. The barn collapsed, shooting black smoke and ash into the careless sky.

A shimmering white tiger leaped from the barn's walls, its coat reflecting the bite of the flames. It didn't pause. It leaned into the wind, head to the ground, silent.

Dormant

2007

As soon as Ellen saw her daughter's car swing up the lane in an explosion of dust, she took off the ring she had been examining in the sunlight and deposited it in the pocket of her barn jacket. Though she hadn't been expecting Minerva, somehow she wasn't surprised at her arrival. It seemed as if it were a moment she had seen coming when Minerva first came into the world.

Ellen stepped out of the greenhouse and walked towards Minerva's car. She did not smile, but she made sure she didn't look grave, either. Whatever had happened would call for neither of those things. Ellen had learned how to look at her daughter and ward off any rage. That was what kept them close—or as close as one could get with Minerva. Johan had never learned how to look at her; he either glared or smiled his lopsided grin, unconscious of which situation called for what. This enraged their daughter often. Only a few times it made her laugh and shake her hands at her sides, the way she always had since she was small. He hadn't learned the art of the in-between.

Minerva practically fell out of the car and rushed to embrace Ellen. She was two inches taller and several pounds heavier than Ellen, so she nearly bowled her over. Ellen had a center of gravity stronger than a man's. She held her ground.

And to what do I owe this pleasure? she asked when Minerva let her go. She didn't even look for Jasper. He rarely came with Minerva on her sporadic visits. He had never been comfortable around Johan. Even after Johan died, he stayed away. Perhaps it was the *feeling* of Johan he was uncomfortable with, more than the man.

Well, Momma, I've left him. For good now. I mean it.

Once again, Ellen controlled her face. This was not the first time Minerva came crashing home with this pronouncement.

What happened?

He never sees me. I try to make him notice me, try to get one reaction from him, and nothing happens. I would have liked it if it was another woman. At least then he would've been afraid of me knowing.

Minerva wrapped her arms around her chest and squinted at the sinking sun. I don't know why he ever married me.

I guess this is the signal for me to sing your praises, right?

Ellen could joke with Minerva if she chose the right moments when Minerva could see the humor—even dark humor—in a situation.

No, Momma, Minerva said. Ellen saw her smiling her father's lop-sided grin.

Ellen walked to the passenger side of the car and opened the door. A worn suitcase and a geranium sat on the floor of the car. Usually, Minerva's escapes were haphazard, which always told Ellen it was only for a certain time. This desertion was well-planned and well-packed. Perhaps this meant it was over. She hefted the suitcase in one hand and cradled the geranium with the other. Minerva stood and continued to look at the sunset.

Help me with the door, Nervy, Ellen said when she reached the porch, wondering if her daughter would laugh at the name Jeffrey had given her the moment she arrived from the hospital. Minerva turned and gave Ellen a teenager's smirk, but she climbed onto the porch and opened the front door.

Ellen set the suitcase by the stairs and placed the geranium among the other houseplants she had just taken in for the winter. It needed a drink, she saw, so she went into the kitchen and filled a glass with water. When she returned to the living room, Minerva was standing by the plants and watching them in fascination.

They look so happy together, Minerva said. I wish I was a geranium.

I doubt you'd like it, Ellen said, leaning over to douse the plant with water. I doubt you'd appreciate it when I trim and pluck the dead bits off.

When Ellen straightened, she saw Minerva looking around the

room in surprise. Ellen surveyed the room, trying to think of the last time Minerva had been home, and what had changed since then. Then she remembered.

Momma, it's so—clean.

Ellen barked a laugh. I'm that bad a housekeeper?

Though Ellen groomed herself quite well, her cleanliness didn't always extend to the house. Books, magazines and old receipts cluttered beside chairs, under tables and next to the various doors. When she dusted or swept, she never moved them; she simply ran the cloth or the broom around them. But a few weeks before, Ellen began to truly clean the house she had lived in for over thirty years. She had picked up those strayed mugs and newspapers and made three huge piles in the front yard; one pile was the trash heap, the second pile was the give-away heap, the third was the keep or give-to-Minerva heap. More than once, Ellen wondered what her husband's sisters would say if they saw these piles of her family's life upon the ground they held as hallowed space. But none of them ever came by, anyway. The only people that saw the piles were two of the men who rented her fields, and they only grinned and took some of her give-away items.

She called the renters a few days later to help her move the furniture out of the house, having seen on television that there were several sunny days ahead. She felt comfortable leaving them out at night. Once everything was out, she swept and scrubbed everything twice. It took two twelve-hour days. Ellen could have arranged a place to stay at night, but she had found Johan's camping equipment and set up camp a few yards from the house. Those two nights were the most restful she'd had in quite awhile. She sat by a small campfire, a quilt wrapped around her shoulders, photo albums clustered around her feet. Some of them were hers; others were of Johan's family. She'd studied everyone's faces, hoping to see what went on in their minds as the camera flashed. Even when she looked at her own face, she found herself mystified by her awkward smile, her uneven teeth.

When she finished cleaning and sorting out the furniture into three piles, she called the renters back and they moved everything she wanted to keep back into the house. Ellen knew they knew what was coming, but they only smiled when they left. She was sure they were conjecturing with their wives and neighbors about who would get to buy what field or pasture, but they had the decency to keep their tongues tied until that moment arrived.

Momma, what's going on? Her daughter's face mirrored faces that Ellen had seen more than once when Minerva was a teenager. A mixture of shock, dismay and confusion danced along her lips, reddened her cheeks and furrowed that smooth brow.

Nervy, I'm selling everything. Ellen's left hand found her left pocket. Her thumb and forefinger tested the sharpness of the stones against the cool grace of the metal ring.

You are not.

Nervy, I'm tired. I love this place, but I don't like being alone. I need to move on with my life.

Why don't you just move to town? Rent the farmhouse out? I'm sure you could find someone.

I'd rather just be clear of it all. Let some young buck and his wife have it. Let them make their own history.

What do the aunts and uncles say about this? Don't they have a say?

No. Your grandpoppa signed this place and all the land to your father. It was his, and now it's mine.

That seems a bit—

Selfish? Ellen laughed. She had thought of everyone's arguments long beforehand. For all their noises about family and history, Johan's brothers and sisters had had nothing to do with the farm once they left. Gretta's sons had helped with the farm work when they were young, but Johan had to pay his sister for it. Other than Huldah, Ellen rarely saw any of the others. Tobias came only to string up the Christmas lights. He wouldn't even stay the night.

It may be selfish, but I don't see anyone deigning to take my place, or move in with me—Ellen shot a look at Minerva, knowing that her daughter would never do either of those things. Minerva reddened and looked down.

Momma, how are you going to pay for yourself? Whatever you'll make will be eaten by taxes or debt.

I've already taken care of that, she said, grinning. The old-fashioned way. She pulled out the ring she had been exploring in her pocket since Minerva appeared.

The ring lay delicately in her palm. The gold was platinum, almost translucent; the stone was a simple ruby that shone an opaque red in the semi-darkness of the house. Before Minerva arrived, Ellen had looked at it in the deepening sunset, and had watched as the ruby hungrily absorbed every shaft of light then flashed out, like the fire that had consumed the brush when she had camped in Johan's stained tent. This ring outshone the silver band Johan had given her. Their relationship had been similar to the ring: simple, strong, battered and ungraceful at times.

~

Harold had stumbled a bit among the furniture on her lawn before giving her the new ring. Ellen had made a move to catch him, but before she could grab his hand he straightened and smiled that wisp of a smile she had noticed and liked the first time she walked into his clinic for an interview.

Doing some redecorating, I see, he said.

No, cleaning.

Ah.

They stood in the forested shade of the kitchen table, the china closet, stacks of chairs, three bedsteads, a low-slung couch, two re-upholstered living room chairs, several end tables, bookshelves, three dressers, a dining room table, a desk with scratches generations old, lamps, pillows and piles of quilts. Ellen realized how dirty she must look: her hair underneath a stained bandanna, one of Johan's sweatshirts that hung like a maternity dress, a pair of sweatpants she'd found under Minerva's old bed, rolled to the knees. She had always made an effort to look well in front of Harold. Partially because of her duty to his clinic—she'd seen more than one receptionist in elastic waist skirts and ill-fitting blouses—and partially because of him. She had known him for years before she became his receptionist, but it wasn't until she knew him professionally that she felt a warmth whenever he was near. This was why she never touched his shoulder or patted his arm, though she was a person who loved to touch anyone who needed the feel of her capable hands. She was afraid of what that touch would do to her. She was afraid Johan would find out, would see the way she encountered Harold outside the office. If he had noticed anything, he didn't say it.

Ellen never knew if Harold had noticed; if he felt anything in return. As they stood together in that strange forest, she realized he had. Because of the way he looked at her, as if she was twenty-five years younger and wore an evening gown, she knew.

This might come as a surprise, he said. But, I was wondering if you would marry me. He looked down, almost as if he was preparing himself for rejection. His left hand traveled to the stump of his amputated right arm, rubbing the cloth wrapped around it like a newborn.

Ellen laughed, stepped around the coffee table that stood between them, and touched his face. That took a lot of guts, I'm assuming, she said.

Harold glanced up. Is that a yes?

~

Minerva's face crinkled with laughter. So, old Dr. Diener finally made his move after all this time!

How on earth—

Come on, Momma, her daughter said, scooping up the ring and

studying it, approval written on her face. I figured it out a long time ago—even before Poppa died. Poppa said something to me about it once. We'd seen you together, talking at church or someplace when I was thirteen or so. Nervy, he said, that bastard is going to go for your momma before I'm cold.

Ellen glanced at her right hand where the other ring now resided. I never knew, about anything, she sighed.

About his feelings? Or yours?

Ellen kept her eyes trained on her right hand, lips pressed together as if she would never open them again. Minerva pressed her new ring in that hand. I guess he waited a bit longer, she said.

Her daughter flopped onto the sofa with a sigh. Relieved that Minerva had taken the news so well, Ellen relaxed enough to examine her carefully. She looked tired. Her clothes that always were on the verge of tightness around her breasts and thighs looked almost baggy; her hair had grown into shag that framed her face in a strangely beautiful way. She couldn't decide whether she was happy or sad, which was unusual for Minerva. She was like her father in that way—either angry or depressed or delirious with happiness. Ellen remembered Johan had gained a kind of similar balance before he died. When the doctor said that there was nothing more to do, Johan did not shout at him like he had in the past. Instead, it was Ellen who slapped the inexpressive face of a doctor renowned for his miraculous work. It was as if he'd decided to accept it long ago. It was as if he'd kept up his anger for Ellen's sake all along.

Are you—sick? Ellen's felt her throat constrict. She wondered if she would be able to find strength for one more death—the last death of her family besides her own. She had been surprised how strong she had been when Jeffrey died. She had wept and screamed at the God she doubted existed, but she had put her grief aside to support Johan and Minerva.

When Johan died, she was almost relieved. Not that he was gone from her life, but because his end had been painful. Ellen had realized then why some wives and mothers killed their husbands and children who were in the same state. She saw how the pain of the person usurped the desire to have them near no matter what. She didn't have the guts to do it, though. It was something she didn't have the strength to do. The day Johan died, he whimpered and writhed and didn't know she was there. She let the nurses give him more and more morphine so that his pain would lessen.

Ellen had hoped his face would relax after death, the way she had heard people talk about, but his face was frozen in the agony. It took the art of the local undertaker to sculpt a smile out of her husband's face.

No, Momma. Minerva stood and put her arm through Ellen's. I guess I do know why Jasper married me, and it had nothing to do with what I was—or am. He just liked the idea of me, more than the reality of me, if that makes any sense. I should have realized—he said as much once before the wedding.

You seem more relaxed, which is good.

I think I am. Not happy, but I feel okay.

I suppose you're hungry.

Definitely.

$\approx$

Minerva hadn't been present at Johan's death, although Ellen had called several times before he was gone. She had arrived at the church just before the funeral, and sat stiffly in the seat beside the gravesite. Afterwards, she strode away before anyone could offer any condolences and sat in the car until Jasper, who'd had the decency to come to the funeral as well, despite the strained relationship, climbed in and drove her away.

A few weeks later, after the casseroles and soups from the church had run out, and Johan's sisters and brothers returned to their lives, Ellen had time to meditate on her daughter's behavior. When she was young and then a teenager, Minerva and Johan had a rocky relationship. She yelled, he yelled; here were many days of silence between them. She had never worshipped her father the way other girls did; she rarely fought with Ellen, unlike other girls did, which made Ellen happy yet disturbed at the same time. But Johan and Minerva seemed easy enough in each other's presence most of the time. They had the same sense of humor. They had the same tempers. They had no idea how similar they were.

During college, something changed. She was rarely home save for holidays. When she called, she only talked if Ellen answered the phone. At least, that's what Ellen suspected, because Johan complained about the Damned Fool that Calls and Hangs Up. The summer after her junior year, Minerva had time to come home for harvest. She obviously didn't want to be there, though she helped out around the house and the farm without complaint as she had for years. She took food to her father and cousins; brought them home at night and ran errands. When Ellen returned from her job at the clinic and took over, she would wander out by herself for hours at a time, but somehow she knew when she would be needed. Ellen sometimes saw her climbing around the equipment, examining every inch of them as though they were parts of a science experiment. Ellen found this odd. She had never had much interest in farming; she had done what she was told, but no more.

Ellen was bringing out a load of laundry to hang up when she saw Minerva sitting in front of one of the gravity wagons, facing the spout to let the grain swirl out into a sieve or an auger.

This was the wagon in which Jeffrey had died. The gate that held the wheat at bay sprung open while Jeffrey was in the wagon. The weight of one kernel, seeming so small and innocuous, massed and became a funnel that grabbed his feet, legs, torso and head and suffocated him. Johan had not used it for years after, but was forced to when the tire of the other wagon had sprung a leak and there was no time to fix it. After that season, the wagon was commissioned again. The only reason it stood on the yard that day was because it was full of seed wheat, waiting to be siphoned into one of the grain bins.

Ellen stood behind one of the outbuildings and watched her daughter sit so still in front of this thing of life and death. She set the laundry down. She wanted to touch her daughter's head, rub her shoulders, and smooth down the rumpled t-shirt that was too small for her. Instead, she watched her daughter rise and place a palm against the frame, as if she was blessing it. Minerva ran her hands along the walls, the spout, the giant chains and wheel that held the door of the spigot closed.

Minerva began to pound the handle on the wheel, the door, the frame. Softly at first, then harder and louder and thundered and screamed against the metal that merely echoed cunningly. Minerva looked wildly around her; Ellen stepped back into the shadows. A pile of rusted machine parts lay mixed with waving weeds and stray shafts of wheat. She strode to the mound and pulled out what once was a field cultivator shank and returned to the wagon.

Minerva's body threw itself forward with each strike, her shirt riding farther up her back, revealing skin that had not seen sun in a long time. Ellen remembered spreading suntan lotion all over that back during old summers. She remembered how that back turned a golden brown that shimmered against the light that dripped through the trees in the evening.

The great wheel began to turn; the chains creaked so loud the sound covered the wind. Minerva threw the shank to the side and began to push the wheel barehanded, her hair loosened from the awkward ponytail and shading her face from Ellen's eyes. Finally the gate began to open; it was small at first, so that only a few kernels slid through at a time. But Minerva kept pushing the great wheel. The wagon began to yawn, so that a shower, then a torrent broke through its spigot. Minerva's feet, then legs were swallowed by the rush.

Ellen stumbled to her daughter through the brush that stood between them. She grabbed Minerva around the waist and pulled her away. Ellen's legs faltered and they both fell into the dirt carved with tractor tire tracks. She held her tight, this only living child. She would not let her go. She imagined fall, then winter winds gliding over their bodies; she saw deep snow cover and cradle them into spring, when tender grasses would shoot up between her shoulder blades. Summer would come again, but she would still be holding on.

After dinner, Ellen and Minerva managed to get the little-used wood stove lit and sat on the sofa doomed to the flames in a few weeks. Ellen had been on the verge of sending it with the other items going to the dump, since it would be an embarrassment to see it in Ulysses' only thrift store, but she realized there would be a lack of comfortable furniture between now and the day she would move. Then she would burn the couch—a final goodbye to her life as it was. She had some blankets to throw over its stains and pillows to hide the sagging springs when buyers came by.

Only a few had come so far. The real estate agent—a new agent in the area, which meant there wouldn't be any gossip in Ulysses—assured her that more would come. Farmers came for the fields and the equipment, not the farmstead. Ellen knew the house needed a lot of work. The carpeting should be replaced; the linoleum had to be ripped up; hardwood on the floor would make the entire house glow, at least on the inside. The agent suggested she do this before the buyers came, because it might make the house more appealing and would up the asking price. However, Ellen was turned off by the contractor's bid. She knew if one of the old-timers got the farmstead, either it would be turned into an elaborate tool shed or it would stand empty for years before someone simply burned it down. Why spend all that money and effort for something no one would appreciate?

Why do you want to leave this? Minerva's hand flew around her head, a meadowlark looking for a place to land.

Why don't you stay here? Ellen countered.

Minerva laughed and leaned against Ellen's shoulder. You know why. I never really belonged, she said, her voice muffled by Ellen's sweater. Neither did Jeffrey. We were born to the wrong family. We weren't what Poppa wanted.

Was I out of the equation?

No—you wanted us, but you have a knack of wanting everyone. It's a beautiful trait, Momma.

I'm not sure how I feel about that statement.

Minerva sat up. I can't explain it! It's good, believe me. I certainly don't have it. Maybe Jeffrey did. I never figured it out.

Jeffrey was a different soul—your father loved him—but he didn't understand him. Your father had a hard time dealing with people who are hard to figure out.

How did you stay with him? Your problems in that relationship make mine look frivolous.

Ellen wanted to be angry. She wanted to shake her daughter and shout: *How dare you refer to the life of your parents—That Relationship! You know nothing about it! You have no right to dismiss him like that!*

But she could not. She had to steel herself between her words and her emotions. She had to be in-between.

You don't know what our relationship was, she said carefully, like one steps between rows of wheat that's just come out of dormancy. There's a catch of fear as you tread among them; a misstep will cripple what the farmer has spent months nourishing.

I know what I saw, Minerva said stiffly.

That was the only time it happened, I promise you.

Minerva made a sound of disbelief at Ellen's statement, and then dropped into silence. Ellen leaned back and rested her head on the sofa. She closed her eyes and thought about wheat. Over the thirty-six years she lived in this place, she had sat for hours watching it in every stage of growth and death. She wondered how people first found it and crafted it into what she saw. She never doubted evolution's presence in the world. She knew, through Johan, that wheat was initially another kind of grass. That over time it slowly developed through the years; that it had evolved into what now carpeted the earth. She figured people and animals had come along the same way.

When she pressed him as to who decided it would become more, he paused before saying: It was probably an accident, you know? Just like other inventions. Then I guess God realized that was a good idea and took it like it was his own.

Then he gave her that lopsided grin that had drawn her to him in the beginning. You'd better keep it to yourself that I have such blasphemous thoughts.

Ellen always wondered how so many faces could reside in Johan's body. He was, at turns, happy and joking, sad and quiet, disgusted by the world, and filled with a deep-welled rage that he tried to control with every rope of his body. He didn't want it, that potential violence; it had chosen him. Ellen had usually been able to protect her children from it. Only a few times it had crested towards them, but she had been able to become a breaker in those moments, so that all her children felt was a heavy rush of water that spilled over their thighs. It was painful, she knew. But it could have been worse.

Minerva was in bed when Johan came home with the tractor and gravity wagon. Ellen waited for him on the porch. The air was thick with fireflies. She watched them as they rose and descended over the lawn and pasture like the final pulse of a dying star. When they were young, Minerva and Jeffrey would race the fireflies up and down the yard with their Mason jars. Even though Jeffrey was six years older than Minerva, he always took her desires seriously. If she wanted to grab fireflies, he obliged. If she wanted to camp out in the pasture, he went with her. When she woke in the middle of the night and wanted to go home, he trundled her back to the house. Jeffrey was born with an old soul. He didn't need to be the moody teenager she had always heard about. He was often angry, he was often sad, he was sometimes annoying, but even his anger and sadness seemed to have a breath in it unlike any other.

A month before he died, Ellen caught him smearing something

heavy and brown into his long dreadlocks. It had the scent of something fetid and exotic. What are you doing? she demanded.

I'm putting henna in my hair.

It looks like dirt.

It sort of is.

Ellen had heard that the best way to deal with a teenager who is doing something supposedly scandalous was to simply accept it. She followed this anonymous advice, although she made sure he cleaned it all up, and yelled at him for staining the bathroom floor and then the crumbles of henna she found in his sheets the following morning.

When he washed his hair the next day and let it dry in the sun, it looked like bronze. She laughed and ran her hand over it. It reminds me of your Aunt Huldah's hair, she whispered. Oh, she said, feeling bad for comparing his hair to a woman's, I didn't mean—

Momma, don't worry. Jeffrey smiled and said: Men shouldn't be ashamed of being compared to women. They should take it as a compliment.

Thankfully, Johan only made a curt comment about it the next evening after supper: Well, at least it's clean for once.

Ellen listened to the tractor idle. An idling tractor had always made her a tinge nervous. It was the fear of the sudden silence afterwards. You don't know what will happen next.

Johan cut the engine. She heard his boots scraping through the gravel. They stopped. She heard him curse under his breath: Scheisse. She willed him to stand a moment more, to corral the rage, pin it against the hedgerows and wait for the anger to subside. The boots started moving again. He wound around the house and stopped. Ellen knew she could see him more than he could see her, because of the porch light that burned behind her back. He had suddenly aged, she realized. His shoulders had stooped; his stomach that used to be full with fat had turned slack like an utter devoid of milk. His arms were still the same: thick and muscled, his fingers short and stubby. They were fitted with calluses upon calluses.

Johan's fingers had not been so tough when they were first married. They had still been rough, but the protective flesh did not come until years later. When they were first married, Ellen loved it when he plunged them inside her. They were determined explorers. Then it started to hurt to have them there. The calluses were harsh and unyielding. They no longer explored gently; their skin did not meld with her walls. They seemed to want to hunt rather than search. For several months she said nothing about it. She thought maybe it was because of Minerva's recent birth. Her body was still mending. Then it was too much. One night, when his hand slid between her thighs, she stopped him.

No, she had said, embarrassed. They never discussed their sex life with each other. It hurts. It hurts when you do that.

His breath stopped. His hand rested between the crux of her thighs; his fingers tangled in her pubic hair. Then he jerked his hand away. He rolled away from her. Ellen wanted to explain, but her voice was trapped.

What happened to the wagon? he asked, his voice coiled and deceptively even.

The gate opened, she said.

How did the gate open?

Someone opened it. She wondered if he would think it was a prank, something no one could control. But he knew she and Minerva had been there all day.

You mean Minerva.

Ellen's silence was enough.

Why didn't you stop her? What, did she think it was some kind of sick joke?

I'm sure she did not think it was a joke.

Where the hell were you, Ellen?

I was here.

Why didn't you stop her? His fingers closed and released, closed and released.

I could not stop her.

Could you not—or would you not? Were you in on it? Are you getting back at me?

No, she said.

She heard the screen door open. Don't talk to her like that, Minerva said.

Ellen didn't turn around. She heard a low growl she had not heard in many years. She wondered if her daughter could feel the tiger's flanks press upon her legs.

I will talk to anyone however I want to!

It's not her you want to yell at.

I'll get to you soon, girl!

Johan stepped towards the porch. Ellen touched his thigh. She felt his muscles shake beneath the denim. Later, she realized that was when she knew his cancer would return. He had known it too, she assumed. He wasn't angry at either of them; he was angry because he knew he wasn't going to beat it when it resumed its post in his body. He could fight anyone except himself. His body would triumph in the end.

Why did you grease the chain that day? Why did you make him unload it alone? It didn't need to be done. You could've waited one more day. It took me forever to make that gate move, but he could have opened it eventually. It didn't need to be greased. Minerva's breath rose and fell roughly, as if she was strangling herself. I read the police report, you know, I read it because I'd heard you could do that.

Watch yourself.

I read the report, and the report mentioned that day you nearly choked him, and that grandmomma had filed it and then rescinded it because you said you were sorry, and there was speculation that you abused us and maybe—

Shut your mouth! Shut that disgusting mouth!

Everyone thought it, Poppa! No one said anything to you, but someone told me a few months ago—and that's when I read the report. You killed him, right? You killed him.

Johan stumbled up the steps. Ellen rose and grabbed his hand. He pushed her down. She fell backward onto the walkway. She heard the screen door close. She heard him rip it open. Ellen got up and pushed him back with her arm. He took it and began to squeeze. His eyes were wild; they saw nothing but the mouth of the open door.

Johan—you're hurting me. Don't you go in there. You're hurting me, Johan.

He drew his eyes from the door. He did not recognize her. Ellen felt her circulation close, her skin cells fighting his fingers' grip.

Don't tell me what I do here, he shouted. You're all against me, I know it! He threw her arm away from him. Ellen could see Minerva standing in the living room, swaying like a forgotten blade of grass. She wanted to shout at her, to make her run away from this moment, to forget about it.

Ellen said instead: Johan, if you touch her, if a hair falls from her head, if you even breathe on her I will leave you, and never set foot in this house again.

They stood in the stillness of an engine just cut. Ellen could feel the muscles of her husband, of her daughter; of her own fix into that moment of time. It was as if they could not press these muscles any further than the now that had decided to slide cement through their bones. As if the now would mummify their flesh that would let thousands of years stream past.

Then she heard it: *Herein*, said the Voice.

Johan's head jerked. He had heard it as well.

Herein, the Voice repeated with a hint of impatience.

Go away! Johan shouted. He took a step towards the door. You have no business here! You belong with the craziness of my sister, not here!

He was answered by a low growl. *Aussteigen*, Johan, the Voice said. *Herein*, Ellen.

Ellen thought she saw a flash of while, a shadow of tail disappear into the kitchen. She walked into the house and shut the door. She led Minerva to bed. She heard the engine of the pickup spark to life and crunch the gravel as it sped beyond the yard light that was crowded with insects.

Minerva got up and helped Ellen with the early morning rituals. She made sandwiches for lunch, brewed ice tea, helped with laundry. Then Ellen had to leave for the clinic. She knew Minerva would be gone when she returned. She lingered on the porch. Her hair, still damp from the shower, clung to the back of her neck, like a swimmer holding on to the edge of a lifeboat.

Bye, Momma, Minerva said, acting like nothing had happened.

You'll take out their lunch?

Yeah.

Your poppa's not back yet.

I'll take my car.

Drive safe, was all Ellen could muster.

I will.

That night, Minerva was gone. The only things Ellen could guess she took with her were her overnight bag and one of Ellen's best geraniums.

Ellen made supper and waited for Johan's return. The pickup finally rolled onto the yard at one in the morning. She heard him enter the mudroom, take off his clothes and step into the shower. Ellen knew if she was not in the next room he wouldn't have bothered with any of it. He would have sat down at the table, reeking with sweat and grease and covered in dust and chaff.

She heard him at the door of the kitchen. He waited. She realized he was waiting for her voice to let him in: Come in before your supper dries out.

He walked into the kitchen, opened the oven door and pulled out the plate. *Scheisse*, he growled, since the plate was hot. He didn't let go, but carried it to the table and placed it across from Ellen. Johan sat and looked at her arm that was slowly turning purple.

I'm sorry, he said, looking into her eyes.

She knew he was sorry he hurt her. That he would never squeeze her flesh like that again. But she didn't believe he was sorry for anything else. She had stopped believing he was sorry years before for anything he did or said. Ellen had often wondered when she finally disbelieved him, why she stayed with him.

As she sat with her daughter now, she knew why she stayed: it was from her ability to hope he would become the man he tried and failed to be. Because a week after she had told him he hurt her when he placed his fingers inside her, she found a bottle of hand lotion under the bathroom sink. She never saw him use it, but every night the air was filled with a scent that reminded her of the soil after a soaking rain. Even now she still imagined him roving his lotioned hands over her body at night.

His entire family had tried to be people they would never be. Their ghosts wandered the house with the hope that one day someone would take that from them so they would not have to pursue that failed experiment further.

Minerva had fallen asleep. Ellen got up, closed the drafts of the stove and walked to the front door. She imagined the ghosts of this house waiting at the door, ready to leave and finally rest; glad to lie dormant with the soulless wheat, without the burden of resurrection.

Shaken in the Water, Part 7

1997

Agnes slipped out of her granny house in the graying morning and slowly walked along the roads that had surrounded her life. The roads curved every hundred miles or so to adjust to the arc of the earth. Those sections came up like the faint soul of a spot on a sheet; unnoticeable until a body got her nose close enough to the fabric. The only reason Agnes even knew this was because Johan had mentioned it offhandedly as they drove to church the previous Sunday. For some reason it stuck with her, those curves in the land that stretched north and south, east and west, seeming to be as straight as God—only they weren't. Like God, they knew better.

Agnes walked back to that place and stood in the little curved triangle. The section beyond belonged to Gerald Wiens. She wondered if he knew he had a few inches more than his cousin, Glen, across the road.

She carefully examined this land that had been below her since birth. That part of the country was higher than that farther east, rising slowly to meet the mountains hundreds of miles west. It was a blank piece of paper, with only the windrows and roads almost exactly one mile apart from each other that mentioned people came and went from the surface. Agnes realized the land had little need of her company that morning or any other.

It was a humid morning, and by the time she reached the semi-shade of the trees that crowded around land that once had held a barn and a soddy, her dress was soaked with sweat and her hair felt like a woolen cap without a lining. She went to the nearly-dead creek and splashed water on her hands and face, grinning at the silliness of an elderly woman walking in this heat alone and without a sunhat. Agnes pulled off her head covering. Her thin white rope of hair slunk past her shoulders and clung to her back.

She stepped out of her shoes and leaned against a tree to pull off her stockings. The whiteness of her toes shocked her; the yellowness of her nails disgusted her, so she quickly sank them into a puddle. Her hands wandered to her throat and unbuttoned her blouse, then her skirt. They fell to the ground silently, as though they were ready to go. Next, she undid the clasps of her corset. When the wind slid over her back she nearly screamed—not in pain, but relief. For many years she had lived with the pain her birthmark had given her; she forgot what it was like to be without the pain.

Agnes took a step away from the shelter of the trees. The sun broke through the clouds like a blessing. She remembered a day when the sun had looked like the head of the Lord; the day that she could feel each season that flowed over this tiny shroud of earth. Agnes looked at the space where a mountain of a barn had stood and burned. She felt her nipples that no longer sagged with the lips of children harden and grow. That forgotten heat rammed between her hips and traveled up her core until it spread itself through to her arms that stretched out of their own accord. That heat was a sharp red that forced itself out of her body in song:

Ein' feste Burg ist unser Gott,
Ein gute Wehr und Waffen;
Er hilft uns frei aus aller Not,
Die uns jetzt hat betroffen—

Agnes' voice was cut short by a growl in the bramble. A quick chill ran over her shoulders. Yes? she said, her voice weaker than she liked.

Herein, said a Voice.

The Voice was unmistakable; tuneless as if it had never heard a sound in its life. Agnes wondered if she was having a stroke. Her poppa had died of one in the middle of church when she was forty. The men who had sat beside him in his last seconds carried him away; eight of them held him high on their shoulders, as if he was already in a casket, and marched him out of the sanctuary. The elder's voice continued to drone upon their exit. Agnes wondered what she was supposed to do—if she had imagined the entire thing. She stared at the scuffed floor and noted the swirls in the wood that looked like inverted funnel clouds; she remembered Poppa holding her to his breast as the wind tried to part them.

Dangerous! he had yelled in her ear. *Dangerous!*

Liar! she screamed back. *Liar!*

Agnes wondered how it would look for people to find her body, stripped in the sunlight. She looked at her clothes, scattered debris in the muck.

Herein, the Voice repeated. Don't make me ask again.

She decided she did not care how they found her, or how shocked the community would be when it was reported. In fact, she wished she could be there. Johan would seethe under every glance no matter how innocent; Tobias would duck his head in shame at the thought of his mother's breasts open to the world; her daughters would weep more for her state of undress than the fact that she was gone. Huldah and Ellen would be different. Huldah would grin at the sky. Ellen would smile, shake her head in bemusement. They would understand.

All right! she crowed. All right! I'm ready now, Nora. I'm finished!

Agnes marched towards the round of stones that once held a barn firmly to the ground. She wondered what she would see next.

Acknowledgments

Thanks to Julia Fierro at Sackett Street Writers' Workshop and Garrett Robinson and Stephen Marlowe at Foxhead Books for their support and feedback; Kirsten Beachy, Chad Gusler, Alisha Huber, Pam Mandigo, Tonya Osinkosky, Andrew Jenner, Anna Maria Johnson, Sarah Chun and Alex Peterson for the many comments on many drafts; Carolyn Ferrell, Christine Schutt and my classmates at Sarah Lawrence College—your friendship and guidance was priceless; Mary Sprunger, Harvey Yoder and Richard Kyle for their historical perspective. To the guy who posed as Moses in the personal ad: I don't remember where I saw it, but I knew there was a story in there and stole it. I hope you found someone. Thanks to my friends and family—you are part of my many blessings. Finally, thanks to my husband Tom, who always knows what I often forget.

Mennonites

The Mennonites are a complex people with different interpretations of faith and cultural heritage. There are many branches of Mennonites: Amish, Old Order Mennonite and Holdeman Mennonite, Mennonite Brethren and Mennonite Church USA.

What holds Mennonites together is the 16th century Anabaptist movement that was a radical part of the Protestant Reformation. Mennonites and similar groups were known as "Anabaptists" because they refused to baptize infants and re-baptized adults—criminal acts at the time. Menno Simons, a former Dutch priest, was one of the early leaders of the movement, thus the term "Mennonite" came into use. Due to persecution from the ruling churches and authorities of Europe, Mennonites scattered east and west. Some Mennonites migrated to the New World as early as 1683. Others went to Russia before immigrating to the United States in the 1870s or to Canada in the 1920s. A few more slipped out of Russia with the retreating German army during World War II.

Mennonites follow a Confession of Faith: to be in community with others, to model one's life after Christ's and to refrain from violence, both in daily life and in military service. Like all faiths, the way in which this is interpreted differs from group to group.

Although there is a real Ulysses, Kansas, the Ulysses and its particular breed of Mennonites in this novel exist on no map except that of the imagination. They will be recognized as the Russian Mennonites of the 1870s migration, with the exceptions of plain dress and selection of elders by lot.

Unlike some of the women in the novel, Russian Mennonite women did not wear the white head coverings and simple dresses one sees on contemporary Amish and Old Order Mennonite women. However, a number of Russian Mennonites joined the Holdeman church post-migration in the 1870s. Modern Holdeman men have beards while the women wear homemade dresses and black head coverings. Amish and conservative Mennonites wear varying forms of plain dress, but it is no longer in the mainstream.

The selection of religious leaders by lot is often used in Old Order Mennonite and Amish congregations. This is based on how Matthias was selected to replace Judas after the Crucifixion of Christ in Acts 1:23-26: *So they nominated two men: Joseph called Barsabbas (also known as Justus) and Matthias. Then they prayed, "Lord, you know everyone's heart. Show us which of these two you have chosen to take over this apostolic ministry, which Judas left to go where he belongs." Then they cast lots, and the lot fell to Matthias; so he was added to the eleven apostles.*

Low German

Platdietsch, or Low German, was a dialect spoken by Russian Mennonites at home and among friends. High German was reserved for church and other official occasions. Like most dialects, there are different variations in grammar and spellings of Low German. Low German vocabulary in this novel comes from either the *Kjenn Jie Noch Plautdietsch?* website by Herman Rempel or the wonderful tome *Mennonite Low German Dictionary/Mennonitisch-Plattdeutsches Wörterbuch* by Jack Thiessen. Christopher Dick assisted in further translation. In the United States, High and Low German slipped out of use in the Russian Mennonite community because of anti-German sentiment during both World Wars. The hymns and Bible quotes in the novel are in High German. Both High and Low German are used interchangeably elsewhere.

About the Author

Jessica Penner has been published in *Bellevue Literary Review*, Center for Mennonite Writing, *Rhubarb*, and the anthology *Tongue Screws and Testimonies*. She has won honorable mentions in fiction and nonfiction from *Open City* and *Bellevue Literary Review*, and was nominated for a Pushcart Prize. *Shaken in the Water* is her first novel. She lives in Virginia.